New York Times Bestselling
Author Lisa Kleypas
is . . .

"Wonderfully refreshing."
Johanna Lindsey

"Delightful!"
Jill Barnett

"A delicious treat for romance readers."
Mary Jo Putney

"A real joy."
Kathleen E. Woodiwiss

"One of today's leading lights in romantic
fiction."
Seattle Times

"A master of her craft."
Publishers Weekly (★Starred Review★)

"Wonderful . . . gratifying and delightful."
Denver Rocky Mountain News

By Lisa Kleypas

CHASING CASSANDRA • DEVIL'S DAUGHTER
HELLO STRANGER • DEVIL IN SPRING
MARRYING WINTERBORNE • COLD-HEARTED RAKE
SCANDAL IN SPRING • DEVIL IN WINTER
IT HAPPENED ONE AUTUMN
SECRETS OF A SUMMER NIGHT
AGAIN THE MAGIC
WHERE'S MY HERO?
(with Kinley McGregor and Julia Quinn)
WORTH ANY PRICE • WHEN STRANGERS MARRY
LADY SOPHIA'S LOVER • SUDDENLY YOU
WHERE DREAMS BEGIN
SOMEONE TO WATCH OVER ME
STRANGER IN MY ARMS • BECAUSE YOU'RE MINE
SOMEWHERE I'LL FIND YOU
THREE WEDDINGS AND A KISS
(with Kathleen E. Woodiwiss, Catherine Anderson,
and Loretta Chase)
PRINCE OF DREAMS • MIDNIGHT ANGEL
DREAMING OF YOU • THEN CAME YOU
ONLY WITH YOUR LOVE

LISA KLEYPAS

Secrets of a Summer Night

The Wallflowers, Book 1

AVONBOOKS

An Imprint of HarperCollinsPublishers

Excerpt from *Devil in Disguise* copyright © 2021 by Lisa Kleypas.

This edition of *Secrets of a Summer Night* contains an altered version of the content that appeared in the original 2004 edition.

SECRETS OF A SUMMER NIGHT. Copyright © 2004, 2021 by Lisa Kleypas. All rights reserved. Printed in the United States of America. No part of this book may be used or reproduced in any manner whatsoever without written permission except in the case of brief quotations embodied in critical articles and reviews. For information, address HarperCollins Publishers, 195 Broadway, New York, NY 10007.

First Avon Books mass market printing: July 2021

Print Edition ISBN: 978-0-06-314261-9
Digital Edition ISBN: 978-0-06-314273-2

Cover design by Patricia Barrow
Cover art by Alan Ayers
Author photograph by Danielle Barnum Photography

Avon, Avon & logo, and Avon Books & logo are registered trademarks of HarperCollins Publishers in the United States of America and other countries.

HarperCollins is a registered trademark of HarperCollins Publishers in the United States of America and other countries.

21 22 23 24 25   QGM   10 9 8 7 6 5 4 3 2 1

Secrets of a Summer Night

Chapter 1

London, 1843
The end of the season

A marriage-minded girl could overcome practically any obstacle, except the lack of a dowry.

Annabelle swung her foot impatiently beneath the frothy white mass of her skirts while she kept her expression composed. During her past three failed seasons, she had become accustomed to being a wallflower. Accustomed, but not resigned. More than once it had occurred to her that she deserved far better than to sit at the side of the room in a spindly chair. Hoping, hoping, hoping, for an invitation that would never come. And trying to pretend that she didn't care—that she was perfectly happy to be watching others dancing and being courted.

Letting out a long sigh, Annabelle fiddled with the tiny silver dance card that hung from a ribbon on her wrist. The cover slid open to reveal a book of near-translucent ivory leaves that spread out in a fan. A girl was supposed to pencil the names of her dance partners on those delicate slips of ivory. To Annabelle, the fan of empty cards seemed to resemble a row of teeth, grinning at her mockingly. Snapping the silver case shut, she glanced at the three girls who sat next to her, all endeavoring to look similarly unconcerned with their fates.

She knew exactly why they were there. Miss Evangeline Jenner's considerable family fortune had been made from gambling, and her origins were common. Moreover, Miss Jenner was painfully shy and possessed a stutter, which made the prospect of conversation a session of torture for both participants.

The other two girls, Miss Lillian Bowman, and her younger sister Daisy, had not yet become acclimated to England—and from the looks of things, it would take them a long time. It was said that the Bowmans' mother had brought the girls from New York because they hadn't been able to get any suitable offers there. The soap bubble heiresses, they were mockingly referred to, or occasionally, the dollar princesses. Despite their elegantly angled cheekbones and tip-tilted dark eyes, they would find no better luck here unless they could find an aristocratic sponsor to vouch for them and teach them how to fit in with British society.

It occurred to Annabelle that in the past few months of this miserable season, the four of them—herself, Miss Jenner, and the Bowmans—had often sat together at balls or soirées, always in the corner or against the wall. And yet they had rarely spoken to each other, trapped in the silent tedium of waiting. Her gaze caught that of Lillian Bowman, whose velvety dark eyes contained an unexpected gleam of humor.

"At least they could have made the chairs more comfortable," Lillian murmured, "when it's obvious we're going to occupy them all evening."

"We should have our names engraved on them," Annabelle replied wryly. "After all the time I've spent in it, I *own* this chair."

A muffled giggle came from Evangeline Jenner, who lifted a gloved finger to push back a vivid red curl that had fallen over her forehead. The smile made her round blue eyes sparkle and her cheeks turn pink beneath a scattering of gold freckles. It seemed that a sudden sense of kinship had temporarily caused her to forget her shyness. "It m-makes no sense that you're a wall-flower," she told Annabelle. "You're the most beautiful girl here—men should be f-falling all over themselves to dance with you."

Annabelle lifted her shoulder in a graceful half shrug. "No one wants to marry a girl without a dowry." It was only in the fantasy realm of novels that dukes could marry poor girls. In reality, dukes and viscounts and the like were burdened with the massive financial responsibility of maintaining large estates and extended families, and helping the tenantry. A wealthy peer needed to marry into money just as badly as a poor one did.

"No one wants to marry a *nouveau-riche* American girl, either," Lillian Bowman confided. "Our only hope of belonging anywhere is to marry a peer with a solid English title."

"But we have no sponsor," her younger sister, Daisy, added. She was a petite, rather elfin version of Lillian, with the same fair skin, heavy dark hair, and brown eyes. An impish smile touched her lips. "If you happen to know of some nice duchess who would be willing to take us under her wing, we would be much obliged."

"I don't even *want* to find a husband," Evangeline Jenner confided. "I'm merely s-s-suffering through the season because there is nothing else for me to do. I'm too old to stay at school any longer, and my father . . ." She broke off abruptly, and sighed. "Well, I have only one more season to go, then I'll be twenty-three and a confirmed spinster. How I'm looking f-forward to it!"

"Is twenty-three the measure of spinsterhood these days?" Annabelle asked with half-feigned alarm. She rolled her eyes heavenward. "Good Lord, I had no idea that I was so far past my prime."

"How old are you?" Lillian Bowman asked curiously.

Annabelle cast a glance to the right and left, to make certain they were not being overheard. "Twenty-five next month."

The revelation earned three rather pitying

glances, and Lillian replied consolingly, "You don't look a day more than twenty-one."

Annabelle clutched her fingers around her dance card until it was concealed in her gloved hand. Time was slipping away quickly, she thought. This, her fourth season, was drawing rapidly to a close. And one simply did not embark on a fifth season—it would be ludicrous. She had to catch a husband, and soon. Otherwise, they could no longer afford to keep Jeremy at school . . . and they would be forced to move from their modest terrace and find a boardinghouse to reside in. And once the downhill slide began, there was no climbing back up.

In the six years since Annabelle's father had died of a heart ailment, the family's financial resources had dwindled to nothing. They had tried to camouflage their increasingly desperate straits, pretending they had a half dozen servants instead of one overworked cook-maid and an aging footman . . . turning their faded gowns so that the underside of the fabric was facing outward . . . selling the stones in their jewelry and replacing them with paste. Annabelle was heartily tired of their constant efforts to deceive everyone, when it seemed that everyone already knew they were on the brink of disaster. Lately, Annabelle had even begun to receive discreet offers from married men, who told her meaningfully that she had only to ask for their help, and it would be given immediately. There was no need to describe the compensations that such "help" would require.

Annabelle was well aware that she had the makings of a first-rate mistress.

"Miss Peyton," Lillian Bowman asked, "what kind of man would be the ideal husband for you?"

"Oh," Annabelle said with irreverent lightness, "any peer will do."

"*Any* peer?" Lillian asked skeptically. "What about good looks?"

Annabelle shrugged. "Welcome, but not necessary."

"What about passion?" Daisy inquired.

"Decidedly *un*welcome."

"Intelligence?" Evangeline suggested.

Annabelle shrugged. "Negotiable."

"Charm?" Lillian asked.

"Also negotiable."

"You don't want much," Lillian remarked dryly. "As for me, I would have to add a few conditions. My peer would have to be dark-haired and handsome, a wonderful dancer . . . and he would *never* ask permission before he kissed me."

"I want to marry a man who has read the entire collected works of Shakespeare," Daisy said. "Someone quiet and romantic—better yet if he wears spectacles—and he should like poetry and nature, and I shouldn't like him to be too experienced with women."

Her older sister lifted her eyes heavenward. "We won't be competing for the same men, apparently."

Annabelle looked at Evangeline Jenner. "What

kind of husband would suit you, Miss Jenner?"

"Evie," the girl murmured, her blush deepening until it clashed with her fiery hair. She struggled with her reply, extreme bashfulness warring with a strong instinct for privacy. "I suppose . . . I would like s-s-someone who was kind and . . ." Stopping, she shook her head with a self-deprecating smile. "I don't know. Just someone who would l-love me. Truly love me."

The words touched Annabelle, and filled her with sudden melancholy. Love was a luxury she had never allowed herself to hope for—a distinctly superfluous issue when her very survival was so much in question. However, she reached out and touched the girl's gloved hand with her own. "I hope you find him," she said sincerely. "Perhaps you won't have to wait for long."

"I want you to find yours first," Evie said, with a bashful smile. "I wish I could help you somehow."

"It seems that we all need help, in one form or another," Lillian commented. Her gaze slid over Annabelle with friendly speculation. "Hmm . . . I wouldn't mind making a project of you."

"What?" Annabelle arched her brows, wondering whether she ought to be amused or offended.

Lillian proceeded to explain. "There are only a few weeks left in the season, and this is your last, I assume. Practically speaking, your aspirations of marrying a man who is your social equal will vanish at the end of June."

Annabelle nodded warily.

"Then I propose—" Suddenly Lillian fell silent in midsentence.

Following the direction of her gaze, Annabelle saw a dark figure approaching, and she groaned inwardly.

The intruder was Mr. Simon Hunt—a man whom none of them wanted anything to do with—and with good reason.

"Parenthetically," Annabelle said in a low voice, "my ideal husband would be the exact opposite of Mr. Hunt."

"What a surprise," Lillian murmured sardonically, for they all shared the sentiment.

One could forgive a man for being a climber, if he possessed a sufficient quantity of gentlemanly grace. However, Simon Hunt did not. There was no making polite conversation with a man who always said exactly what he thought, no matter how unflattering or objectionable his opinions.

Perhaps one might call Mr. Hunt goodlooking. Annabelle supposed that some women might find his robust masculinity appealing— even she had to admit that there was something compelling about the sight of all that bridled power contained in a crisp formal scheme of black-and-white evening clothes. However, Simon Hunt's arguable attractions were completely overridden by the churlishness of his character. There was no sensitive aspect to his nature, no idealism or appreciation of elegance . . . he was all pounds and pence, all selfish, grasping calculation. Any other man in his situation would have had the decency to be embarrassed by his own lack of refinement— but Hunt had apparently decided to make a virtue of it. He loved to mock the rituals and graces of aristocratic civility, his cold black eyes glittering with amusement—as if he were laughing at them all.

No doubt many people shared Annabelle's dislike of Simon Hunt, but to the dismay of London's upper tiers, he was there to stay. In the past few years he had become incomparably rich, having acquired majority interests in companies that manufactured agricultural equipment, ships, and locomotive engines. Despite Hunt's coarseness, he was invited to upperclass parties because he was simply too wealthy to be ignored. Hunt personified the threat that industrial enterprise posed to the British aristocracy's centuries-old entrenchment in estate farming. Therefore, the peerage regarded him with concealed hostility even as they unwillingly allowed him access to their hallowed social circles. Worse still, Hunt made no pretense at humility, but instead seemed to enjoy forcing his way into places where he wasn't wanted.

Annabelle sensed the other wallflowers' relief as Hunt ignored them and turned his attention exclusively to her. "Miss Peyton," he said. His obsidian gaze seemed to miss nothing; the carefully mended sleeves of her gown, the fact that she had used a spray of pink rosebuds to conceal the frayed edge of her bodice, the paste pearls dangling from her ears. Annabelle faced him with an expression of cool defiance.

"Good evening, Mr. Hunt."

"Will you favor me with a dance?" he asked without prelude.

"No, thank you."

"Why not?"

"My feet are tired."

One of his dark brows arched. "From doing what? You've been sitting here all evening."

Annabelle held his gaze without blinking. "I have no obligation to explain myself to you, Mr. Hunt."

"One waltz shouldn't be too much for you to manage."

Despite Annabelle's efforts to stay calm, she felt a scowl tugging at the little muscles of her face. "Mr. Hunt," she said tautly, "has no one ever told you that it isn't polite to try and badger a lady into doing something that she clearly has no desire to do?"

He smiled faintly. "Miss Peyton, if I ever worried about being polite, I'd never get anything I wanted. I merely thought you would enjoy a temporary respite from being a perpetual wallflower. And if this ball follows your usual pattern, my offer to dance is likely the only one you'll get."

"Such charm," Annabelle remarked in a tone of mocking wonder. "Such artful flattery. How could I refuse?"

There was a new alertness in his eyes. "Then you'll dance with me?"

"*No,*" she whispered sharply. "Now go away. Please."

Instead of slinking away in embarrassment at the rebuff, Hunt grinned. "What is the harm in one dance? I'm a fairly accomplished partner—you may even enjoy it."

"Mr. Hunt," she muttered, in rising exasperation, "the notion of being partnered with you in any way, for any purpose whatsoever, makes my blood run cold."

Leaning closer, Hunt lowered his tone so that no one else could hear. "Very well. But I'll leave you with something to consider, Miss Peyton. There may come a time when you won't have the luxury of turning down an honorable offer from someone like me . . . or even a dishonorable one."

Annabelle's eyes widened, and she felt a flush of outrage spread upward from the neckline of her bodice. Really, it was too much—having to sit against the wall all evening, then be subjected to insults from a man she despised. "Mr. Hunt, you sound like the villain in a very bad play."

That elicited another grin, and he bowed with sardonic politeness before striding away.

Rattled by the encounter, Annabelle stared after him with narrowed eyes.

The other wallflowers breathed a collective sigh of relief at his departure.

Lillian Bowman was the first to speak. "The word 'no' doesn't seem to make much of an impression on him, does it?"

"What was that last thing he said, Annabelle?" Daisy asked curiously. "The thing that made your face turn all red."

Annabelle stared down at the silver cover of her dance card, rubbing her thumb over a tiny spot of tarnish on the corner. "Mr. Hunt implied that someday my situation might become so desperate that I would consider becoming his mistress."

If she hadn't been so worried, Annabelle would have laughed at the identical looks of owlish astonishment on their faces. But instead of exclaiming in virginal outrage, or tactfully letting the matter drop, Lillian asked the one question that Annabelle wouldn't have expected. "Was he right?"

"He was right about my desperate situation," Annabelle admitted. "But not about my becoming his—or anyone's—mistress. I would marry a beet farmer before I sank to that."

Lillian smiled at her, seeming to identify with the note of grim determination in Annabelle's voice. "I like you," she announced, and leaned back in her chair, crossing her legs with a negligence that was rather inappropriate for a girl in her first season.

"I like you, too," Annabelle replied automatically, prompted by good manners to reply in kind—but as the words left her mouth, she was surprised to discover that they were true.

Lillian's assessing gaze moved over her as she continued. "I should hate to see you end up trudging behind a mule and plow in a beet field—you were meant for better things than that."

"I agree," Annabelle said dryly. "What are we to do about it?"

Although the question was intended to be facetious, Lillian seemed to take it seriously. "I was getting to that. Before we were interrupted, I was about to make a proposition: We should make a pact to help each other find husbands. If the right gentlemen won't pursue us, then we'll pursue *them*. The process will be vastly more efficient if we join forces rather than forge ahead individually. We shall start with the eldest—which appears to be you, Annabelle— and work down to the youngest."

"That hardly works out to *my* advantage," Daisy protested.

"It's only fair," Lillian informed her. "You've got more time than the rest of us."

"What kind of 'help' do you mean?" Annabelle asked.

"Whatever is required." Lillian began to scribble industriously in her dance card. "We'll supplement each other's weaknesses and give advice and assistance when needed." She glanced up with a cheerful grin. "We'll be like a Rounders team."

Annabelle regarded her skeptically. "You're referring to the game in which gentlemen take turns whacking a leather ball with a flat-sided bat?"

"Not only gentlemen," Lillian replied. "In New York, ladies may play also, as long as they don't forget themselves in the excitement."

Daisy smiled slyly. "Such as the time Lillian became so incensed by a bad call that she pulled a sanctuary post out of the ground."

"It was already loose," Lillian protested. "A loose post could have presented a danger to one of the runners."

"Particularly while you were hurling it at them," Daisy said, meeting her older sister's frown with a sweet smirk.

Smothering a laugh, Annabelle glanced from the pair of sisters to Evie's vaguely perplexed expression. She could easily read Evie's thoughts—that the American sisters were going to require a lot of training before they would attract the attention of eligible peers. Returning her attention to the Bowman sisters, she couldn't help smiling at their expectant faces. It was not at all difficult to imagine the pair flailing at balls with sticks and running around the playing field with their skirts hitched up to their knees. She wondered if all American girls possessed such a plenitude of spirit . . . no doubt the Bowmans would terrify any proper British gentleman who dared to approach them.

"Somehow I've never thought of husband-hunting as a team sport," she said.

"Well, it should be!" Lillian said emphatically. "Think of how much more effective we'll be. The only potential difficulty is if two of us take an interest in the same man . . . but that doesn't seem likely, given our respective tastes."

"Then we'll agree never to compete for the same gentleman," Annabelle said.

"And f-furthermore," Evie broke in unexpectedly, "we shall do no harm to anyone."

"Very Hippocratic," Lillian said approvingly.

"I happen to think she's right, Lillian," Daisy protested, misunderstanding. "Don't browbeat the poor girl, for heaven's sake."

Lillian scowled in sudden annoyance. "I said 'Hippocratic,' not 'hypocritical,' you dunce."

Annabelle interceded hastily, before the two began to quarrel. "Then we must all agree on the plan of action—it won't do any good for any of us to be at cross-purposes."

"And we'll tell each other everything," Daisy said with relish.

"Even i-intimate details?" Evie asked timidly.

"Oh, *especially* those!"

Lillian smiled wryly and slid an appraising glance over Annabelle's gown. "Your clothes are atrocious," she said bluntly. "I'm going to give you a few of my gowns. I've got trunks full that I've never worn, and I'll never miss them. My mother will never notice."

Annabelle shook her head immediately, at once grateful for the offer yet mortified by her conspicuous financial straits. "No, no, I couldn't accept such a gift, although you are very generous—"

"The pale blue one, with the lavender piping," Lillian murmured to Daisy, "do you remember it?"

"Oh, that would look heavenly on her," Daisy said enthusiastically. "It will suit her much better than you."

"Thanks," Lillian retorted, flashing her a comical glare.

"No, really—" Annabelle protested.

"And that green muslin with the white lace trim down the front," Lillian continued.

"I can't take your gowns, Lillian," Annabelle insisted in a low voice.

The girl looked up from her notes. "Why not?"

"For one thing, I couldn't afford to repay you. And it won't be any use. Fine feathers won't make my lack of a dowry any more appealing."

"Oh, money," Lillian said, in the careless manner that could only come from someone who had a great deal of it. "You're going to repay me by giving me something infinitely more valuable than cash. You're going to teach Daisy and me how to be . . . well, more like you. Teach us the right things to say and do—all the unspoken rules that we seem to break every minute of the day. If possible, you might even help to find us a sponsor. And then we'll be able to walk through all the doors that are currently closed to us. As for your lack of a dowry . . . you just get the man on the hook. The rest of us will help you reel him in."

Annabelle stared at her in amazement. "You're actually serious about this."

"Of course we are," Daisy replied. "What a relief it will be for us to have something to do, rather than sit against the wall like idiots! Lillian and I have been driven to near madness by the boredom of the season."

"S-So have I," Evie added.

"Well . . ." Annabelle looked from one expectant face to another, unable to keep from grinning. "If the three of you are willing, then so am I. But if we're to make a pact, shouldn't we sign it in blood or something?"

"Heavens, no," Lillian said. "I should think we can all agree to something without having to open a vein over it." She gestured with her dance card. "Now, I suppose we should make a list of the most promising candidates left after the past season. And a sadly picked-over lot they are by now. Shall we list them in order of rank? Starting with dukes?"

Annabelle shook her head. "We may as well not bother with dukes, as I'm not aware of any eligible ones who are under seventy years old and have any teeth remaining."

"So intelligence and charm are negotiable, but not teeth?" Lillian said slyly, making Annabelle laugh.

"Teeth are negotiable," Annabelle replied, "but *highly* preferred."

"All right, then," Lillian said. "Passing over the category of gummy old dukes, let's progress to earls. I know of Lord Westcliff, for one—"

"No, not Westcliff." Annabelle winced as she added, "He's a cold fish—and he has no interest in me. I practically threw myself at him when I came out four years ago, and he looked at me as if I were something that had stuck on his shoe."

"Forget Westcliff, then." Lillian raised her brows questioningly. "What about Lord St. Vincent? Young, eligible, handsome as sin—"

"It wouldn't work," Annabelle said. "No matter how compromising the situation, St. Vincent would never propose. He has compromised, seduced, and utterly ruined at least a dozen women—honor means nothing to him."

"There's the earl of Eglinton," Evie suggested hesitantly. "But he is quite p-p-portly, and at least fifty years old—"

"Put him on the list," Annabelle insisted. "I can't afford to be particular."

"There's Viscount Rosebury," Lillian remarked with a little frown. "Although he's rather an odd sort, and so . . . well, *droopy*."

"As long as he's firm in the pocketbook, he can be droopy everywhere else," Annabelle said, causing the other girls to snicker. "Write him down, too."

Ignoring the music and the couples that swirled in front of them, the four of them worked diligently on the list, occasionally making each other laugh so hard that they drew curious glances from passersby.

"Quiet," Annabelle said, making an effort to sound stern. "We don't want anyone to suspect what we're planning . . . and wallflowers aren't supposed to be laughing."

They all attempted to assume grave expressions, which set off fresh spasms of giggles. "Oh, look," Lillian gasped, regarding their ever-growing list of matrimonial prospects. "For once our dance cards are full." Considering the roster of bachelors, she pursed her lips thoughtfully. "It occurs to me that some of these gentlemen will probably be attending

Westcliff's end-of-season party in Hampshire. Daisy and I have already been invited. What about you, Annabelle?"

"I'm acquainted with one of his sisters," Annabelle said. "I think I can get her to invite me. I'll *beg*, if necessary."

"I'll put in a word for you as well," Lillian said confidently. She smiled at Evie. "And I'll have her extend an invitation to you, too."

"How fun this will be!" Daisy exclaimed. "The plan is set, then. In a fortnight we'll invade Hampshire and find a husband for Annabelle." They all reached out and clasped hands, feeling silly and giddy and more than a little encouraged. *Perhaps my luck is about to change,* Annabelle thought, and closed her eyes with a brief prayer of hope.

Chapter 2

Simon Hunt had learned at an early age that since fate had not blessed him with noble blood, wealth, or unusual gifts, he would have to wrest his fortune from an often uncharitable world. He was ten times more aggressive and ambitious than the average man. People usually found it far easier to let him have his way rather than stand against him. Although Simon was domineering, perhaps even ruthless, his sleep at night was never troubled by pangs of conscience.

His father had been a butcher, providing comfortably for a family of six and enlisting Simon as his assistant when he was old enough to wield the heavy chopping blade. Years of working in his father's shop had given Simon the massive arms and brawny shoulders of a butcher. It had always been expected that he would eventually manage the family business, but at the age of twenty-one, Simon had disappointed his father by leaving the shop in search of a different livelihood. Upon investing his small accumulation of savings, Simon had quickly discovered his true talent in life— making money.

Simon loved the language of economics, the elements of risk, the interplay of trade and industry and politics . . . and he had realized immediately that before long the growing British railway network would be the primary means for banks to conduct their business efficiently. The remittance of cash and securities, the creation of fast-developing investment opportunities, would depend heavily on the service of the railroad. Following his instincts, Simon invested every cent he had in railroad speculation. Now, at thirty-three, he owned controlling portions of three manufacturing companies, a nine-acre foundry, and a shipyard. He was a guest—albeit an undesired one—in aristocratic ballrooms, and he sat shoulder to shoulder with peers on the boards of six companies.

After years of relentless work, he had gotten almost everything he had ever wanted. However, if someone had asked whether he was a happy man, Simon would have snorted at the question. Happiness, that elusive result of success, was a sure sign of complacency. By his very nature, Simon would never be complacent, or satisfied; nor did he want to be.

All the same . . . in the deepest, most private corner of his neglected heart, there was one wish Simon couldn't seem to extinguish.

He shot a covert glance across the ballroom, experiencing as always the peculiar sharp pang that the sight of Annabelle Peyton produced. With all the women that were available to him—and there were more than a few—no one had ever seized his attention with such all-encompassing thoroughness. Annabelle's appeal went beyond mere physical beauty, though God knew she'd been blessed with a surplus. Were there an ounce of poetry in Simon's soul, he might have thought of dozens of rapturous phrases to describe her charms. But he was common to the core, and he could not find words accurately to describe his attraction. All he knew was that sight of Annabelle in the glittering light of the chandeliers was very nearly knee-weakening.

Simon had never forgotten the first moment that he had seen her standing outside a panorama, digging through her purse with a little pucker on her forehead. The sun had picked out streaks of gold and champagne in her hair and made her skin glow. There had been something so delicious . . . so touchable . . . about her, the velvety skin and shining blue eyes, and the slight frown that he had longed to soothe away.

He had been altogether certain that Annabelle would have been married by now. The evidence that the Peytons had fallen on hard times had not signified to Simon, who had assumed that any peer with his brains intact would see her worth and claim her at once. But as two years had passed, and Annabelle had remained unwed, a fragile tendril of hope had awakened inside Simon. He saw a touching valiance in her determined search for a husband, the self-possession with which she wore her increasingly threadbare gowns . . . the clear value that she placed on herself, despite her lack of a dowry. The artful way she approached the process of husband-hunting brought to mind nothing so much as a seasoned gambler playing his last few cards in a losing game. Annabelle was smart, careful, uncompromising, and still beautiful, although lately the threat of poverty had lent a certain hardness to her eyes and mouth. Selfishly, Simon was not sorry for her financial hardship—it created an opportunity that he never would have had otherwise.

The problem was that Simon had not yet figured out how to make Annabelle want him, when she was so obviously repulsed by everything he was. Simon was well aware that there were few graces to his character. Moreover, he had no ambition to become a gentleman any more than a tiger aspired to become a house cat. He was merely a man with a great deal of money and all the accompanying frustration of realizing that it could not buy the thing he most wanted.

So far, Simon's strategy had been to wait patiently, knowing that desperation would eventually drive Annabelle to do things that she had never considered doing before. Privation had a way of presenting a situation in a whole new light. Soon Annabelle's game would end. She would be faced with the choice of marrying a poor man or becoming the mistress of a wealthy one. And in the latter case, his bed would be the one she ended up in.

"A tasty little tart, isn't she?" came a comment from nearby, and Simon turned toward Henry Burdick, whose father, a viscount, was reputedly on his deathbed. Caught in the interminable wait before his father kicked off and finally yielded the title and family fortune, Burdick spent the majority of his time gambling and skirt-chasing. He followed Simon's gaze to Annabelle, who was engaged in a lively conversation with the wallflowers around her.

"I wouldn't know," Simon returned, feeling a jolt of antipathy for Burdick and all his ilk, who'd been given all manner of privileges on a silver platter since the day they were born. And usually did nothing to justify fate's imprudent generosity.

Burdick smiled, his face florid from too much drink and rich food. "I intend to find out soon," he commented.

Burdick was hardly in the minority. No small number of men had set their sights on Annabelle, with the anticipation of a wolf pack trailing after a wounded prey. At the moment that she was at her weakest, and would offer the least resistance, one of them would move in for the kill. However, as in nature, the dominant male would always win out.

The shadow of a smile settled on Simon's hard mouth. "You surprise me," he murmured. "I would have assumed that a lady's predicament would inspire gallantry from gentlemen of your sort—and instead I find you entertaining the ill-bred notions that one would expect from *my* sort."

Burdick emitted a low laugh, missing the feral gleam in Simon's black eyes. "Lady or no, she'll have to choose one of us when her resources finally give out."

"Will none of you offer her marriage?" Simon asked idly.

"Good God, why?" Burdick licked his lips as anticipatory thoughts crossed his mind. "No need to marry the chit when she'll soon be available for the right price."

"Perhaps she has too much honor for that."

"Doubt it," the young aristocrat returned cheerfully. "Women that beautiful, and poor, can't afford honor. Besides, there is a rumor that she's already been giving over the goods to Lord Hodgeham."

"Hodgeham?" Inwardly startled, Simon kept his face expressionless. "What started that rumor?"

"Oh, Hodgeham's carriage has been seen at the mews behind the Peyton house at odd hours of the night . . . and according to some of their creditors, he takes care of their bills now and then." Burdick paused and chortled. "A night between those pretty thighs is worth paying the grocer's account, wouldn't you say?"

Simon's instantaneous response was a murderous impulse to separate Burdick's head from the rest of his body. He wasn't certain how much of the cold, splintering rage was fueled by the image of Annabelle Peyton in bed with Lord Hodgeham, and how much was elicited by Burdick's snide enjoyment of gossip that was very likely untrue.

"I would say that if you're going to slander a lady's reputation," Simon said in a dangerously pleasant tone, "you had better have some hard proof of what you're saying."

"Egads, gossip doesn't require *proof*," the young man replied with a wink. "And time will soon reveal the lady's true character. Hodgeham doesn't have the means to keep a prime beauty like that—before long she'll want more than he can deliver. I predict that at the season's end, she'll sail off to the fellow with the deepest pockets."

"Which would be mine," Simon said softly.

Burdick blinked in surprise, his smile fading as he wondered if he had heard correctly. "Wha—"

"I've watched as you and the pack of idiots you run with have sniffed at her heels for two years," Simon said, his eyes narrowing. "Now you've lost your chance at her."

"Lost my . . . what do you mean by that?" Burdick asked indignantly.

"I mean that I will afflict the most acute kind of pain, mental, physical, and financial, on the first man who dares to trespass on my territory. And the next person who repeats any unsubstantiated rumors about Miss Peyton in my hearing will find it shoved right back in his throat—along with my fist." Simon's smile contained a tigerish menace as he beheld Burdick's stunned face. "Tell that to anyone who may find it of interest," he advised, and strode away from the pompous, gape-jawed little runt.

Chapter 3

Having been returned to her town house by the elderly cousin who sometimes acted as her chaperone, Annabelle strode into the empty, flagstoned entrance hall. She stopped short at the sight of the hat that had been placed on the scallop-edged demilune table against the wall. It was a high-crowned gentleman's hat, gray banded with dark burgundy satin. A distinctive hat, compared to the simple black ones that most gentlemen wore. Annabelle had seen it on far too many occasions, perched on this very table like a coiled snake.

A stylish cane with a diamond-tipped handle leaned against the table. Annabelle entertained a lively desire to use the cane to bash in the crown of the hat—preferably while the owner was wearing it. Instead, she walked up the stairs with a leaden heart while a frown pinched her forehead.

As she neared the second floor where the family rooms were located, a heavyset man came to the top landing. He viewed her with an intolerable smirk, his complexion pink and moist from recent exertion, while a lopsided lock of his combed-over hair dangled like a rooster's crest.

"Lord Hodgeham," Annabelle said stiffly, swallowing against the shame and fury that had lumped in her throat. Hodgeham was one of the few people in the world whom she genuinely hated. A so-called friend of her late father's, Hodgeham paid infrequent calls to the household, but never at regular visiting hours. He came late at night, and against all dictates of decorum, he spent time alone in a private room with Annabelle's mother, Philippa. And in the days after his visits, Annabelle could hardly fail to notice that some of their most pressing bills had been mysteriously paid, and some irate creditor or another had been appeased. And Philippa was uncustomarily brittle and irritable, and disinclined to talk.

It was nearly impossible for Annabelle to believe that her mother, who had always shrunk from impropriety, would allow anyone the use of her body in return for money. Yet it was the only reasonable conclusion to draw, and it filled Annabelle with helpless shame and rage. Her anger was not directed solely at her mother—she was also furious at their situation, and herself for not yet having been able to land a husband. It had taken a long time for Annabelle to realize that, no matter how pretty and charming she was, and no matter how much interest a gentleman displayed, she was

not going to get an offer. At least not a respectable one.

Since her come-out, Annabelle had gradually
been forced to accept that her dreams of some
handsome, cultivated suitor who would fall in
love with her and make all her problems go
away was a naive fantasy. That disillusionment
had sunk in deeply during the prolonged disap-
pointment that was her third season. And now
in her fourth season, the unappealing image of
Annabelle-the-farmer's-wife was alarmingly close
to reality.

Stone-faced, Annabelle attempted to walk
past Hodgeham in silence. He stopped her with
a meaty hand on her arm. Annabelle jerked
back with such antipathy that the force of the
movement nearly caused her to lose her balance. "Don't touch me," she said, glaring into
his florid face.

Hodgeham's eyes appeared very blue against
the ruddiness of his complexion. Grinning, he
rested his hand on the top of the banister, preventing Annabelle from ascending to the landing. "So inhospitable," he murmured, in the
incongruous tenor voice that so many tall men
seemed to be afflicted with. "After the favors I
have done for your family—"

"You've done no favors for us," Annabelle
said tersely.

"You would have been cast into the streets
long ago if not for my generosity."

"Are you suggesting that I should be grateful?" Annabelle asked, her tone saturated with
loathing. "You're a filthy scavenger."

"I've taken nothing that wasn't willingly offered to me." Hodgeham reached out and touched her chin, the damp brush of his fingers making her recoil in disgust. "In truth, it's been tame sport. Your mother is too docile for my taste." He leaned closer, until the odor of his body—stale sweat liberally overlaid with cologne—filled Annabelle's nostrils with a pungent stench. "Perhaps the next time I'll try you out," he murmured.

No doubt he expected Annabelle to cry, or blush, or plead. Instead, she leveled a cold stare at him. "You vain old fool," she said evenly, "if I were to become someone's mistress, don't you think I could get someone better than you?"

Hodgeham eventually twisted his lips into a smile though Annabelle was pleased to see that it had taken some effort. "It's unwise to make an enemy of me. With a few well-placed words, I could ruin your family beyond all hope of redemption." He stared at the frayed fabric of her bodice and smiled contemptuously. "If I were you, I shouldn't be quite so disdainful, standing there in rags and paste jewels."

Annabelle flushed and knocked his hand away angrily as he reached out in an attempt to grope her bodice. Chuckling to himself, Hodgeham descended the stairs, while Annabelle waited in frozen silence. After she had heard the sound of the front door open and close, she hastened downstairs and turned the key in the lock. Breathing hard from anxiety and lingering outrage, she flattened her palms on the heavy oak door and leaned her forehead against one of the panels.

"That does it," she mumbled aloud, trembling with fury. No more Hodgeham, no more unpaid bills . . . they had all suffered enough. She would have to find someone to marry immediately—she would find the best prospect she could at the Hampshire hunting party and finally be done with it. And failing that . . .

She slid her hands slowly along the door panel, her palms leaving streaking imprints on the grainy wood. If she couldn't get someone to marry her, she could become some man's mistress. Athough no one seemed to want her as a wife, there seemed to be an infinite number of gentlemen willing to keep her in sin. If she was clever, she could earn a fortune. But she flinched at the thought of never again being able to go out in good society . . . being scorned and ostracized and valued only for her skills in bed. The alternative, living in virtuous poverty and taking in sewing or washing, or becoming a governess, was infinitely more perilous—a young woman in that position would be at *everyone's* mercy. And the pay wouldn't be enough to sustain her mother, or Jeremy, who would also have to go in service. It didn't seem that the three of them could afford Annabelle's morality. They lived in a house of cards . . . and the merest agitation would cause it to collapse.

The following morning, Annabelle sat at the breakfast table with a porcelain cup clasped in her icy fingers. Although she had just finished her tea, the ceramic was still warm from the sturdy brew. There was a tiny chip in the glaze, and she rubbed the pad of her thumb over it repeatedly, not looking up as she heard her mother, Philippa, enter the room.

"Tea?" she asked in a careful monotone, and heard Philippa's murmured assent. Pouring another cup from the pot before her, Annabelle sweetened it with a small lump of sugar and lightened it with a liberal splash of milk.

"I don't take it with sugar any longer," Philippa said. "I've come to prefer it without."

The day when her mother stopped liking sweets was the day they began serving ice water in hell. "We can still afford sugar for your tea," Annabelle replied, stirring the cup with a few brisk swirls of her spoon. Glancing upward, she slid the cup and saucer to Philippa's place at the table. As she had expected, her mother looked sullen and haggard, with shame writhing behind her bitter facade. Once she would have found it inconceivable that her dashing, high-spirited mother—always so much prettier than anyone else's mother—could have worn such an expression. And as she stared at Philippa's taut face, Annabelle realized that her own facade was very nearly as world-weary, her mouth holding the same edge of disenchantment.

"How was the ball?" Philippa asked, holding her face close to her own tea so that the steam wafted over her face.

"The usual disaster," Annabelle said, softening the honesty of her reply with a deliberately light laugh. "The only man who asked me to dance was Mr. Hunt."

"Dear heaven," Philippa murmured, and drank a scalding mouthful of tea. "Did you accept him?"

"Of course not. There would be no purpose to it. When he looks at me, it is clear that he has anything but marriage in mind."

"Even men such as Mr. Hunt do eventually marry," Philippa countered, glancing up from her porcelain cup. "And you would be an ideal wife for him . . . you could perhaps be a softening influence, and help to ease his way into decent society—"

"Good Lord, Mama—it sounds as if you are encouraging me to accept his attentions."

"No . . ." Philippa picked up her spoon and needlessly stirred her tea. "Not if you truly find Mr. Hunt objectionable. However, if you could manage to bring him to scratch, we would all certainly be well provided for . . ."

"He is not the marrying kind, Mama. Everyone knows it. No matter what I did, I could never get a respectable offer from him." Annabelle dug through the sugar bowl with a tiny pair of tarnished silver tongs, searching for the smallest lump she could find. Extracting a morsel of raw brown sugar, she dropped it into her cup and drowned it with fresh tea.

Philippa drank her tea, her gaze carefully averted as she jumped to a new thread of conversation that Annabelle perceived had a disagreeable connection to the last. "We haven't the means to keep Jeremy in school for his next

term. I haven't paid the servants in two months.
There are bills—"

"Yes, I know all of that," Annabelle said,
flushing slightly with a swift burn of annoyance. "I'll find a husband, Mama. Very soon."
Somehow she forced a shallow smile to her face.
"How do you feel about a jaunt to Hampshire?
Now that the season is coming to a close, many
people will be leaving London in search of new
amusements—in particular, a hunt given by
Lord Westcliff at his country estate."

Philippa glanced at her with new alertness.
"I wasn't aware that we had received an invitation from the earl."

"We haven't," Annabelle replied. "Yet. But
we will . . . and I have a feeling that good things
await us in Hampshire, Mama."

Chapter 4

Two days before Annabelle and her mother
left for Hampshire, a towering stack of
boxes and parcels arrived. It took the footman
three trips to convey them from the entrance
hall to Annabelle's room upstairs, where he
piled them in a mountain beside the bed. Un-
wrapping them carefully, Annabelle discovered at least a half dozen gowns that had never
been worn . . . taffeta silks and muslins in rich
colors, and matching jackets lined in butter-
soft chamois, and a ball gown made of heavy
ivory silk with spills of delicate Belgium lace at
the bodice and sleeves. There were also gloves,
shawls, scarves, and hats, of such quality and
beauty that they nearly made Annabelle want
to weep. The gowns and accessories must have
cost a fortune—undoubtedly nothing to the
Bowman girls, but to Annabelle, the gift was
overwhelming.

Picking up the note that had been delivered

along with the parcels, she broke the wax seal
and read the decisively scrawled lines.

*From your fairy godmothers, otherwise
known as Lillian and Daisy. Here's to a
successful hunt in Hampshire.*

*P.S. You're not going to lose your nerve,
are you?*

She wrote back:

Dear Fairy Godmothers,

*Nerve is the only thing I've got left.
Thank you endlessly for the gowns. I
am in ecstasy at finally being able to
wear pretty clothes again. It is one of my
many failings, to love beautiful things so
dearly.*

                    Your devoted Annabelle

*P.S. Am returning the shoes, however,
as they are far too small. And I'd always
heard that American girls had large feet!*

Dear Annabelle,

*Is it a failing to love beautiful things? That
must be an English notion, as we are certain that it has never occurred to anyone
in Manhattanville. Just for that remark
about feet, we're going to make you play*

Rounders with us in Hampshire. You will love whacking balls with sticks. There is nothing quite so satisfying.

Dear Lillian and Daisy,

I will consent to Rounders only if you can persuade Evie to join in, which I highly doubt. And though I won't know until I've tried it, I can think of lots of things more satisfying than whacking balls with sticks. Finding a husband comes to mind . . .

By the way, what does one wear to play Rounders? A walking costume?

Dear Annabelle,

We play in our knickers, of course. One can't run properly in skirts.

Dear Lillian and Daisy,

The word "knickers" is unfamiliar to me. Can you possibly be referring to under-garments? Surely you are not suggesting that we shall romp about outdoors in our drawers like savage children . . . ?

Dear Annabelle,

The word is derived from "Knickerbock-ers"—a level of New York society from *which we are ritually excluded. In America, "drawers" belong inside a piece of furniture. And Evie says yes.*

Dear Evie,

I did not trust my eyes when the Bowman sisters wrote to inform me that you have agreed to play Rounders in knickers. Have you really said so? I am hoping that you will deny it, as I had made my acceptance contingent upon yours.

Dear Annabelle,

It is my belief that this association with the Bowmans will help to cure me of my shyness. Rounders-in-knickers seems just the way to begin. Have I shocked you? I've never shocked anyone before, not even myself! I do hope that you are impressed by my willingness to jump into the spirit of things.

Dear Evie,

Impressed, amused, and somewhat apprehensive about what scrapes these Bowmans will land us in. Where, pray tell, are we to find a place where we may play Rounders-in-knickers unobserved? Yes, I am thoroughly shocked, you shameless hussy.

Dear Annabelle,

I am coming to believe that there are two kinds of people . . . those who choose to be masters of their own fate and those who wait in chairs while others dance. I would rather be one of the former than the latter. As to how and when Rounders game shall take place, I am satisfied to leave such details to the Bowmans.

With all fondness,
Evie the hussy

During the flurry of these and other playful notes that were sent back and forth, Annabelle began to experience something she had forgotten long ago . . . the delight of having friends. As her past friends had moved into the hallowed existence of married couples, she had been left behind. Her wallflower status, not to mention her lack of money, had created a chasm that friendship could not seem to bridge. In the past few years she had come to be increasingly self-reliant, and had even made efforts to avoid the company of the girls with whom she had once talked and giggled and shared secrets.

However, in one fell swoop she had acquired three friends with whom she had something in common, despite their radically different backgrounds. They were all young women with hopes and dreams and fears . . . each of them entirely familiar with the sight of a gentleman's polished black shoes walking by their row of chairs in search of more promising quarry. The wallflowers had nothing to lose by helping each other, and everything to gain.

"Annabelle," came her mother's voice from the doorway, as she carefully packed the boxes of new gloves into a valise, "I have a question, and you must answer it honestly."

"I am always honest with you, Mama," Annabelle replied, looking up from her task. Guilt swept over her as she beheld Philippa's lovely, careworn face. Dear God, she was tired of Philippa's guilt, and her own. She felt pity and despair for the sacrifice that her mother had made in sleeping with Lord Hodgeham. And yet, in the back of Annabelle's mind, the unseemly thought occurred to her that if Philippa had chosen to do such a thing, why couldn't she have at least set herself up properly as a real mistress instead of settling for the petty little wads of cash that Lord Hodgeham gave her?

"Where did those clothes come from?" Philippa asked, pale but earnest as she stared directly into Annabelle's eyes.

Annabelle frowned. "I've already told you, Mama—they came from Lillian Bowman. Why are you staring at me like that?"

"Did these clothes come from a man? Perhaps from Mr. Hunt?"

Annabelle's mouth fell open. "You're actually asking if I . . . with *him*? Good Lord, Mama! Even if I had the inclination, I haven't had the slightest opportunity. How in heaven's name did you come up with such an idea?"

Her mother met her gaze without blinking. "You've mentioned Mr. Hunt quite often this season. Far more than any other gentlemen. And these gowns are obviously quite costly . . ."

"They are not from him," Annabelle said firmly.

Philippa seemed to relax, but a question remained in her eyes. Unaccustomed to having anyone look at her with suspicion, Annabelle picked up a hat and set it at a smart angle over her forehead. "They're not," she repeated.

Simon Hunt's mistress . . . Turning toward the looking glass, Annabelle saw an oddly frozen expression on her face. She supposed that her mother was right—she had mentioned Hunt quite often of late. There was something about him that made thoughts of him linger in Annabelle's mind long after they had seen each other. No other man of her acquaintance possessed Hunt's charismatic, wicked appeal, nor had any man ever been so openly interested in her. And now, in the last few weeks of a failed season, she found herself contemplating things that no decent young woman should ever think about. She knew that without much effort, she could become Hunt's mistress, and all her troubles would be over. He was a wealthy man—he would give her whatever she wanted, pay her family's debts, and provide her with beautiful clothes, jewels, her own carriage, her own house . . . all that in return for sleeping with him.

The thought sent a sharp quiver through her abdomen. She tried to imagine being in bed with Simon Hunt, what things he might demand of her, his hands on her body, his mouth—

Flushing deeply, she forced the image aside and toyed with the silk rose adornments on the corded band of her hat. If she became Simon Hunt's mistress, he would own her completely, in bed and out of it, and the thought of being so completely at his mercy was appalling. A mocking voice in her head asked, "Is your honor so important to you? More important than your family's welfare? Or even your own survival?"

"Yes," Annabelle said under her breath, staring at her own pale, purposeful reflection. "Right now it is." She couldn't answer for later. But until every last hope was exhausted, she still had her self-respect . . . and she would fight to keep it.

Chapter 5

It was easy to see why the name of Hampshire was derived from the Old English word "hamm," referring to a water meadow. The county was rich with such meadows, not to mention heath and lush woodland that had once been earmarked as royal hunting grounds. With its contrast of dramatic scarps and deep green vales, and rivers flush with trout, Hampshire offered activities for every sportsman. The earl of Westcliff's estate, Stony Cross Park, was set like a jewel in a fertile river valley that scored gently through acres of forest. It seemed that there were always guests at Stony Cross Park, for Westcliff was an accomplished host as well as an avid hunter.

From all appearances, Lord Westcliff deserved his reputation of immaculate honor and high principles. He was not the sort to be involved in scandal, as he seemed to have little tolerance for the intrigues and slippery morality of London society. Instead, he spent much of his time in the country, shouldering his responsibilities and caring for his tenants. On occasion he traveled to London to further his business interests or involve himself in a political matter that demanded his attention.

It was on one of these trips that Annabelle had met the earl, when they had been introduced at a soirée. Although he was not classically handsome, Westcliff was not without attractions. He was only of medium height, but he possessed the powerful form of a seasoned sportsman and an air of unmistakable virility. All that, combined with an immense personal fortune and one of the oldest earldoms in the peerage, made him the most desirable matrimonial catch in England. Naturally, Annabelle had wasted no time in beginning a determined flirtation with him when they had first met. However, Westcliff was inured to such attentions from eager young women and had immediately labeled her as a husband hunter—which had stung, even though it was the truth.

Ever since Annabelle had been rebuffed by Westcliff, she had made an effort to avoid him. She did happen to like his younger sister, Lady Olivia, a softhearted girl who was of an age with Annabelle and had been tainted by scandal in her past. And it was thanks to Lady Olivia's kindness that Annabelle and Evie had been invited to this party. For the next three weeks, both the four-legged and the two-legged varieties of prey would be under siege at Stony Cross Park.

"My lady," Annabelle exclaimed, as Lady

Olivia came to welcome them. "How kind of you to invite us! London was positively stifling—the refreshing climate of Hampshire is precisely what we needed."

Lady Olivia smiled. Although she was a small and rather unassuming girl with average features, she seemed extraordinarily pretty on this occasion, her face glowing with happiness. According to Lillian and Daisy, Lady Olivia was betrothed to an American millionaire. *"Is it a love match?"* Annabelle had asked in her last letter to them, and Lillian had written back that it reportedly was.

Bringing her mind back to the present, Annabelle smiled as Lady Olivia took her hands in a welcoming clasp. "And you are precisely what *we* needed," Lady Olivia exclaimed with a laugh. "The place is overrun with males in search of sport—I informed the earl that we simply *had* to invite some women to keep the atmosphere reasonably civilized. Come, let me accompany you to your rooms."

Picking up the skirts of the new salmon pink muslin from Lillian, Annabelle followed Lady Olivia up the front steps into the entrance hall. "How is Lord Westcliff?" Annabelle asked as they ascended one side of the grand double staircase. "In good health, I hope?"

"My brother is quite well, thank you. Although I fear he is driving himself to distraction with plans for my wedding. He insists on overseeing every detail."

"A reflection of his great affection for you, I'm certain," Philippa said.

Lady Olivia laughed wryly. "It is more a reflection of his great need to control everything within his reach. I'm afraid that it won't be easy to find a bride who will be strong-willed enough to manage him."

Catching her mother's meaningful sideways glance, Annabelle shook her head slightly. It would do no good to encourage Philippa's hopes in that direction. However . . . "I happen to know of a strong-willed and quite charming young woman who is yet unmarried," she commented. "An American, as a matter of fact."

"Are you referring to one of the Bowman sisters?" Lady Olivia asked. "I have not yet made their acquaintance, though their father has stayed at Stony Cross before."

"Both sisters are delightful in every regard," Annabelle said.

"Excellent," Lady Olivia exclaimed. "We may yet find a match for my brother."

Reaching the second floor, they paused to glance at the people milling about the entrance hall below. "I'm afraid there are not as many unmarried men here as one could wish for," Lady Olivia commented. "But there are a few . . . Lord Kendall comes to mind. If you like, I will introduce you to him when the opportunity presents itself."

"Thank you, I would enjoy that *very* much."

"I'm afraid he is somewhat reticent, though," Lady Olivia added. "He may not appeal to someone as high-spirited as you, Annabelle."

"On the contrary," Annabelle said quickly, "I find reticence to be a most attractive quality in a man. Gentlemen with dignified reserve are so much more pleasant than those who are forever swaggering and boasting about themselves." *Like Simon Hunt*, she thought darkly, whose high self-opinion couldn't be more obvious.

Before Lady Olivia could reply, her gaze was caught from afar by that of a tall golden-haired gentleman who had come to stand in the entrance hall below. He stood in a cultivated slouch, resting his shoulder against a column, his hands thrust into his coat pockets. Annabelle knew instantly that he was an American. His irreverent grin and blue eyes, and the relaxed way he wore his elegant clothes, gave him away. Moreover, Lady Olivia blushed and seemed to require an extra breath or two, from the way he was looking at her. "Do pardon me," she said absently. "I . . . my fiancé . . . he seems to require me for something . . ." And she drifted away with a dreamy over-the-shoulder comment about their room being the fifth on the right. Instantly, a housemaid appeared to show them the rest of the way, and Annabelle heaved a sigh.

"There will be vicious competition for Lord Kendall," she fretted aloud. "I hope he hasn't already been taken."

"He can't be the *only* unmarried gentleman here," Philippa remarked hopefully. "One must not forget Lord Westcliff himself."

"Don't entertain any hope in that direction," Annabelle told her wryly. "The earl was distinctly underwhelmed by me when we met."

"That was a great lapse in judgment on his part," came her mother's indignant reply.

Smiling, Annabelle reached down and squeezed Philippa's gloved hand. "Thank you, Mama. But I had better set my sights on a far more attainable target."

As guests continued to arrive, some went immediately to their rooms to refresh themselves with a midday nap, in anticipation of the supper and welcome dance that would be held later. Gossip-minded ladies congregated in the parlor and card room, while the gentlemen played billiards or smoked in the library. After their maid finished unpacking their clothes, Philippa decided to doze in their room. It was a small but lovely bedchamber, with flowered French paper on the walls and windows swathed in pale blue silk.

Too impatient and excited to sleep, Annabelle reflected that Evie and the Bowman sisters had probably arrived. Even so, they would want some time to restore themselves after traveling. Rather than endure hours of enforced inactivity, Annabelle decided to explore the grounds outside the manor. It was a warm, sunlit day, and she craved exercise after the long carriage ride. Changing into a blue muslin day dress shaped with rows of tiny box pleats, she left her room.

She slipped out a side entrance, passing a few servants on the way, and walked into a gentle flood of sunlight. There was something wonderful about the atmosphere at Stony Cross Park. One could easily imagine it as some magical place set in some far-off land. The surrounding forest was so deep and thick as to be primeval in appearance, while the twelve-acre garden behind the manor seemed too perfect to be real.

Annabelle skirted the edge of the terraced gardens at the back of the manor and followed a graveled path set between raised beds of poppies and geraniums. The atmosphere soon became thick with the perfume of flowers, as the path paralleled a drystone wall covered with tumbles of pink and cream roses.

Wandering more slowly, Annabelle crossed through an orchard of ancient pear trees, sculpted by decades into fantastic shapes. Farther off, a canopy of silver birch led to woodland beds that appeared to melt seamlessly into the forest beyond. The graveled path ended in a small circle, where a stone table had been centered. Drawing closer, Annabelle saw the thick stubs of two melted candles that had been burned directly on the stone surface. She smiled a bit wistfully, realizing that the privacy of the clearing must have been the perfect setting for some romantic interlude.

Inured to the dreamy atmosphere around them, a line of five fat white ducks waddled across the graveled circle, heading to a raised pool on the other side of the garden. It appeared that the ducks had been long accustomed to the multitude of visitors at Stony Cross Park, for they ignored Annabelle completely as they passed by. They quacked loudly in anticipation of reaching the artificial pond, their progress so comically animated that Annabelle couldn't help laughing.

Before her amusement had faded, she heard the crunch of a heavy footstep on the gravel. It was a man, who was evidently returning from a walk in the forest. He had lifted his head to stare at her with an arrested expression, his dark gaze meeting hers.

Annabelle froze.

Simon Hunt, she thought, shocked beyond the power of speech to see him there at Stony Cross. She had always associated him with town life—she usually saw him indoors, at night, confined by walls and windows and starched neckties. However, in these day-lit natural surroundings, he seemed a different creature altogether. His broad-shouldered build, so irreconcilable with the narrow cut of evening clothes, seemed utterly right for the rough weave of a hunting coat and the shirt that had been left open at the throat, no cravat anywhere in sight. He was darker than usual, his skin burnished amber from a great deal of time spent out of doors. The sun glanced off his close-cropped hair, striking a rich shimmer from thick locks that were not quite black, but an intense shade of brown. His features, finely delineated by sunlight, were hard and prominent and striking. The few touches of softness in his face . . . the thick crescents of his dark lashes, the lush curve of his lower lip, were all the more intriguing for their uncompromising setting.

Hunt and Annabelle stared at each other in silent bemusement, as if someone had posed a question that neither of them knew how to answer.

The moment lengthened uncomfortably, until Simon Hunt finally spoke. "A pretty sound, that," he said softly.

Annabelle struggled to find her voice. "What is?" she asked.

"Your laughter."

Annabelle experienced a sharp little ache in her midriff that was neither pain nor pleasure. The disarming stab of sensation was unlike anything she had ever experienced before. Unconsciously she put her fingers over the spot just beneath her ribs. Hunt's gaze shot to her hand before easing slowly back up to her face. He moved nearer to the stone table, closing some of the distance between them.

"I hadn't expected to see you here." His gaze moved over her in a disconcertingly thorough sweep. "But of course, it's the logical place for a woman in your situation."

Annabelle narrowed her eyes. "In my situation?"

"Trying to catch a husband," he clarified.

"You may set your mind at ease, Mr. Hunt, as I have no intention of separating you from your precious freedom. You're the very last on the list."

"What list?" Hunt contemplated her in the tense silence that followed, working it out for himself. "Ah. You've actually made a list of potential husbands?" Amusement danced in his eyes. "It's a relief to hear that I'm not in the running, as I have resolved to avoid being padlocked into marriage at all cost. But I can't seem to stop myself from asking . . . who is at the top of the list?"

Annabelle refused to answer. Even as she cursed her own tendency to fidget, she could not keep from reaching over to the lumpen stub of a candle and picking at it with the edges of her fingernails.

"Why are you here?" she asked.

"I'm a friend of Westcliff's," he said easily.

"The two of you are as different as chalk from cheese."

"As it happens, the earl and I do have some common interests. We both like to hunt, and we share a remarkable number of political beliefs. Unlike most peers, Westcliff does not allow himself to be chained by the restrictions of aristocratic life."

"Good Lord," Annabelle mocked, "you seem to view nobility as a condition of imprisonment."

"I do, as a matter of fact."

"Then I can hardly wait to incarcerate myself and dispose of the keys."

That made Hunt laugh. "You would probably do quite well as a peer's wife."

Recognizing that his tone was far from complimentary, Annabelle frowned at him. "If you dislike the peerage so much, I wonder that you spend so much time among them."

His eyes glinted wickedly. "They have their uses. And I don't dislike them—it's just that I have no desire to be one of them. In case you haven't noticed, the peerage—or at least the way of life they've known 'til now—is dying."

Annabelle reacted with a wide-eyed glance, genuinely shocked by the statement. "What do you mean?"

"Most landholding peers are losing their fortunes, seeing them divided and shrunken by ever-increasing numbers of relatives who require support . . . and then there is the transformation of the economy to contend with. The rule of the great landowner is fast coming to an end. Only men like Westcliff—who is open to new ways of doing things—will weather the change."

"With your invaluable assistance, of course," Annabelle said.

"That's right," Hunt said with such self-satisfaction that she couldn't help laughing.

"Have you ever considered making at least a pretense of humility, Mr. Hunt? Just for the sake of politeness?"

"I don't believe in false modesty."

"People might like you more if you did."

"Would you?"

Her nails dug into the soft pastel-colored wax, and she flashed Hunt a quick glance to measure the depth of mockery in his eyes. To her bewilderment, there was none. He seemed seriously interested in her answer. As he watched her intently, she felt a dismaying tide of pink creep over her face. She was not at all comfortable in this situation, conversing alone with Simon Hunt while he lounged beside her like a lazy, inquisitive pirate. Her gaze fell to the large hand he had braced on the table, the fingers long and clean and sun-browned, with nails cut so short that the crescents of white were barely visible.

"'Like' may be going a bit far," Annabelle said, releasing her biting grip on the candle. The more she tried to control her flush, the worse it became, until it surged into her hairline. "I suppose I could tolerate your company more easily if you would try to behave like a gentleman."

"For example?"

"To begin with, the . . . the way you like to correct people . . ."

"Isn't honesty a virtue?"

"Yes . . . but it hardly makes for the best conversation!" Ignoring his low laugh, she continued. "And the way you talk so openly about money is vulgar, especially to those in higher circles. Nice people pretend that they don't care about money, or how to earn it, or invest it, or any of the other things you like to discuss."

"I've never understood why the enthusiastic pursuit of wealth should be held in such disdain."

"Perhaps because such pursuit is accompanied by so many vices . . . greed, selfishness, duplicity—"

"Those aren't my faults."

Annabelle raised her brows. "Oh?"

Smiling, Hunt shook his head slowly, the sunlight glittering on his sable locks. "If I were greedy and selfish, I would keep most of the profits from my businesses. However, my partners will tell you that they have been handsomely rewarded for their investments. And my employees are well paid by anyone's standards.

As for being duplicitous—I think it's fairly obvious that I have the opposite problem. I'm truthful—which is very nearly unpardonable in civilized society."

For some reason, Annabelle could not help grinning back at the ill-bred scoundrel. She pushed away from the table and dusted her skirts. "I'm not going to waste any more of my time telling you how to be polite when it's perfectly obvious that you don't wish to be."

"Your time wasn't wasted," he said, coming around to her. "I'm going to lend some deep consideration to changing my ways."

"Don't bother," she said, the smile lingering on her lips. "You're a hopeless cause, I'm afraid. Now, if you'll excuse me, I'm going to continue my walk through the garden. Have a pleasant afternoon, Mr. Hunt."

"Let me come with you," he said softly. "You can lecture me some more. I'll even listen."

She wrinkled her nose at him impudently. "No, you won't." She started off on the gravel path, aware of his gaze on her back until she disappeared into the pear orchard.

Chapter 6

*J*ust before supper on the first evening of the party, Annabelle, Lillian, and Daisy met in the downstairs receiving room, a spacious area set with clusters of chairs and tables where many of the guests had chosen to congregate.

"I should have known that dress would look a hundred times better on you than me," Lillian Bowman said gleefully, hugging Annabelle and holding her at arm's length to gaze at her. "Oh, it's torture, being friends with someone so ravishing."

Annabelle was wearing another of her new gowns, a yellow silk with fluttering tulle skirts caught up at narrow intervals with tiny bunches of silk violets. Her hair was pinned at the back of her head in an intricately braided plait. "I have many flaws," Annabelle informed Lillian with a smile.

"Really? What are they?"

Annabelle grinned. "I'm hardly going to admit them if you haven't already noticed."

"Lillian tells everyone about her flaws," Daisy said, her brown eyes twinkling. "She's *proud* of them."

"I do have a terrible temper," Lillian acknowledged smugly. "And I can curse like a sailor."

"Who taught you to do that?" Annabelle asked.

"My grandmother. She was a washerwoman. And my grandfather was the soap maker from whom she bought her supplies. Since she worked near the docks, most of her customers were sailors and dockers, who taught her words so vulgar that it would curl your hair ribbons to hear them."

Laughter rustled in Annabelle's chest. She was thoroughly charmed by the mischievous spirit of two girls who were unlike anyone she had ever known before. Unfortunately, it was difficult to imagine either Lillian or Daisy being happy as the wife of a peer. Most gentlemen of the aristocracy wanted to marry a girl who was serene, regal, self-effacing . . . the kind of wife whose sole purpose was to make her husband the focus of admiring attention.

Evie entered the room with the reluctance of a mouse who had been thrown into a sack of cats, but her face relaxed as she saw Annabelle and the Bowmans. Murmuring something to her dour-looking aunt, she headed toward them with a smile.

Annabelle slipped her arm behind Evie's slender waist. "How lovely you look tonight," she said. Evie's hair had been piled at the crown of her head in a mass of gleaming red curls and fastened with pearl-tipped pins. The scattering of amber freckles across her nose only increased her appeal, as if nature had given in to a moment of whimsy and sprinkled a few flecks of extra sunlight over her.

Evie leaned into her partial hug as if she was seeking comfort. "Aunt F-Florence says I look like a f-flaming torch with my hair pinned up like this," she said.

Daisy scowled at the comment. "Your aunt Florence should hardly make such statements when *she* looks like a hobgoblin."

"Daisy, hush," Lillian said sternly.

Annabelle kept her gloved arm around Evie's waist, reflecting that from what little the girl had related to her, Aunt Florence appeared to take heartless delight in shredding what little confidence Evie possessed. After Evie's mother had died at a young age, the family had taken the unfortunate girl into its respectable bosom—and the ensuing years of criticism had left Evie's self-confidence decidedly battered.

Evie's smile contained a flash of amusement as she regarded the Bowman sisters. "She's not a h-hobgoblin. I've always thought of her as m-more of a troll."

Annabelle laughed in delight at the little jab. "Tell me," she said, "have any of you seen Lord Kendall yet? I was told that he is one of the very few unmarried men here—and aside from Westcliff, the only bachelor with a title."

"The competition for Kendall is going to be brutal," Lillian remarked. "Fortunately, Daisy and I have come up with just the plan to entrap an unsuspecting gentleman into marriage." She crooked her finger for them to come closer.

"I'm afraid to ask," Annabelle said, "but how?"

"You will entice him into a compromising situation, at which time the three of us will conveniently happen along and 'catch' you together. And then the gentleman will be honor-bound to ask for your hand in marriage."

Evie looked at Annabelle dubiously. "It's rather underh-handed, isn't it?"

"There's no 'rather' about it," Annabelle replied. "But I'm afraid that I can think of nothing better, can you?"

Evie shook her head. "No," she admitted. "The question is, are we all s-so desperate to catch husbands that we'll resort to any means, be they fair or foul?"

"I am," Annabelle said without hesitation.

"So are we," Daisy said cheerfully.

Evie regarded the three of them uncertainly. "I can't toss aside *all* scruples. That is, I sh-shouldn't care to deceive a man into doing something that he—"

"Evie," Lillian interrupted impatiently, "men *expect* to be deceived in these matters. They're happiest that way. If one were straightforward with them, the whole prospect of marriage would be too alarming, and none of them would ever do it."

Laughing, Annabelle returned her attention to Evie, who wore a nonplussed frown. "Evie," she said gently, "until now, I've always tried to do things the right way. But it hasn't gotten me very far—and at this point, I am willing to try something new . . . aren't you?"

Still not seeming entirely convinced, Evie surrendered with a nod of resignation.

"That's the spirit," Annabelle said encouragingly.

As they conversed, there was a minor stir in the crowd as Lord Westcliff appeared. Seeming entirely comfortable in the position of managing things, he deftly paired gentlemen with ladies in preparation for the procession to the dining room. Although Westcliff was not the tallest man in the room, he had a magnetic presence that was impossible to ignore. Annabelle wondered why some people possessed such a quality—something unnameable that lent significance to every gesture they made and every word they spoke. Glancing at Lillian, she saw that the American girl had noticed it, too.

"There's a man who thinks well of himself," Lillian said dryly. "I wonder what—if anything—could ever set him back on his heels."

"I can't imagine," Annabelle replied. "But I would like to be there if it happens."

Evie drew closer and nudged her arm lightly. "There is Lord K-Kendall, in the corner."

"How do you know that he is Kendall?"

"Because he is surrounded by a dozen unmarried women who are circling him like sh-sharks."

"Good point," Annabelle said, staring at the young man and his milling entourage. William, Lord Kendall, seemed befuddled by the inordinate amount of female attention he was receiving. He was a fair-haired, slightly built young man, his lean face adorned by a pair of perfectly polished spectacles. The reflection of the glass lenses flashed as his perplexed gaze moved from face to face. The passionate interest being shown to a man of Kendall's timid demeanor proved that there was no aphrodisiac more effective than end-of-season bachelorhood. Whereas Kendall had been supremely uninteresting to these same girls last January, by June he had acquired an irresistible allure.

"He looks like a nice man," Annabelle said thoughtfully.

"He looks like he'll spook easily," Lillian commented. "If I were you, I'd try to appear as bashful and helpless as possible when you meet him."

Annabelle gave her an ironic glance. " 'Helpless' has never been my forte. I'll try for bashful, but I can't promise anything."

"I don't foresee that you'll have any problem in diverting Kendall's interest from those girls to you," Lillian replied confidently. "After supper, when the ladies and gentlemen return here for tea and conversation, we'll find some way to introduce you."

"How should I . . ." Annabelle began, and paused as she felt a soft prickle along the nape of her neck, as if someone had drawn the fronds of a fern across her skin. Wondering what had caused it, she reached up to touch the back of her neck, and suddenly found her gaze caught by Simon Hunt's.

Hunt was standing across the room, leaning one shoulder negligently against the side of a flat pilaster, while a group of three men around him were engaged in conversation. It was clear that he had noticed her interest in Kendall.

Hell's bells, she thought in vexation, and deliberately turned her back to him. She wouldn't put it past Hunt to cause trouble for her. "Have you noticed that Mr. Hunt is here?" Annabelle asked her friends in a low voice, and saw their eyes widen.

"*Your* Mr. Hunt?" Lillian sputtered, while Daisy whipped her head around to catch a glimpse of him.

"He's not mine!" Annabelle protested, making a comical face. "But yes, he's standing on the other side of the room. I saw him earlier today, actually. He claims to be a close friend of the earl's." She frowned and predicted darkly, "Mr. Hunt will do everything possible to wreck our plans."

"Would he really be so s-selfish as to prevent you from marrying?" Evie asked in amazement. "With the intention of making you into his . . . his . . ."

"Kept woman," Annabelle finished for her. "It's hardly outside the realm of possibility. Mr. Hunt has a reputation for stopping at nothing to have his way."

"That may be true," Lillian commented, her mouth firming with determination. "But he's not going to have *you*—I swear it."

Supper was a magnificent presentation, with gigantic silver tureens and platters carried in a ceaseless procession around the three long tables in the dining room. Annabelle could scarcely credit that the guests would dine like this every night, but the gentleman on her left—the parish vicar—assured her that this was commonplace for Westcliff's table. "The earl and his family are renowned for their balls and supper parties," he said. "Lord Westcliff is the most accomplished host of the peerage."

Annabelle was not inclined to argue. It had been a long time since she had been served such exquisite food. The lukewarm offerings at the London soirées and parties couldn't begin to compare to this feast. In the past few months the Peyton household had not been able to afford much more than bread, bacon, and soup, with the occasional helping of fried sole or stewed mutton.

Hungrily she consumed a bowl of soup made with champagne and Camembert, followed by delicate veal strips coated in herb-dressed sauce, and tender vegetable marrow in cream . . . fish baked in paper cases, which let out a burst of fragrant steam when opened . . . tiny buttered potatoes served on beds of watercress . . . and, most delightful of all, fruit relish served in hollowed-out orange rinds.

Annabelle was so engrossed in the meal that several minutes passed before she noticed that Simon Hunt had been seated near the head of Lord Westcliff's table. Lifting a glass of diluted wine to her lips, she glanced discreetly at him. Hunt was exquisitely dressed as usual, in a formal black coat and a rich pewter-shaded waistcoat, its silk weave gleaming with a quiet luster. His sun-darkened skin contrasted sharply with the starched white linen at his throat, the knot of his cravat as precise as a knife blade. His heavy dark hair needed an application of pomade . . . already a thick forelock had fallen over his forehead. It bothered Annabelle for some reason, that unruly lock. She wanted to push it back from his face.

As Hunt's gaze met hers, Annabelle was perturbed by the realization that she had been staring at him. Staring, and fantasizing. Although they were sitting far apart from each other, she was aware of an immediate, electric connection between them . . . there was an arrested expression on his face, and she wondered what he saw that fascinated him so. Coloring violently, she tore her gaze away and dug her fork into a casserole of leeks and mushrooms blanketed with shavings of white truffle.

After supper, the ladies retired to the parlor for coffee and tea while the gentlemen remained at the tables for port. In the traditional style, the group would eventually reunite in the drawing room. As clusters of women laughed and chatted easily in the parlor, Annabelle sat with Evie, Lillian, and Daisy. "Have you found out anything about Lord Kendall?" she asked, hoping that one of them might have gleaned some gossip from the dinner conversation. "Is there anyone in particular whom he might have taken an interest in?"

"The field seems to be open so far," Lillian replied.

"I asked Mother what she knew about Kendall," Daisy supplied, "and she said that he has a sizable fortune and is unencumbered by debt."

"How would she know?" Annabelle asked.

"At Mother's request," Daisy explained, "our father commissioned a written report on every eligible peer in England. And she's memorized it. She says that the ideal suitor for either one of us would be a poverty-stricken duke whose title would guarantee the Bowmans' social success, while our money would ensure his cooperation in the marriage." Daisy's smile turned sardonic, and she reached over to pat her older sister's hand as she added, "They made up a rhyme about Lillian, back in New York . . . 'Marry Lillian, you'll get a million.' The saying became so popular that it was one of the reasons we had to leave for London. Our family looked like a bunch of gauche, overly ambitious idiots."

"And we're not?" Lillian asked wryly.

Daisy crossed her eyes. "I'm only fortunate that we left before they could make up a rhyme about me."

"I have," Lillian said. "Marry Daisy, and you can be lazy."

Daisy gave her a speaking glance, and her sister grinned. "Never fear," Lillian continued, "eventually we will succeed in infiltrating London society, and then we'll marry Lord Heavydebts and Lord Shallowpockets, and finally assume our places as ladies of the manor."

Annabelle shook her head with a sympathetic

smile, while Evie left with a murmur, presumably to attend to her private needs. Annabelle almost felt sorry for the Bowmans, for it was becoming apparent that their chances of marrying for love were no greater than hers.

"Is it both your parents' ambition for you to marry a title?" Annabelle asked. "What is your father's opinion on the matter?"

Lillian shrugged nonchalantly. "For as long as I can remember, Father has never had an opinion about anything regarding his children. All he wants is to be left alone so he can make more money. Whenever we write him, he disregards the contents of the letter, unless we happen to be asking to draw more funds from the bank. And then he'll respond with a single line—'Permission to draw.'"

Daisy seemed to share her sister's cynical amusement. "I think Father is pleased by Mother's matchmaking, as it keeps her too busy to bother him."

"Dear me," Annabelle murmured. "And he never complains about your requests for more money?"

"Oh, never," Lillian said, and laughed at Annabelle's patent envy. "We're hideously rich, Annabelle—and we have three older brothers, all unmarried. If you like, I'll have one shipped across the Atlantic for your inspection."

"Tempting, but no," Annabelle replied. "I don't want to live in New York. I would rather be a peer's wife."

"Is it really so wonderful, being a peer's

wife?" Daisy asked plaintively. "Living in one of these drafty old houses with bad plumbing, and having to learn all the endless rules about the proper way to do *everything* . . ."

"You're no one if you're not married to a peer," Annabelle assured her. "In England, nobility is everything. It determines how others treat you, the schools your children attend, the places you're invited . . . every facet of your life."

"I don't know . . ." Daisy began, and was interrupted by Evie's precipitate return.

Although Evie displayed no obvious signs of being in a hurry, her blue eyes were lit with urgency, and excited color had gathered at the crests of her cheeks. Taking the chair she had previously occupied, she perched on the edge of the seat and leaned toward Annabelle, stammering and whispering. "I h-had to turn 'round and hurry back to tell you . . . *he's alone!*"

"Who?" Annabelle whispered back. "Who is alone?"

"Lord Kendall! I saw him at the b-b-back terrace. Just sitting there at one of the tables by himself."

Lillian frowned. "Perhaps he's waiting to meet someone. If so, it would hardly do Annabelle any good to go dashing up to him like a bitch in heat."

"Might you be able to come up with a more flattering metaphor, dear?" Annabelle asked mildly, and Lillian flashed her a grin.

"Sorry. Just proceed with care, Annabelle."

"Point taken," Annabelle said with an answering smile, standing and straightening her skirts deftly. "I'm going to investigate the situation. Good work, Evie."

"Good luck," Evie replied, and they all crossed their fingers as they watched her leave the room.

Annabelle's heartbeat escalated as she walked through the house. She knew full well that she was treading through an intricate maze of social rules. A lady should never deliberately seek out a gentleman's company; but if they crossed paths accidentally, or happened to find themselves on the same settee or conversation chair, they could exchange a few pleasantries. They should never spend time alone unless they were riding horses or being conveyed in an open carriage. And if a girl chanced to meet a gentleman while heading out to view the gardens, she must take pains to ensure that the situation did not appear compromising in any way.

Unless, of course, she wanted to be compromised.

Drawing close to the long row of French doors that opened onto the wide flagstone terrace, Annabelle saw her quarry. As Evie had described, Lord Kendall was sitting alone at a round table, leaning back in his chair with one leg stretched carelessly before him. He seemed to be enjoying a momentary respite from the overheated atmosphere of the house.

Quietly Annabelle strode to the nearest door and slipped through it. The air was lightly scented with heather and bog myrtle, while the sounds of the river beyond the gardens provided a soothing undercurrent. Keeping her head down, Annabelle rubbed her temples with her fingers as if she were afflicted with a nagging headache. When she was ten feet away from Kendall's table, she looked up and made herself jump a little, as if she was startled to see him there.

"Oh," she said. It was not at all difficult to sound breathless. She was nervous, knowing how important it was to make the right impression on him. "I didn't realize that someone was out here . . ."

Kendall stood, his spectacles twinkling in the light of the terrace torch. His form was slim to the point of being insubstantial, his coat hanging from his padded shoulders. Despite the fact that he was approximately three inches taller than Annabelle, she would not have been surprised to learn that they were the same weight. His posture was at once diffident and oddly tense, like that of a deer poised for a sudden, bounding retreat. As she stared at him, Annabelle had to admit silently that Kendall was not the kind of man whom she would have had any natural attraction to. On the other hand, she didn't like pickled herring, either. But if she was starving and someone handed her a jar of pickled herring, she was hardly going to turn her nose up at it.

"Hullo," Kendall said, his voice cultured and soft, though a bit high-pitched. "There's no need to be alarmed. Really, I'm harmless."

"I'll reserve judgment on that," Annabelle said, smiling, then wincing as if the effort had pained her. "Forgive me for disturbing your privacy, sir. I wanted a breath of fresh air." She inhaled until her breasts pressed becomingly at the seams of her bodice. "The atmosphere inside the house was rather oppressive, wasn't it?"

Kendall approached with his hands half-raised, as if he feared she might collapse to the terrace. "May I fetch you something? A glass of water?"

"No, thank you. A few moments outside will restore me to rights." Annabelle sank gracefully into the nearest chair. "Although . . ." She paused and tried to look self-conscious. "It wouldn't do for us to be seen out here unchaperoned. Especially as we haven't even been introduced."

He made a slight bow. "Lord Kendall, at your service."

"Miss Annabelle Peyton." She glanced at the empty chair nearby. "Do have a seat, please. I promise, I shall hurry away as soon as my head clears."

Kendall obeyed cautiously. "No need for that," he said. "Stay as long as you wish."

That was encouraging. Mindful of Lillian's advice, Annabelle pondered her next remark with great care. Since Kendall was being exhaustively pursued by a score of women, she would have to distinguish herself by pretending that she was the only one who was *not* interested in him. "I can guess why you came out here alone," she said with a smile. "You must be desperate to avoid being mobbed by eager women."

Kendall threw her a glance of surprise. "As a matter of fact, yes. I must say, I have never attended a party with such excessively friendly guests."

"Wait until the end of the month," she advised. "They'll be so friendly by then that you'll need a whip and a chair to hold them off."

"You seem to be suggesting that I'm some sort of matrimonial target," he commented dryly, giving voice to the obvious.

"The only way you could be more of a target is if you drew white circles on the back of your coat," Annabelle said, making him chuckle. "May I ask what your other reasons for escaping to the terrace are, my lord?"

Kendall continued to smile, looking far more comfortable than he had at first. "I'm afraid I can't hold my liquor. There is only so much port that I am willing to drink for the sake of being social."

Annabelle had never met a man who was willing to admit such a thing. Most gentlemen equated manliness with the ability to drink a sufficient quantity of liquor to inebriate an elephant. "Does it make you ill, then?" she asked sympathetically.

"Sick as a dog. I've been told that tolerance improves with practice—but it seems a rather pointless objective. I can think of better ways to pass the time."

"Such as . . ."

Kendall contemplated the question with great care. "A walk through the countryside. A book that improves the mind." His eyes contained a sudden friendly twinkle. "A conversation with a new friend."

"I like those things, too."

"Do you?" Kendall hesitated, while the sounds of the river and the sway of the trees seemed to whisper through the air. "Perhaps you might join me on a walk tomorrow morning. I know of several excellent ones around Stony Cross."

Annabelle's sudden eagerness was difficult to contain. "I would enjoy that," she replied. "But dare I ask—what about your entourage?"

Kendall smiled, revealing a row of small, neat teeth. "I don't expect that anyone will bother us if we depart early enough."

"I happen to be an early riser," she lied. "And I love to walk."

"Six o'clock, then?"

"Six o'clock," she repeated, standing from her chair. "I must go back inside—my absence will soon be remarked on. I am feeling much better, however. Thank you for your invitation, my lord." She allowed herself to send him a little flirting grin. "And for sharing the terrace."

As she went back inside, she closed her eyes briefly and let out a sigh of relief. It had been a good introduction—and far easier than she had anticipated to attract Kendall's interest. With a bit of luck—and some help from her friends—she might be able to catch a peer; and then everything would be all right.

Chapter 7

When the after-supper visiting was concluded, most of the guests began to retire for the evening. As Annabelle walked through one of the arched entrances of the drawing room, she saw that the other wallflowers were waiting for her. Smiling at their expectant faces, she went with them to a niche where they could exchange a few private words.

"Well?" Lillian demanded.

"Mama and I are going on a walk with Lord Kendall tomorrow morning," Annabelle said.

"Alone?"

"Alone," Annabelle confirmed. "In fact, we're meeting at daybreak, to avoid being accompanied by a herd of husband hunters."

Were they in a more private setting, they might have all squealed with glee. Instead, they settled for exchanging triumphant grins, while Daisy stamped her feet in an exuberant little victory dance.

"Wh-what is he like?" Evie asked.

"Shy, but pleasant," Annabelle replied. "And he seems to have a sense of humor, which I hadn't dared to hope for."

"All that, and teeth, too," Lillian exclaimed.

"You were right about him being spooked easily," Annabelle said. "I am certain that Kendall would not be attracted to a strong-willed woman. He's cautious and soft-spoken. I'm trying to be demure—although I should probably feel guilty for the deception."

"All women do that during courtship—and men, too, for that matter," Lillian said prosaically. "We try to conceal our defects and say the things we think the other one wants to hear. We pretend that we're always lovely and sweet-tempered and that we don't mind the other's nasty little habits. And then after the wedding, we lower the boom."

"I don't think that men have to pretend quite as much as women do, however," Annabelle replied. "If a man is portly, or has brown teeth, or is somewhat dull-witted, he's still a catch as long as he is a gentleman and has some money. But women are held to far more exacting standards."

"Which is why we're all w-wallflowers," Evie said.

"Not for long," Annabelle promised with a smile.

Evie's aunt Florence came from the ballroom, looking witchlike in a black dress that did not flatter her sallow complexion. There was little family resemblance between Evie, with her round face and red hair and freckled complexion, and her ill-tempered aunt, who was a dry little wisp of a woman. "Evangeline," she said sharply, throwing the group a disapproving glance as she gestured to the girl. "I've warned you not to disappear like that—I've searched everywhere for you, for at least ten minutes, and I don't recall you asking for permission to meet with your friends. And of all the girls for you to associate with . . ." Chattering angrily, Aunt Florence stalked toward the grand staircase, while Evie sighed and fell into step behind her. As they watched, Evie stuck her hand behind her back and waggled her fingers to wave good-bye.

Lillian tucked her arm into Daisy's. "Come, dear, before Mother realizes that we've disappeared." She glanced at Annabelle with an inquiring smile. "Will you come walk with us, Annabelle?"

"No, thank you. My mother will meet me at the foot of the stairs in just a moment."

"Good night, then." Lillian's dark eyes glowed as she added, "By the time we awaken tomorrow, you'll have already gone on your walk with Kendall. I'll expect a full report at breakfast."

Annabelle saluted her playfully and watched the two of them depart. She meandered slowly to the grand staircase and paused in the shadow at the base of the curving structure. It seemed that Philippa, as usual, was taking an interminable length of time to finish a conversation back in the drawing room. Annabelle didn't mind waiting, however. Her head was filled with thoughts, including conversational gambits that might amuse Kendall during their walk tomorrow and ideas of how to secure his attention to herself, in spite of the many other girls who would be pursuing him during the next few weeks.

If she was clever enough to make Lord Kendall like her, and if the wallflowers succeeded in their plan of entrapment, what would it be like to be the wife of such a man? Probably very pleasant. Life would be comfortable and secure, and she would never again have to worry about whether or not there was enough food for the table. And most importantly, Jeremy's future would be assured, and her mother would never again have to endure the foul attentions of Lord Hodgeham.

Heavy footsteps approached as someone descended the staircase. Standing at the banister, Annabelle glanced upward with a slight smile, and suddenly she froze. Incredibly, she found herself being confronted by a fleshy face surmounted by a dangling crest of iron gray hair. *Hodgeham?* But it couldn't be!

He reached the nadir of the stairs and stood before her, looking unbearably smug. As Annabelle stared into Hodgeham's cold blue eyes, the food she had eaten earlier seemed to gather into a spiky ball that rolled around her stomach.

As she thought of her mother, who was soon to meet her at this very spot, fury boiled swiftly. This grossly insolent man, who styled himself their benefactor and subjected her mother to his disgusting attentions in return for his stingy handfuls of coins, had now come to persecute them at the worst possible time. There was no more certain guarantee of torment for Philippa at this party than Hodgeham's presence. At any moment he might betray his relationship with her—he could ruin them so easily, and they had no means of keeping him silent.

"Why, Miss Peyton," Hodgeham murmured, his chubby face turning pink with malevolent pleasure. "What a pleasant coincidence that you should be the first guest I encounter at Stony Cross Park."

Queasy chills coursed over Annabelle as she forced herself to hold his gaze. Hodgeham smiled, seeming aware of the hostile fear that engulfed her. "After the rigors of the journey from London," he continued, "I elected to have supper in my room. So sorry to have missed you earlier. However, there will be many opportunities for us to visit in the coming weeks. Your charming mother is here with you, I presume?"

Annabelle would have given anything to be able to answer "no." Her heart was beating so hard that it seemed to drive the breath from her lungs . . . she fought to think and speak above the insistent hammering. "Don't go near her," she said, amazed that her voice was steady. "Don't speak to her."

"Ah, Miss Peyton, you wound me . . . I, who have been your family's only friend in these difficult times when others have deserted you."

She stared at him without blinking, without moving, as if she was face-to-face with a venomous snake that was poised to strike.

"A happy coincidence, is it not, that we find

ourselves attending the same party?" Hodgeham asked. He laughed quietly, the movement causing his combed-over hair to slip in an oily banner across his low forehead. He smoothed it back with his plump palm. "Fortune has indeed smiled on me, to provide proximity between myself and a woman whom I esteem so highly."

"There will be no proximity between you and my mother," Annabelle said, clenching her fist hard to keep from driving it into his gloating face. "I warn you, my lord, if you bother her in any way—"

"Dear girl, did you think that I was referring to Philippa? You are too modest. I meant *you*, Annabelle. I have long admired you. Yearned, in fact, to demonstrate the nature of my feelings for you. Now it seems that fate has presented us with the perfect opportunity to become more familiar with each other."

"I would rather sleep in a pit of snakes," Annabelle replied coldly, but there was a catch in her voice, and he smiled at the sound.

"At first you will protest, of course. But then you'll do the sensible thing . . . the wise thing . . . and you'll see the advantages of becoming my friend. I can be a valuable friend, my dear. And if you please me, I will reward you handsomely."

Annabelle tried desperately to think of a way to destroy any hope he might have of making her his mistress. The fear that he might trespass on another man's province was likely the only thing that would keep Hodgeham away from her. Annabelle forced her lips into a scornful smile. "Does it appear that I'm in need of your so-called friendship?" she asked, fingering the folds of her fine new gown. "You're mistaken. I already have a protector—a far more generous one than you. So you had better leave me—and my mother—completely alone. Or you will answer to him."

She saw the progression of emotions across Hodgeham's face, initial disbelief followed by anger, and then suspicion. "Who is he?"

"Why should I tell you?" Annabelle asked with a cool smile. "I would much rather let you wonder."

"You're lying, you devious bitch!"

"Believe what you like," she murmured.

Hodgeham's meaty hands half curled as if he was longing to seize her and shake a confession from her. Instead, he regarded her with a fury-mottled complexion. "I'm not done with you yet," he muttered, spittle flecking his fleshy lips. "Not by half." He left her with crude abruptness, too incensed to bother with a show of courtesy.

Annabelle stood without moving. Her fury faded, leaving behind a stinging anxiety that settled in her bones. In the coming days he would be watching her closely, scrutinizing every word and action to ascertain whether or not she had been lying about having a protector. But no matter what, she could not allow him to reveal the arrangement that he had shared with her mother. It would kill Philippa, and certainly it would ruin Annabelle's chances of marriage.

Her mind swam with feverish thoughts, and she stood motionless and taut-framed, until a quiet voice nearly startled her out of her slippers.

"Interesting. What were you and Lord Hodgeham arguing about?"

Blanching, Annabelle whirled around to behold Simon Hunt, who had approached her with catlike quietness. His shoulders blocked the profusion of glittering light from the drawing room. In his utter self-possession, he seemed infinitely more threatening than Hodgeham.

"What did you hear?" Annabelle blurted out, cursing inwardly as she heard the defensiveness in her own voice.

"Nothing," he said smoothly. "I merely saw your face as the two of you talked. Obviously, you were upset about something."

"I was not upset. You misinterpreted my expression, Mr. Hunt."

He shook his head, and stunned her by reaching out with a single fingertip to touch the upper part of her arm that was not covered by her glove. "You turn splotchy when you're angry." Looking down, Annabelle saw a pale pink patch of color, a sign of her skin's wont to color unevenly during times of distress.

A quiver ran through her at that glancing brush of his fingertip, and she stepped back from him.

"Are you in trouble, Annabelle?" Hunt asked softly.

He had no right to ask something in that gentle, almost concerned manner . . . as if he was someone she could turn to for help . . . as if she could ever allow herself to do so.

"You would like that, wouldn't you?" she retorted. "Any predicament of mine would delight you to no end—then you could step in with an offer of help and take advantage of the situation."

His eyes were narrow and intent. "What kind of help do you need?"

"Nothing from you," she assured him curtly. "And don't use my first name. I'll thank you to address me properly from now on—or better yet, don't speak to me at all." Unable to bear his speculative gaze for another moment, she swept past him. "Now if you'll excuse me . . . I must go find my mother."

Lowering herself to the chair beside the vanity table, Philippa stared at Annabelle with an ashen face. Annabelle had waited until they were safely enclosed in the privacy of their room before she had told Philippa the disastrous news. It seemed to take her mother a full minute to assimilate the information that the man whom she detested and feared most was a guest at Stony Cross Park. Annabelle had half expected her mother to dissolve into tears, but Philippa surprised her by tilting her head to the side and staring into the shadowy corner of the room with an odd, weary smile. It was a smile that Annabelle had never seen on her face before, a whimsical bitterness that indicated there was never any use in trying to improve one's situation, as fate would invariably have its way.

"Shall we leave Stony Cross Park?" Annabelle murmured. "We can go back to London immediately."

The question hovered in the air for what seemed to be minutes. When Philippa responded, she sounded dazed and contemplative. "If we did that, there would be no hope at all of your marrying. No . . . our only choice is to see this through. We are going to walk with Lord Kendall tomorrow morning—I won't allow Hodgeham to ruin your chances with him."

"He will be a constant source of trouble," Annabelle said quietly. "If we don't go back to town, it will turn into a nightmare here."

Philippa turned toward her then, still smiling in that discomforting way. "My dear, if you don't find someone to marry, then when we return to London, the real nightmare will begin."

Chapter 8

Bedeviled by worry, Annabelle slept for a total of two, perhaps three hours. When she awoke in the morning, her eyes were shadowed, and her face was pale and weary. "Hell's bells," she muttered, soaking a cloth in cold water and pressing it to her face. "This will not do. I look a hundred years old this morning."

"What did you say, dear?" came her mother's sleepy query. Philippa was standing behind her, dressed in a worn robe and threadbare slippers.

"Nothing, Mama. I was talking to myself." Annabelle scrubbed her face roughly to bring some color to her cheeks. "I didn't sleep well last night."

Coming beside Annabelle, Philippa regarded her closely. "You do look a bit tired. I'll send for some tea."

"Send for a large pot," Annabelle said. Peering closely at her red-veined eyes in the looking glass, she added, "*Two* pots."

Philippa smiled sympathetically. "What shall we wear for our walk with Lord Kendall?"

Annabelle wrung out the cloth before draping it on the washstand. "Our older gowns, I think, as it may be rather muddy on some of the forest paths. But we can cover them with the new silk shawls from Lillian and Daisy."

After downing a cup of steaming tea and taking a few hasty bites of cold toast that a maid had brought from downstairs, Annabelle finished dressing. She studied herself critically in the looking glass. The blue silk shawl knotted over her bodice did much to conceal the worn bodice of the biscuit-colored gown beneath. And her new bonnet, also from the Bowmans, was wonderfully flattering, its periwinkle-shaded lining bringing out the blue of her eyes.

Yawning widely, Annabelle went with Philippa to the back terrace of the manor. The hour was early enough that most of the guests at Stony Cross Park were still abed. Only a few gentlemen who were bent on trout fishing had troubled themselves to arise. A small group of men ate breakfast at the outside tables, while servants awaited nearby with rods and creel baskets. The peaceful scene was undercut with an annoying clamor that was most unexpected for this hour.

"Dear heaven," she heard her mother exclaim. Following her appalled gaze, Annabelle looked toward the other end of the terrace, which had been overrun by a cacophony of frantically chattering, squealing, laughing, aggressively posturing girls. They were surrounding something that remained unseen in the middle of the tightly packed congregation. "What are they all here for?" Philippa asked in bewilderment.

Annabelle sighed and said resignedly, "An early-morning hunt, I suspect."

Philippa's jaw sagged as she stared at the clamorous group. "You don't mean to say . . . do you think that poor Lord Kendall is caught up in the midst of that?"

Annabelle nodded. "And from the looks of things, there won't be much left of him when they're finished."

"But . . . but he arranged to go walking with *you*," Philippa protested. "*Only* you, with me as the chaperone."

As a few of the girls noticed Annabelle standing on the other side of the terrace, they crowded more tightly around their prey, as if to shield him from their view. Annabelle shook her head slightly. Either Kendall had foolishly told someone of their plans, or else the marriage frenzy had reached such a pitch that he could not venture out of his room without attracting a mob of women, no matter what the hour.

"Well, don't just stand there," Philippa urged. "Go and join the group, and try to attract his attention."

Annabelle watched glumly as her mother departed. Distracted by a muffled laugh from nearby, she turned toward the sound. Simon Hunt was lounging at the terrace balcony, a china cup nearly engulfed in his broad hand as he leisurely drank coffee. He was dressed in rugged garments similar to those of the other fishermen, made of tweed and rough twill, with a worn linen shirt left open at the throat. The mocking gleam in his eyes made no secret of his interest in the situation.

Annabelle found herself drifting nearer to him. Coming to stand a few feet away from him, she leaned both her elbows on the balcony, gazing out at the mist-shrouded morning. Hunt rested his back against it, facing the manor wall.

Feeling the need to jab at his irritating self-confidence, Annabelle murmured, "Lord Kendall and Lord Westcliff aren't the only bachelors at Stony Cross, Mr. Hunt. One wonders why *you* are not pursued to the degree that they are."

"That's obvious," he said pleasantly, lifting the cup to his lips and draining its contents. "I'm not a peer, and I would make a devil of a husband." He gave her a shrewd sideways glance. "As for you . . . despite my sympathy for your cause, I wouldn't advise making a play for Kendall."

"My *cause?*" Annabelle repeated, taking immediate offense to the word. "What do you define as my cause, Mr. Hunt?"

"Why, yourself, of course," he said softly. "You want what's best for Annabelle Peyton. But Kendall doesn't fall in that category. A match between you and him would be a disaster."

She turned her head to stare at him with slitted eyes. "Why?"

"You'd run roughshod over him until his gentlemanly soul was left in a battered pile at your feet."

Annabelle itched to knock the superior smile from his face—she, who had never before contemplated inflicting physical harm to anyone. Her anger was hardly mitigated by the fact that he was right. She knew quite well that she was far too spirited for a man as docile and civilized as Kendall. But that was none of Simon Hunt's business . . . and it wasn't as if Hunt or any other man was going to offer her a better alternative!

"Mr. Hunt," she said sweetly, her gaze poisonous, "why don't you go and—"

"Miss Peyton!" A faint exclamation came from several yards away, and Annabelle saw Lord Kendall's slight form emerging from the mass of females. He looked disheveled and vaguely harassed as he pushed his way over to her. "Good morning, Miss Peyton." He paused to straighten the knot of his cravat and adjust his skewed spectacles. "It seems that we were not the only ones who had taken it in our heads to walk this morning." Giving Annabelle a sheepish glance, he asked, "Shall we make an attempt nonetheless?"

Annabelle hesitated, inwardly groaning. There was little she could accomplish on a walk with Kendall when they'd be accompanied by at least two dozen women. One might as well try to have a quiet conversation in the midst of a flock of screaming magpies. On the other hand, she couldn't very well refuse Kendall's invitation . . . even a minor rejection could be off-putting to him, and he might never ask again.

She gave him a bright smile. "I would be delighted, my lord."

"Excellent. There are some fascinating species of flora and fauna I would like to show you. As an amateur horticulturist, I've made a careful study of Hampshire's native vegetation . . ."

Enthusiastic girls surrounded him.

"How I *love* plants," one of them gushed. "There isn't a single plant that I don't find absolutely charming."

"And the outdoors would be *so* dull without them," another girl enthused.

"Oh, Lord Kendall," yet another beseeched, "you simply must explain what the difference is between a flora and a fauna . . ."

The crowd of girls carried Kendall away as if he was being swept out to sea by an irresistible current.

Kendall threw a helpless glance over his shoulder as he was nudged strongly toward the terrace steps. "Miss Peyton?"

"I'm coming," Annabelle called back, cupping her fingers on either side of her mouth to make herself heard.

His reply, if he made one, was impossible to hear.

Lazily, Simon Hunt set his empty cup on the nearest table, and murmured something to a servant who was holding his fishing gear. The servant nodded and retreated, while Hunt fell into step beside Annabelle. She stiffened as she noticed him walking side by side with her.

"What are you doing?"

Hunt shoved his hands comfortably into the pockets of his tweed fishing coat. "I'm going with you. Whatever happens at the trout stream won't be half so interesting as watching you compete for Kendall's attention. Besides, my horticultural knowledge is sadly lacking. I may learn something."

Suppressing an ill-tempered reply, Annabelle resolutely followed Kendall and his entourage. They all walked down the terrace steps and took a path that led into the forest, where towering beeches and oaks presided over thick quilts of moss, fern, and lichen. At first Annabelle ignored Simon Hunt's presence beside her, trudging stonily behind Kendall's admiring throng. Kendall was being put to great exertion, obliged to help one girl after another to step over what seemed to be minor obstacles. A fallen tree, its circumference no bigger than Annabelle's arm, became such an overwhelming impediment that they all required Kendall's assistance to step over it. Each girl became progressively more helpless until the poor fellow was practically obliged to carry the last one over the log while she squealed in pretend-dismay and locked her arms around his neck.

Walking far behind, Annabelle refused to take Simon Hunt's arm when he offered it and stepped over the log by herself. He smiled slightly as he glanced at her set profile. "I would have expected you to have made your way up to the front by now," he remarked.

She made a scornful sound. "I'm not going to waste my efforts battling with that group of feather-wits. I'll wait for a more opportune moment to make Kendall notice me."

"He's already noticed you. He'd have been blind not to. The question is why you think that you'll have any luck wrestling a proposal out of Kendall, when you haven't managed to bring anyone up to scratch in the two years that I've known you."

"Because I have a plan," she said crisply.

"Which is?"

She gave him a derisive glance. "As if I would tell you."

"I hope it's something conniving and underhanded," Hunt said gravely. "You don't seem to have much success with the ladylike approach."

"Only because I have no dowry," Annabelle retorted. "If I had money, I'd have been married years ago."

"I have money," he said helpfully. "How much do you want?"

Annabelle gave him a sardonic glance. "Having a fair idea of what you'd require in return, Mr. Hunt, I don't want a shilling from you."

"It's nice to hear you're so discriminating about the company you keep." Hunt reached out to hold back a branch for her. "Having heard a rumor to the contrary, I'm glad it's not true."

"Rumor?" Annabelle stopped in the middle

of the path and whirled to face him. "About me? What could anyone possibly say about me?"

Hunt remained silent, watching her perturbed face as she worked it out for herself.

"Discriminating . . ." she murmured. "About the company I keep? . . . Is that supposed to imply that I've had some inappropriate . . ." She stopped abruptly as the nasty, florid image of Hodgeham sprang into her brain. Hunt had to notice the swift departure of color from her cheeks and the tiny indentations that dug between her brows. Giving him a cold glance, Annabelle turned away, her footsteps measured and heavy on the foliage-padded path.

Hunt kept pace with her, while Kendall's distant voice drifted back to them, lecturing his avid listeners on the plants they passed. Rare orchids . . . celandines . . . several varieties of fungi. The speech was punctuated every few seconds with crows of wonder from his enraptured audience. ". . . these lower plants," Kendall was saying, having paused briefly to indicate a haze of moss and lichen covering a hapless oak, "are classified as bryophytes, and require wet conditions to thrive. Were they to be deprived of the woodland canopy, they would surely perish out in the open . . ."

"I've done nothing wrong," Annabelle said shortly, wondering why Hunt's opinion mattered in the least. Still, it bothered her enough to wonder who had told him the rumor—and specifically, what it had been about. Was it possible that someone had seen Hodgeham visiting her home at night? That was bad. A reputation-destroying piece of gossip like that was impossible to defend oneself against. "And I have no regrets."

"That's a pity," Hunt said easily. "Having regrets is the only sign that you've done anything interesting with your life."

"What are *your* regrets, then?"

"Oh, I don't have regrets, either." A wicked glint appeared in his dark eyes. "Not for the lack of trying, of course. I keep doing unspeakable things in the hopes that I'll be sorry for them later. But so far . . . nothing."

In spite of her inner turmoil, Annabelle couldn't help chuckling. A long branch intersected the path, and she reached out to push it aside.

"Allow me," Hunt said, moving to hold it back for her.

"Thank you." She pushed by him, glancing at Kendall and the others in the distance, and suddenly felt a stinging prickle at the inner side of her foot. "Ouch!" Stopping on the path, she hitched the hem of her skirt up to investigate the source of the discomfort.

"What is it?" Hunt was beside her immediately, one large hand grasping her elbow to secure her balance.

"There is something scratchy in my shoe."

"Let me help," he said, sinking to his haunches and taking hold of her ankle. It was the first time a man had ever touched any part of her leg, and Annabelle went scarlet.

"*Don't* touch me there," she protested in a violent whisper, nearly losing her balance as she jerked backward. Hunt didn't loosen his grip. To keep from toppling over, Annabelle was forced to hold on to his shoulder. "Mr. Hunt—"

"I see the problem," he murmured. She felt him pluck at the veil of cotton stocking that covered her leg. "You've stepped in some prickly fern." He held something up for her inspection—a sprig of pale, chafflike scales that had worked their way into the cotton weave over her instep.

Flooding with burning color, Annabelle maintained her stabilizing grasp on his shoulder. The surface of his shoulder was astonishingly hard, the plane of bone and resilient muscle unsoftened by any layer of padding in his coat. Her stunned mind was having difficulty accepting the fact that she was standing in the middle of the woods with Simon Hunt's hand on her ankle.

Seeing her mortification, Hunt grinned suddenly. "There are more bits of chaff in your stocking. Shall I remove them?"

"Be quick about it," she said in an aggrieved tone, "before Kendall turns around and sees you with your hand up my skirts."

With a muffled laugh Hunt bent to his task, deftly picking the last of the prickly scales from her stocking. While he worked, Annabelle stared at the place on the back of his neck where the obsidian locks of hair curled slightly.

Reaching for the discarded slipper, Hunt placed it on her foot with a flourish. "My rustic Cinderella," he said, and rose to his feet. As his gaze passed over the blooming pink surface of her cheeks, friendly mockery flickered in his dark eyes. "Why did you wear such ridiculous shoes for a walk in the woods? I would have thought you'd have the good sense to put on a pair of ankle boots."

"I don't have any ankle boots," Annabelle said, annoyed by the implication that she was some feather-wit who couldn't select the appropriate footwear for a simple walk. "My old ones fell to pieces, and I couldn't afford a new pair."

Surprisingly, Hunt did not take advantage of the opportunity to mock her further. His face became impassive as he studied her for a moment. "Let's join the others," he said eventually. "They've probably discovered a variety of moss we haven't yet seen. Or God help us, a mushroom."

The pinching tightness eased from her chest. "I'm hoping for some lichen, myself."

That elicited a faint smile, and he reached out to snap off a slender branch that protruded across the pathway. Following gamely, Annabelle picked up her skirts and tried not to think of how nice it would be to be sitting on the manor terrace with a tray of tea and biscuits before her. They reached the summit of a shallow incline and were greeted with a surprising vista of bluebells that blanketed the forest floor. It was like stumbling into a dream, vivid blue haze seeping between the trunks of oak and beech and ash. The smell of bluebells was everywhere, the perfumed air feeling heavy and rich in her lungs.

Pausing by a slender tree trunk, Annabelle

curled her arm around it loosely and stared at the stands of flowers with surprised pleasure. "Lovely," she murmured, her face gleaming in the shadow cast by the canopy of ancient, interlaced branches.

"Yes." But Hunt was looking at her.

Uneasy, she pushed away from the tree trunk and made her way to Kendall, whose gaze alighted on Simon Hunt's dark form.

The two men exchanged nods, Hunt looking self-assured, Kendall appearing somewhat wary. "I see that we've attracted yet more company," Kendall murmured.

Annabelle gave Kendall her most dazzling smile. "Of course we have," she said. "You're the Pied Piper, my lord. Wherever you go, people follow."

He blushed, pleased by the bit of nonsense, and murmured, "I hope that you have enjoyed the walk so far, Miss Peyton."

"Oh, I have," she assured him. "Although I will admit to having blundered into a patch of prickly fern. The fault was entirely mine—I'm afraid I wore the wrong kind of shoes." She stuck out her foot to show Kendall one of her light slippers, making certain to display a few inches of trim ankle.

Kendall clicked his tongue in dismay. "Miss Peyton, you need something far sturdier than those slippers for a tromp through the forest."

"You're right, of course." Annabelle shrugged, continuing to smile. "It was silly of me not to realize the terrain would be so rugged. I'll try to choose my steps more carefully on the way back. But the bluebells are so heavenly, I'd wade through a field of prickly fern to reach them."

Reaching down to a stray cluster of bluebells, Kendall broke off a sprig and tucked it into the ribbon trim of her bonnet. "They're not half so blue as your eyes," he said. His gaze dropped to her ankle, which was now covered by the hem of her skirts. "You must take my arm when we walk back, to avoid further mishap."

"Thank you, my lord." Annabelle gazed up at him admiringly. "I'm afraid that I missed some of your earlier remarks about ferns, my lord. You had mentioned something about . . . spleenwort, wasn't it? . . . and I was *thoroughly* fascinated . . ."

Kendall obligingly proceeded to explain all one would ever want to know about ferns . . . and later, when Annabelle chanced to glance back in Simon Hunt's direction, he was gone.

Chapter 9

"Are we really going to do this?" Annabelle asked somewhat plaintively, as the wallflowers strode along the forest path with baskets and hampers in hand. "I thought that all our talk of Rounders-in-knickers was merely amusing banter."

"Bowmans *never* banter about Rounders," Daisy informed her. "That would be sacrilegious."

"You like games, Annabelle," Lillian said cheerfully. "And Rounders is the best game of all."

"I like the kind that is played at a table," Annabelle retorted. "With proper clothes on."

"Clothing is vastly overrated," came Daisy's airy reply.

Earlier that morning, Annabelle had privately attempted to sway Evie to her side, unable to fathom that the girl truly intended to strip down to her drawers out in the open. But Evie was rashly determined to fall in with the

Bowmans' plans, seeming to consider it as part of a self-devised program to embolden herself. "I w-want to be more like them," she had confided to Annabelle. "They're so free and daring. They fear nothing."

"Maybe it will be f-fun?" Evie had suggested, and Annabelle had responded with a speaking glance, making her laugh.

The weather, of course, had decided to cooperate fully with the Bowmans' plans, the sky open and blue, the air stirred by a soft breeze. Laden with baskets, the four girls walked along a sunken road, past wet meadows sprinkled with red sundew blossoms and vivid purple violets.

"Keep an eye out for a wishing well," Lillian said briskly. "Then we're supposed to cross the meadow on the other side of the lane and cut through the forest. There's a dry meadow at the top of the hill. One of the servants told me no one ever goes there."

"Naturally it would be uphill," Annabelle said without rancor. "Lillian, what does the well look like? Is it one of those little white-washed things with a pail and a pulley?"

"No, it's a big muddy hole in the ground."

"There it is," Daisy exclaimed, hastening to the sloshing brown hole, which was being replenished from a bank beside it. "Come, all of you, we must each make a wish. I even have pins we can toss into it."

"How did you know to bring pins?" Lillian asked.

Daisy grinned. "Well, as I sat with Mama

and all the dowagers while they were sewing yesterday afternoon, I made our Rounders ball." She unearthed a leather ball from her basket and held it up proudly. "I sacrificed a new pair of kid gloves to make it—and it was no easy task, I tell you. Anyway, the old ladies were watching me stuff it with wool snippets, and when one of them could bear it no longer, she came out and asked me what in heaven's name I was making. Of course I couldn't tell them it was a Rounders ball. I'm sure Mama guessed, but she was too embarrassed to say a word. So I told the dowager that I was making a pincushion."

All the girls snickered. "She must have thought it was the ugliest pincushion in existence," Lillian remarked.

"Oh, there's no doubt of that," Daisy replied. "I think she felt quite sorry for me. She gave me some pins for it, and said something under her breath about poor bumbling American girls who have no practical skills whatsoever." Using the edge of her nail, she pried the pins out of the leather ball and gave them over.

Setting down her own basket, Annabelle held a pin between her thumb and forefinger, and closed her eyes. Whenever the opportunity presented itself, she always made the same wish . . . to marry a peer. Strangely, however, a new thought entered her head, just as she cast the pin into the well.

I wish I could fall in love.

Surprised by the willful, wayward notion, Annabelle wondered how it was that she could have wasted a wish on something that was obviously so ill-advised.

Opening her eyes, Annabelle saw that the other wallflowers were staring into the well with great solemnity. "I made the wrong wish," she said fretfully. "Can I have another?"

"No," Lillian said in a matter-of-fact tone. "Once you've thrown in your pin, it's done."

"But I didn't mean to make that particular wish," Annabelle protested. "Something just popped into my head, and it wasn't at all what I had planned."

"Don't argue, Annabelle," Evie advised. "You d-don't want to annoy the well spirit."

"The what?"

Evie smiled at her perplexed expression. "The resident spirit of the well. He's the one to whom y-you make a petition. But if you annoy him, he may decide to demand a terrible price for granting your wish. Or he may drag you into the well with him, to live there forever as his c-consort."

Annabelle stared into the brown water. She cupped her hands around the sides of her mouth to help direct her voice. "You don't have to grant my rotten wish," she told the unseen spirit loudly. "I take it back!"

"Don't taunt him, Annabelle," Daisy exclaimed. "And for heaven's sake, step back from the edge of that well!"

"Are you superstitious?" Annabelle asked with a grin.

Daisy glowered at her. "There's a reason for superstitions, you know. At *some* point in time, *something* bad happened to *someone* who was standing right next to a well, just as you are." Closing her eyes, she concentrated intently, then tossed her own pin into the water. "There. I've made a wish for your benefit—so there's no need for you to complain about having wasted one."

"But how do you know what I wanted?"

"The wish I made is for your own good," Daisy informed her.

Annabelle groaned theatrically. "I *hate* things that are for my own good."

A good-natured squabble followed, in which each girl made suggestions as to what would be best for the other, until finally Lillian commanded them to stop, as they were interfering with her concentration. They fell silent just long enough to allow Lillian and Evie to make their wishes, then they made their way across the meadow and through the forest. Soon they reached a lovely dry meadow, grassy and sun-drenched, with shade extending from a grove of oak at one side. The air was balmy and rarefied, and so fresh that Annabelle sighed blissfully. "This air has no substance to it," she said in mock-complaint. "No coal smoke or street dust whatsoever. Much too thin for a Londoner. I can't even feel it in my lungs."

"It's not that thin," Lillian replied. "Every now and then the breeze carries a distinct hint of *eau de* sheep."

"Really?" Annabelle sniffed experimentally. "I can't smell a thing."

"That's because you don't have a nose," Lillian replied.

"I beg your pardon?" Annabelle asked with a quizzical grin.

"Oh, you have a regular sort of nose," Lillian explained, "but I have *a nose*. I'm unusually sensitive to smell. Give me any perfume, and I can separate it into all its parts. Before we left New York, I even helped to develop a formula for scented soap, for my father's factory."

"Could you create a perfume, do you think?" Annabelle asked in fascination.

"I daresay I could create an excellent perfume," Lillian said confidently. "However, anyone in the industry would disdain it, as the phrase 'American perfume' is considered to be an oxymoron—and I'm a woman, besides, which throws the caliber of my nose very much into question."

"You mean, men have better noses than women?"

"They certainly think so," Lillian said darkly, and whipped a picnic blanket out of her basket with a flourish. "Enough about men and their protuberances. Shall we sit in the sun for a little while?"

"We'll get freckles," Daisy predicted, flopping onto a corner of the blanket with a pleasured sigh. "And then Mama will have conniptions."

"What are conniptions?" Annabelle asked, entertained by the American word. She dropped to the space beside Daisy. "Do send for me if she has them—I'm curious to see what they look like."

"Mama has them all the time," Daisy assured

her. "Never fear, you'll be well acquainted with conniptions before we all leave Hampshire."

"We shouldn't eat before we play," Lillian said, watching as Annabelle lifted the lid of a picnic basket.

"I'm hungry," Annabelle said wistfully, peering inside the basket, which was filled with fruit, cheese, pâté, thick cuts of bread, and several varieties of salad.

"You're always hungry," Daisy observed with a laugh. "For such a small person, you have a remarkable appetite."

"*I*, small?" Annabelle countered. "If you are one fraction of an inch above five feet tall, I'll eat that picnic basket."

"You'd better start chewing, then," Daisy said. "I'm five feet and one inch, thank you."

"Annabelle, I wouldn't gnaw on that wicker handle quite yet, if I were you," Lillian interceded with a slow smile. "Daisy stands on her toes whenever she's measured. The poor dressmaker has had to recut the hems of nearly a dozen dresses, thanks to my sister's unreasonable denial of the fact that she is short."

"I'm not short," Daisy muttered. "Short women are never mysterious, or elegant, or pursued by handsome men. And they're always treated like children. I refuse to be short."

"You're not mysterious or elegant," Evie conceded. "But you're very pr-pretty."

"And you're a dear," Daisy replied, levering upward to reach into the picnic basket. "Come, let's feed poor Annabelle—I can hear her stomach growling."

They delved into the repast enthusiastically. Afterward, they reclined lazily on the blanket and cloud-watched, and talked about everything and nothing. When their chatter died to a contented lull, a small red squirrel ventured out of the oak grove and turned to the side, watching them with one bright black eye.

"An intruder," Annabelle observed, with a delicate yawn.

Evie rolled to her stomach and tossed a bread crust in the squirrel's direction. He froze and stared at the tantalizing offering, but was too timid to advance. Evie tilted her head, her hair glittering in the sun as if it had been overlaid with a net of rubies. "Poor little thing," she said softly, casting another crust at the timid squirrel. This one landed a few inches closer, and his tail twitched eagerly. "Be brave," Evie coaxed. "Go on and take it." Smiling tolerantly, she tossed another crust, which landed a scant few inches from him. "Oh, Mr. Squirrel," Evie reproved. "You're a dreadful coward. Can't you see that no one's going to harm you?"

In a sudden burst of initiative, the squirrel seized the tidbit and scampered off with his tail quivering. Looking up with a triumphant smile, Evie saw the other wallflowers staring at her in drop-jawed silence. "Wh-what is it?" she asked, puzzled.

Annabelle was the first to speak. "Just now, when you were talking to that squirrel, you didn't stammer."

"Oh." Suddenly abashed, Evie lowered her gaze and grimaced. "I never stammer when

I'm talking to children or animals. I don't know why."

They pondered the puzzling information for a moment. "I've noticed that you never seem to stammer quite as much when you're talking to me," Daisy observed.

Lillian could not seem to resist the comment. "Which category do you fall into, dear? Children, or animals?"

Daisy responded with a hand gesture that was completely unfamiliar to Annabelle.

Annabelle was about to ask Evie if she had ever consulted a doctor about her stammering, but the red-haired girl abruptly changed the subject. "Where is the R-rounders ball, Daisy? If we don't play soon, I'll fall asleep."

Realizing that Evie didn't want to discuss her stammering any longer, Annabelle seconded the request. "I suppose if we're really going to do it, now is as good a time as any."

While Daisy dug in the basket for the ball, Lillian unearthed an item from her own basket. "Look what I've brought," she said smugly.

Daisy looked up with a delighted laugh. "A real bat!" she exclaimed, regarding the flat-sided object admiringly. "And I thought we'd have to use a plain old stick. Where did you get it, Lillian?"

"I borrowed it from one of the stableboys. It seems they sneak away for Rounders whenever possible—they're quite passionate about the game."

"Who wouldn't be?" Daisy asked rhetorically, beginning on the buttons of her bodice.

"Gracious, the day is warm—it will be lovely to shed all these layers."

As the Bowman sisters unfastened their gowns with the casual manner of girls not unaccustomed to disrobing out in the open, Annabelle and Evie regarded each other in a moment of uncertainty.

"I dare you," Evie murmured.

"Oh, God," Annabelle said in an aggrieved tone, and began to unbutton her own dress. She had discovered an unexpected streak of modesty that brought a rush of color to her face. However, she was not going to turn coward when even timid Evie Jenner was willing to join in the rebellion against propriety. Pulling her arms from the sleeves of her dress, she stood and let the heavy overlay fall in a crumpled mound at her feet. Left in her chemise, drawers, and corset, her feet covered only by stockings and thin slippers, she felt a breeze waft over the perspiration-dampened places beneath her arms, and she shivered pleasantly.

The other girls stood and shed their own gowns, which lay heaped on the ground like gigantic exotic flowers.

"Catch!" Daisy said, and tossed the ball to Annabelle, who caught it reflexively. They all walked to the center of the meadow, pitching the ball back and forth. Evie was the worst at throwing and catching, though it was clear that her ineptitude was caused by inexperience rather than clumsiness. Annabelle, on the other hand, had a younger brother who had frequently turned to her as a playmate, and so the mechanics of lobbing a ball were familiar to her.

It was the oddest, lightest feeling, walking outside with her legs unimpeded by the weight of skirts. "I suppose this is what men feel like," Annabelle mused aloud, "being able to stroll here and there in trousers. One could almost envy them such freedom."

"Almost?" Lillian questioned with a grin. "Without question, I *do* envy them. Wouldn't it be lovely if women could wear trousers?"

"I w-wouldn't like it at all," Evie said. "I would die of embarrassment if a man were able to see the shape of my legs and my . . ." She hesitated. ". . . other things," she finished lamely.

"Your chemise is in a sad state, Annabelle," came Lillian's sudden blunt observation. "I hadn't thought to give you new underwear, though I should have realized . . ."

Annabelle shrugged offhandedly. "It doesn't matter, since this is the only time anyone will see it."

Daisy glanced at her older sister. "Lillian, we're abominably shortsighted. I think poor Annabelle drew the short straw when it came to fairy godmothers."

"I haven't complained," Annabelle said, laughing. "And as far as I can tell, the four of us are all riding in the same pumpkin."

After a few more minutes of practice, and a brief discussion of the rules of Rounders, they set out empty picnic baskets in lieu of sanctuary posts, and the game began. Annabelle planted her feet squarely on a spot that had been designated as "Castle Rock."

"I'll pitch," Daisy said to her older sister, "and you catch."

"But I have a better arm than you," Lillian grumbled, taking a position behind Annabelle nevertheless.

Holding the bat over her shoulder, Annabelle swung at the ball Daisy threw. The bat failed to connect, and whistled through the air in a neat arc. Behind her, Lillian expertly caught the ball. "That was a good swing," Daisy encouraged. "Keep watching the ball as it comes toward you."

"I'm not accustomed to standing still while objects are being hurled at me," Annabelle said, brandishing the bat once again. "How many tries do I get?"

"In Rounders, the striker has an infinite number of swings," came Lillian's voice behind her. "Have another go, Annabelle . . . and this time, try to imagine that the ball is Mr. Hunt's nose."

Annabelle received the suggestion with relish. "I'd prefer to aim for a protuberance somewhat lower than that," she said, and swung as Daisy fed her the ball again. This time, the flat side of the bat met the ball with a solid *thwack*. Letting out a whoop of delight, Daisy went scampering after the ball, while Lillian, who had been screeching with laughter, cried out, "Run, Annabelle!"

She did so with a triumphant chortle, skirting the baskets as she rounded toward Castle Rock.

Daisy scooped up the ball and threw it to Lillian, who snatched it from the air.

"Stay at the third post, Annabelle," Lillian called. "We'll see if Evie can bring you back to Castle Rock."

Looking nervous but determined, Evie took the bat and assumed a stance at the striker's place.

"Pretend the ball is your aunt Florence," Annabelle advised, and a grin erupted on Evie's face.

Daisy pitched a slow, easy ball, while Evie flailed with the bat. She missed, and the ball landed with a neat smack in Lillian's palms. Throwing the ball back to Daisy, Lillian repositioned Evie. "Widen your stance and bend your knees a bit," she murmured. "That's a girl. Now watch the ball as it comes, and you won't miss."

Unfortunately Evie did miss, time and again, until her face was pink with frustration. "It's t-too hard," she said, her forehead puckered with worry. "Perhaps I should stop now and give someone else a turn."

"Just a few more tries," Annabelle said anxiously, determined that Evie should hit the ball at least once. "We're in no hurry."

"Don't give up!" Daisy chimed in. "It's just that you're trying too hard, Evie. Relax—and stop closing your eyes when you swing."

"You can do it," Lillian said, pushing a lock

of silky dark hair away from her forehead and flexing her slim, well-toned arms. "You almost connected with the last one. Just *keep . . . watching . . . the ball.*"

Sighing in resignation, Evie dragged the bat back to Castle Rock and lifted it once more. Her blue eyes narrowed as she stared at Daisy, and she tensed in preparation for the next feed. "I'm ready."

Daisy tossed the ball gamely, and Evie swung with grim determination. A thrill of satisfaction shot through Annabelle as she saw the bat strike the ball solidly. It soared into the air, far into the oak grove. They all whooped in jubilation at the splendid strike. Shocked at what she had done, Evie began to jump in the air, squealing, "I did it! I did it!"

"Run around the baskets!" Annabelle cried, and scampered back to Castle Rock. Gleefully Evie circled the makeshift Rounders field, her garments a blur of white. When she reached Castle Rock, the girls continued to jump and scream for no reason at all, other than the fact that they were young and healthy and quite pleased with themselves.

Suddenly, Annabelle became aware of a dark figure rapidly ascending the hill. She fell abruptly silent as she ascertained that there was one—no, two—riders advancing to the dry meadow. "Someone's coming!" she said. "A pair of riders. Hurry, fetch your clothes!" Her low-voiced alarm cut through the girls' jubilation. They stared at each other with wide eyes and burst into panicked action. Shrieking,

Daisy and Evie broke into a dead run toward the remains of the picnic, where they had left their dresses.

Annabelle began to follow, then stopped and turned abruptly as the riders thundered to a halt just behind her. She faced them warily, trying to assess what danger they might present. Looking up at their faces, she felt a bolt of chilling dismay as she recognized them.

Lord Westcliff . . . and even worse . . . Simon Hunt.

Chapter 10

*O*nce Annabelle met Hunt's stunned gaze, she could not seem to look away. It was like one of those nightmares that one always awoke from with a sense of relief, knowing that something so dreadful could never really happen. Were the situation not so completely to her disadvantage, she might have enjoyed the prospect of Simon Hunt rendered absolutely speechless. At first his face was blank, as if he was having tremendous difficulty absorbing the fact that she was standing before him dressed only in a chemise, corset, and drawers. His gaze slid over her, slowly coming to rest on her flushed face.

Another moment or two of suffocated silence, and Hunt swallowed hard before speaking in a rusty-sounding voice. "I probably shouldn't ask. But what the hell are you doing?"

The words unlocked Annabelle from her paralysis. She certainly could not stand there and converse with him while she was clad in her undergarments. But her dignity—or the threads that remained of it—demanded that she not screech idiotically and dash for her clothes the way Evie and Daisy were doing. Settling for a compromise, she strode briskly to her discarded gown and clasped it to her front as she turned to face Simon Hunt once more. "We're playing Rounders," she said, her voice far higher-pitched than usual.

Hunt glanced around the scene before settling on her again. "Why did you—"

"One can't run properly in skirts," Annabelle interrupted. "I should think that would be obvious."

Absorbing that, Hunt averted his face swiftly, but not before she saw the sudden flash of his grin.

Behind her, Annabelle heard Daisy say to Lillian accusingly, "I thought you said that no one ever comes to this meadow!"

"That's what I was told," Lillian replied, her voice muffled as she stepped into the circle of her gown and bent to jerk it upward.

The earl, who had been mute until that point, spoke with his gaze trained studiously on the distant scenery. "Your information was correct, Miss Bowman," he said in a controlled manner.

"Well, then, why are you here?" Lillian demanded accusingly, as if she, and not Westcliff, was the owner of the estate.

The question caused the earl's head to whip around. He gave the American girl an incredulous glance before he dragged his gaze away once more. "Our presence here is purely coincidental. I wished to have a look at the northwest section of my estate today." He gave the word *my* a subtle but distinct emphasis. "While Mr. Hunt and I were traveling along the lane, we heard your screaming. We thought it best to investigate, and came with the intention of rendering aid, if necessary. Little did I realize that you would be using this field for . . . for . . ."

"Rounders-in-knickers," Lillian supplied helpfully, sliding her arms into her sleeves.

The earl seemed incapable of repeating the ridiculous phrase. He turned his horse away and spoke curtly over his shoulder. "I plan to develop a case of amnesia within the next five minutes. Before I do so, I would suggest that you refrain from any future activities involving nudity outdoors, as the next passersby who discover you may not prove to be as indifferent as Mr. Hunt and I."

Despite Annabelle's mortification, she had to repress a skeptical snort at the earl's claim of indifference on Hunt's behalf, not to mention his own. Hunt had certainly managed to get quite an eyeful of her. And though Westcliff's scrutiny had been far more subtle, it had not escaped her that he had stolen a quick but thorough glance at Lillian before he had veered his horse away. However, in light of her current state of undress, it was hardly the time to deflate Westcliff's holier-than-thou demeanor.

"Thank you, my lord," Annabelle said with a calmness that pleased her immensely. "And now, having dispensed such excellent advice, I would ask that you allow us some privacy to restore ourselves."

"With pleasure," Westcliff growled.

Before Simon Hunt departed, he could not seem to keep from looking back at Annabelle as she stood clutching her gown across her chest. Despite his apparent composure, it seemed to her that his color had heightened . . . and there was no mistaking the smoldering of his jet-black eyes. Annabelle longed for the self-possession to stare at him with cool disregard, but instead she felt flushed and disheveled and thoroughly off-balance. He seemed on the verge of saying something to her, then checked himself and muttered beneath his breath with a self-derisive smile. His horse stomped and snorted impatiently, pivoting eagerly as Hunt guided him to gallop after Westcliff, who was already halfway across the field.

Mortified, Annabelle turned to Lillian, who was blushing but admirably self-possessed. "Of all men to discover us like this," Annabelle said in disgust, "it *would* have to be those two."

"You have to admire such arrogance," Lillian commented dryly. "It must have taken years to cultivate."

"Which man are you referring to? . . . Mr. Hunt or Lord Westcliff?"

"Both. Although the earl's arrogance just may edge out Mr. Hunt's—which I call a truly impressive feat."

They stared at each other in shared disdain for their departed visitors, and suddenly Annabelle laughed irrepressibly. "They were surprised, weren't they?"

"Not nearly as surprised as we were," Lillian

rejoined. "The question is, how are we to face them again?"

"How are they to face us?" Annabelle countered. "We were minding our own business—*they* were the intruders!"

"How right you . . ." Lillian began, and stopped as she became aware of a choking noise coming from their picnic spot. Evie was writhing on the blanket, while Daisy stood over her with arms akimbo.

Hurrying to the pair, Annabelle asked Daisy, "What is it?"

"The embarrassment was too much for her," Daisy said.

Evie rolled on the blanket, a napkin concealing her face, while one exposed ear had turned the color of pickled beets. The more she tried to control her giggles, the worse they became, until she gasped frantically for air in between yelps. Somehow she managed to squeak out a few words. "What a s-s-smashing introduction to lawn sports!" And then she was snorting with more spasms of helpless laughter, while the other three stood over her.

Daisy threw Annabelle a significant glance. "*Those*," she informed her, "are conniptions."

Simon and Westcliff rode away from the meadow at a fast gallop, slowing to a walk when they entered the forest and followed a trail that wound through the wooded terrain. It was a good two minutes before either of them was inclined, or indeed able, to speak. Simon's head was whirling with images of Annabelle Peyton's firm, flour-

ishing curves clad in ancient undergarments that
had shrunk from a thousand washings. It was a
good thing that he and she had not found themselves alone in such a circumstance, for Simon
was certain that he wouldn't have been able to
leave her without doing something completely
barbaric.

In Simon's entire life, he had never experienced such potent craving as he had the moment he had seen Annabelle half-undressed
in the meadow. His entire body had been
flooded with the urge to dismount his horse,
seize Annabelle in his arms, and carry her to
the nearest soft patch of grass he could find.
He could not imagine a more unholy temptation than the sight of her voluptuous body. She
had looked so enchantingly mortified, blushing
everywhere. He wanted to remove her ragged
undergarments with his teeth and fingers; and
then he wanted to kiss her from head to toe,
taste her in sweet, soft places that—

"No," Simon muttered, feeling his blood
heat until it scalded the inside of his veins. He
could not allow himself to pursue that line of
thought, or his hard-thrumming desire would
make the rest of the ride damned uncomfortable. When he had gotten his lust under control, Simon glanced at Westcliff, who appeared
to be brooding. That was unusual for Westcliff,
who was not the brooding sort.

The two men had been friends for about five
years, having met at a supper given by a pro-
gressive politician with whom they were both

acquainted. Westcliff's autocratic father had just died, and it had been left to Marcus, the new earl, to take charge of the family's business affairs. He had found the family finances to be superficially sound but ailing underneath, much like a patient who had contracted a terminal disease but still appeared healthy. Alarmed by the steady losses revealed by the account books, Westcliff had recognized that drastic changes had to be made. He had resolved to avoid the fate of other peers who spent their lives presiding over an ever-shrinking family fortune. Unlike the silver-fork novels that depicted countless peers losing their wealth at the gambling tables, the reality was that modern aristocrats were generally not so reckless as they were simply inept financial managers. Conservative investments, old-fashioned views and ill-fated fiscal arrangements were slowly eroding aristocratic wealth and allowing a newly prosperous class of professional men to encroach on the higher levels of society. Any man who chose to disregard the influences of science and industrial advances on the emerging economy was sure to be abandoned in its churning wake . . . and Westcliff had no desire to be included in that category.

When Simon and Westcliff had struck up a friendship, there had been no doubt that each man was using the other to get something he wanted. Westcliff had wanted the benefit of Simon's financial instincts, and Simon had wanted an entree into the world of the privileged class. But as they'd become acquainted with each other, it became apparent that they were alike in many ways.

As Simon had continued to be a regular guest at Stony Cross, and a frequent visitor to Westcliff's London house, Marsden Terrace, the earl's friends had gradually come to accept him into their circle. It had been a welcome surprise for Simon to discover that he was not the only commoner whom Westcliff considered a close friend. The earl seemed to prefer the company of men whose perspectives of the world had been shaped outside the walls of noble estates.

At the moment, the usually coolheaded earl seemed rather more perturbed than the situation warranted.

"Damn," Westcliff finally exclaimed. "I have occasional business dealings with their father. How am I supposed to face Thomas Bowman without remembering that I've seen his daughter in her underwear?"

"Daughters," Simon corrected. "They were both there."

"I only noticed the taller one."

"Lillian?"

"Yes, that one." A scowl crossed Westcliff's face. "Good God, no wonder they're all unmarried! They're heathens even by American standards. And the way that woman spoke to me, as if *I* should have been embarrassed to interrupt their pagan revelry—"

"Westcliff, you sound like a prig," Simon interrupted, amused by the earl's vehemence.

"A few innocent girls scampering about in the meadow is hardly the end of civilization as we know it. And if they had been village wenches, you'd have thought nothing of it. Hell, you probably would have joined them. I've seen you do things with your paramours at parties and balls that—"

"Well, they aren't village wenches, are they? They're young ladies—or at least they're supposed to be. Why in God's name are a bunch of *wallflowers* behaving in such a way?"

Simon grinned at his friend's aggrieved tone. "My impression is that they have become allies in their unwedded state. For most of the past season they sat without speaking to each other, but it seems they've recently struck up a friendship."

"For what purpose?" the earl asked with deep suspicion.

"Perhaps they're merely trying to enjoy themselves?" Simon suggested, interested by the degree to which Westcliff had taken exception to the girls' behavior. Lillian Bowman, in particular, seemed to have bothered him profoundly. And that was unusual for the earl, who always treated women with casual ease. To Simon's knowledge, despite the numbers of women who pursued him in and out of bed, Westcliff had never lost his detachment.

"Then they should take up needlework, or do whatever it is that proper women do to enjoy themselves," the earl growled. "At least they should find a hobby that doesn't involve running naked through the countryside."

"They weren't naked," Simon pointed out. "Much to my regret."

"As you know, I'm not usually one to give advice when it isn't asked for—"

Simon interrupted with a bark of laughter. "Westcliff, I doubt that a day in your life has passed without you giving advice to someone about something."

"I offer advice when it's obviously needed," the earl said with a scowl.

Simon gave him a sardonic glance. "Dispense your words of wisdom, then, as it appears that I'm going to hear them whether I wish to or not."

"It pertains to Miss Peyton. If you're wise, you'll divest yourself of all notions concerning her. She's a shallow bit of goods, and as self-absorbed as any creature I've ever met. The facade is beautiful, I'll grant you . . . but in my judgment there's nothing beneath to recommend it. No doubt you're thinking of taking her as your mistress if she fails in her bid to win Kendall. My advice is, don't. There are women who have infinitely more to offer."

Simon didn't reply for a moment. "What gave you the impression that I had any interest in Miss Peyton?" Simon asked in a noncommittal tone.

"The fact that you nearly fell off your horse when you saw her in her drawers."

That elicited a reluctant smile from Simon. "With a facade like that, I may not give a damn about what's beneath."

"You should," the earl said emphatically. "Miss Peyton is a selfish jade if I've ever seen one."

"Westcliff," Simon asked conversationally, "does it ever occur to you that you might occasionally be wrong? About anything?"

The earl looked perplexed by the question. "Actually, no."

Shaking his head with a rueful grin, Simon spurred his horse to a faster gait.

Chapter 11

As the girls walked back to Stony Cross Manor, Annabelle became uncomfortably aware of a twinge in her ankle. She must have turned it during the Rounders game, though she could not recall the precise moment when it had happened. Sighing heavily, she hefted the basket in her hand and lengthened her stride to keep pace with Lillian, who looked pensive. Daisy and Evie walked a few yards behind them, both of them involved in an earnest conversation.

"What are you worrying about?" Annabelle asked Lillian in a low voice.

"The earl and Mr. Hunt . . . do you think they will tell anyone about having seen us this afternoon? It would put a nasty dent in our reputations."

"I don't think Westcliff would," Annabelle said after a moment's thought. "I was inclined to believe him when he made that remark about amnesia. And he doesn't seem to be a man who is given to gossip."

"What about Mr. Hunt?"

Annabelle frowned. "I don't know. It didn't escape me that he made no promise to remain silent. I suppose he'll keep his mouth closed if he thinks he has something to gain from it."

"You should be the one to ask him, then. As soon as you see Mr. Hunt at the ball tonight, you must go to him and make him promise not to tell anyone about our Rounders game."

Recalling the dance that would take place at the manor that evening, Annabelle groaned. She was relatively—no, positively—certain that she could not bear to face Hunt after what had happened that afternoon. On the other hand, Lillian was right—one couldn't assume that Hunt would be silent. Annabelle would have to deal with him, much as she dreaded the prospect. "Why me?" she asked, although she already knew the answer.

"Because Hunt likes you. Everyone knows that. He'll be much more inclined to do something you ask."

"He won't give something for nothing," Annabelle muttered, while the throbbing in her ankle worsened. "What if he makes some vulgar proposition to me?"

Lillian looked at her with a touch of surprise. "He wouldn't do that, would he?"

"Of course he would. He's a dreadful human being."

"Do you really find Mr. Hunt so repulsive?" Lillian asked. "He's not bad, actually. I'd even go so far as to call him handsome."

"He's so insufferable that I've never really

taken notice of his looks. But I will admit that he's . . ." Annabelle fell into a confused silence as she considered the question.

The word "handsome" was usually applied to people with highly chiseled faces and slender, elegant proportions. But Simon Hunt redefined the word with his bold, audacious black eyes, and the wide mouth that was forever edged with irreverent humor. Even his unusual height and brawn seemed to suit him perfectly, as if nature had recognized that he was not a creature to be formed by half measures.

She rubbed her forehead, which was suddenly as sore as if it had been whacked with a Rounders bat. "Can't we just ignore the whole thing and just hope that he'll have the good taste to keep his mouth shut?"

"Oh, yes," Lillian said sarcastically, "by all means, let's just cross our fingers and wait . . . if your nerves can bear the suspense."

Massaging her temples, Annabelle made a sound of distress. "All right. I'll approach him tonight and ask him to be a gentleman about it. And then I'll stand there and watch while he laughs his head off."

A satisfied grin curved Lillian's mouth. "I'm certain you can come to some agreement with Mr. Hunt."

After they parted company at the manor, Annabelle went to her room for an afternoon nap, which she hoped would restore her to rights before the supper ball. Her mother was nowhere to be seen, most likely having elected to take tea with some of the other ladies in the downstairs parlor. Annabelle was thankful for her mother's absence, which allowed her to change her clothes and wash without having to answer any unwanted questions. Although Philippa was a fond and generally permissive parent, she would not have reacted well to the news that her daughter had been involved in some scrape with the Bowman sisters.

After changing into fresh undergarments, Annabelle slipped beneath the slickly ironed bed linens. To her frustration, the nagging pain of her ankle made it impossible to sleep. Feeling weary and irritable, she rang for a maid to bring a cold footbath, and she sat with her foot soaking for a good half hour. Her ankle was most definitely swollen, leading her to conclude grumpily that it had been a singularly unlucky day. Cursing as she eased a fresh stocking over the pale, puffy flesh, Annabelle dressed herself slowly. She rang for the maid once more when she needed help to tighten her corset and fasten the back of her yellow silk gown.

"Miss?" the maid murmured, her eyes squinting with concern as she glanced into Annabelle's set face. "You look a bit peaked . . . Is there aught I can bring for you? The housekeeper keeps a tonic in her closet for female ailments—"

"No, it's not that," Annabelle said with a wan smile. "It's just a twinge in my ankle."

"Some willowbark tea, then?" the girl suggested, moving behind Annabelle to button the back of the ball gown. "I'll run down and fetch it straightaways, and you can drink it while I do your hair."

"Yes, thank you." Annabelle stood still as the maid's nimble fingers fastened the gown, then she sank gratefully into the chair before the dressing table. She stared at her own strained reflection in the Queen Anne looking glass. "I can't think how I injured it. I'm never clumsy."

The maid fluffed the pale golden tulle that trimmed the sleeves of Annabelle's gown. "I'll hurry with the tea, miss. That will set you to rights."

Just as the maid left, Philippa entered the room. Smiling at the sight of her daughter dressed in the yellow ball gown, she stood behind her, and met her gaze in the looking glass. "You look lovely, darling."

"I feel wretched," Annabelle said wryly. "I turned my ankle during my walk with the wall-flowers this afternoon."

"Must you refer to yourselves that way?" Philippa asked, looking perturbed. "Surely you could think of some more flattering name for your little group—"

"But it suits us," Annabelle said with a grin. "If it makes you feel better, I do say the word with a suitable touch of irony."

Philippa sighed. "I'm afraid my own store of irony is quite depleted at the moment. It isn't easy for me to watch you struggle and scheme, while other girls of your station have so much easier a time of it. Seeing you in borrowed gowns, and knowing the burdens you carry . . . I've thought a thousand times that if only your father hadn't died, and if only we had just a little money . . ."

Annabelle shrugged. "As they say, Mama . . . 'if turnips were watches, I'd have one by my side.' "

Philippa stroked her hair lightly. "Why don't you rest in our room tonight? I'll read to you, while you lie with your ankle propped up—"

"Don't tempt me," Annabelle said feelingly. "I'd like nothing better—but I can't afford to stay up here tonight. I can't miss a single opportunity to make an impression on Lord Kendall." *And negotiate with Simon Hunt*, she thought, feeling hollow with apprehension.

After drinking a large mug of willowbark tea, Annabelle was able to make her way downstairs with scarcely a wince, although the swelling of her ankle had refused to abate. She had time for a brief exchange with Lillian before the guests were led to the dining hall. A touch of sun had left Lillian's cheeks pink and glowing, her brown eyes velvety in the candlelight. "So far, Lord Westcliff has made an obvious effort to ignore the wallflowers," Lillian said with a grin. "You were right—there'll be no trouble from that quarter. Our only potential problem is Mr. Hunt."

"He won't be a problem," Annabelle said grimly. "As I promised earlier, I'll talk to him."

Lillian responded with a relieved grin. "You're a peach, Annabelle."

As they were seated at the supper table, Annabelle was disconcerted to discover that she had been located near Lord Kendall. On any other occasion, it would have been a gratifying boon, but on this particular evening, Annabelle wasn't feeling her best. She was unequal to the task of making intelligent conversation while her ankle was throbbing and her head was aching. To add to her discomfort, Simon Hunt was seated almost directly opposite her, looking maddeningly self-possessed. And making matters even worse, a sense of queasiness kept her from doing justice to the magnificent repast. Bereft of her usual healthy appetite, she found herself picking listlessly at the contents of her plate. Every time she looked up, she found Hunt's shrewd gaze on her and braced herself for some subtle taunt. Mercifully, however, the few remarks he made to her were bland and commonplace, and she was able to suffer through the meal without incident.

A tide of music began to surge from the ballroom as the supper concluded, and Annabelle was thankful that the ball would begin soon. For once she would be entirely happy to sit in the line of wallflowers and rest her feet while others danced. She supposed that she had taken too much sun earlier in the day, as she was feeling unpleasantly light-headed and sore. Lillian and Daisy, by contrast, looked as vibrant and healthy as ever. Unfortunately, poor Evie had gotten a scolding from her aunt that had left her sorely chastened. "The sun makes her freckle," Daisy told Annabelle ruefully. "Aunt Florence told Evie that after our outing she's become as spotty as a leopard, and she's to have nothing more to do with us until her complexion returns to normal."

Annabelle frowned, feeling a wave of sympathy for her friend. "Beastly Aunt Florence," she muttered. "Obviously her sole purpose in life is to make Evie miserable."

"And she's brilliant at it," Daisy agreed. Suddenly she saw something over Annabelle's shoulder that made her eyes turn as round as saucers. "Zounds! Mr. Hunt is coming this way. I am *perishing* of thirst, so I'll just visit the refreshment table, and leave the two of you to, er . . ."

"Lillian told you," Annabelle said grimly.

"Yes, and she and Evie and I are ever so grateful that you're going to talk to him on our behalf." Daisy fled promptly.

Annabelle started as she heard Simon Hunt's deep voice close to her ear. The quiet jeer of his baritone seemed to resonate all the way down her spine. "Good evening, Miss Peyton. I see you're fully clothed . . . for a change."

Gritting her teeth, Annabelle turned to face him. "I must confess, Mr. Hunt, I had expected a rash of insulting comments from you, and yet you managed to behave like a gentleman all through dinner."

"It wasn't easy," he acknowledged gravely. "But I thought I would leave the shocking behavior to you . . ." He paused delicately before adding, ". . . since you seem to be doing so well at it of late."

"My friends and I did nothing wrong!"

"Did I say that I disapproved of your playing Rounders in the altogether?" he asked innocently. "On the contrary—I endorse it whole-heartedly. In fact, I think you should do it every day."

"I wasn't in the 'altogether,'" Annabelle retorted in a sharp whisper. "I was wearing undergarments."

"Is that what they were?" he asked lazily.

She flushed bright red, mortified that he had noticed how ragged her underclothes were. "Have you told anyone about seeing us in the meadow?" she asked tensely.

Obviously, that was the question that he had been waiting for. A slow smile curved his lips. "Not yet."

"Are you planning to tell anyone?"

Hunt considered the question with a thoughtful expression that didn't begin to conceal his enjoyment of the situation. "Not planning to, no . . ." He shrugged regretfully. "But you know how it is. Sometimes these things have a way of slipping out during a conversation . . ."

Annabelle narrowed her eyes. "What will it take to keep you quiet?"

Hunt pretended to be shocked by her bluntness. "Miss Peyton, you should learn to handle these matters with a bit more diplomacy, don't you think? I would have assumed that a lady of your refinement would use some tact and delicacy—"

"I don't have time for diplomacy," she interrupted with a scowl. "And it's obvious that you can't be depended upon to keep silent unless you're offered some kind of bribe."

"The word 'bribe' has such negative connotations," he mused. "I prefer to call it an inducement."

"Call it what you like," she said impatiently. "Let's get on with the negotiations, shall we?"

"All right." Hunt's facade was sober, but laughter flickered in the coffee-colored depths of his eyes. "I suppose I could be persuaded to hold my silence about your scandalous cavorting, Miss Peyton. With sufficient inducement."

Annabelle fell silent, her lashes lowering as she considered what she was about to say. Once the words were out, they couldn't be taken back. Dear Lord, why had it fallen to her to buy Simon Hunt's silence regarding a silly Rounders game that she hadn't even wanted to play in the first place? "If you were a gentleman," she muttered, "this wouldn't be necessary."

A wealth of suppressed laughter made his voice husky and uneven. "No, I'm not a gentleman. But I am compelled to remind you that *I* was not the one running half-naked through the meadow this afternoon."

"Will you *hush*?" she whispered sharply. "Someone will overhear you."

Hunt watched her with fascination, his eyes dark and heathen. "Make your best offer, Miss Peyton."

Staring fixedly at a portion of the wall far beyond his shoulder, Annabelle spoke in a suffocated tone, while the rims of her ears turned so hot that her hair was nearly singed. "If you promise to keep quiet about the Rounders game . . . I'll let you kiss me."

The unaccountable silence that followed her statement was excruciating. Forcing her gaze upward, Annabelle saw that she had surprised Hunt. He was staring at her as if she had just spoken in a foreign language, and he was not quite certain of the translation.

"One kiss," Annabelle said, her nerves shredded from the tension between them. "And don't assume that because I let you do it once, that I would ever consent to it again."

Hunt replied in an unusually guarded manner, seeming to choose his words with great care. "I had assumed that you would offer to dance with me. A waltz or a quadrille."

"I had thought of that," she said. "But a kiss is more expedient, not to mention much faster than a waltz."

"Not the way I kiss."

The soft statement caused her knees to quiver. "Don't be absurd," she replied shortly. "An ordinary waltz lasts for at least three minutes. You couldn't possibly kiss someone for that long."

Hunt's voice thickened almost imperceptibly as he replied. "You know best, of course. Very well—I accept your offer. One kiss, in return for keeping your secret. I'll decide when and where it happens."

"The 'when' and 'where' will be determined by mutual agreement," Annabelle countered. "The whole point of this is to keep my repu-

tation from being compromised—I'm hardly
going to let you jeopardize it by choosing some
inappropriate time or place."

Hunt smiled mockingly. "What a negotiator you are, Miss Peyton. God help us all if you
have any future ambitions to take part in the
business world."

"No, my sole ambition is to become Lady
Kendall," Annabelle returned with poisonous
sweetness. She had the satisfaction of seeing his
smile fade.

"That would be a pity," he said. "For you as
well as Kendall."

"Go to the devil, Mr. Hunt," she said beneath her breath, and walked away from him,
ignoring the violent throb of her sprained ankle.

As she made her way to the back terrace, she
became aware that the injury to her ankle had
worsened, until shooting pains had traveled up
to her knee. "Hell's bells," she muttered. In this
condition, she was hardly going to make progress with Lord Kendall. It was not easy to be
seductive when one was on the verge of shrieking in torment. Suddenly feeling exhausted and
defeated, Annabelle decided that she would return to her room. Now that her business with
Simon Hunt was finished, the best thing to do
would be to rest her ankle and hope it would
improve by morning.

With each step she took, the pain intensi-
fied until she could feel trickles of cold sweat
beneath the rigid stays of her corset. She
had never had an injury like this before. Not

only did her leg hurt, but her head was suddenly swimming, and she ached everywhere. Abruptly, the contents of her stomach began an alarming roil. She needed air . . . she had to go outside in the cool darkness, and sit somewhere until the nausea subsided. The door to the back terrace looked dreadfully far away, and she wondered dazedly how she was going to reach it.

Fortunately, the Bowman sisters had hurried toward her as soon as they saw that her conversation with Simon Hunt had concluded. The expectant smile on Lillian's face died away as she met Annabelle's pain-darkened gaze. "You look terrible," Lillian exclaimed. "My God, what did Mr. Hunt say to you?"

"He agreed to keep quiet," Annabelle replied shortly, continuing to hobble toward the terrace. She could scarcely hear the orchestra music over the ringing in her ears.

"And my ankle hurts," she continued in exasperation. "I sprained it earlier in the day, and now I can hardly walk."

"Why didn't you mention something earlier?" Lillian demanded in instant concern. Her slender arm was unexpectedly strong as she curved it around Annabelle's back. "Daisy, go to the nearest door and hold it open while we slip outside."

The sisters helped her outside, and Annabelle wiped her gloved hand over her sweating forehead. "I think I'm going to be sick," she moaned, while her mouth watered disagreeably, and stinging gall rose in her throat. Her leg ached as if it had been crushed by a carriage wheel. "Oh, Lord, I *can't*. I can't be sick now."

"It's all right," Lillian said, guiding her inexorably toward a flower bed that lined the side of the terrace steps. "No one can see you, dear. Be as sick as you want. Daisy and I are here to take care of you."

"That's right," Daisy chimed in from behind her. "True friends never mind holding your hair back while you cast up your crumpets."

Annabelle would have laughed, had she not been overcome with a spasm of mortifying nausea. Fortunately, she had not eaten much during supper, so the process was mercifully quick. Her stomach erupted, and she had no choice but to surrender. Gasping and spitting into the flower bed, she moaned weakly. "I'm sorry. I'm so sorry, Lillian—"

"Don't be ridiculous," came the American girl's calm reply. "You'd do the same for me, wouldn't you?"

" 'Course I would . . . but you would never be so silly . . ."

"You're not being silly," Lillian said gently. "You're sick. Now take my handkerchief."

Still leaning over, Annabelle received the lace-trimmed square of linen gratefully, but recoiled at the scent of perfume. "*Ugh*, I can't," she whispered. "The smell. Do you have one that isn't scented?"

"Drat," Lillian said apologetically. "Daisy, where is your handkerchief?"

"Forgot it," came the succinct reply.

"You'll have to use this one," Lillian told Annabelle. "It's all we've got."

A masculine voice entered the conversation. "Take this one."

Chapter 12

Too dizzy to notice what was happening around her, Annabelle received the clean handkerchief that was thrust in her hand. It was mercifully free of any smell except for the crisp hint of starch. After wiping her perspiring face, then her mouth, Annabelle managed to straighten and face the newcomer. Her sore stomach did a slow, agonizing revolution at the sight of Simon Hunt. It seemed that he had followed her out to the terrace just in time to witness her humiliating nausea. She wanted to die. If only she could conveniently expire right then, and forever obliterate the knowledge that Simon Hunt had seen her cast up her crumpets in the flower bed.

Hunt's face was impassive, save for the frown indentations between his brows. Quickly he reached out to steady her as she swayed before him. "In light of our recent agreement," he murmured, "this is most unflattering, Miss Peyton."

"Oh, go away," Annabelle moaned, but she

found herself leaning hard against the strong support of his body as another wave of illness washed over her. She clamped the handkerchief to her mouth and breathed through her nose, and mercifully the feeling passed. But the most debilitating weakness she had ever felt swept over her, and she knew that if he had not been there, she would have crumpled to the ground. Good Lord, what was wrong with her?

Hunt immediately adjusted his hold, bracing her easily. "I thought you looked pale," he remarked, gently stroking back a lock of hair that had fallen over her damp face. "What's the matter, sweetheart? Is it just your stomach, or do you hurt somewhere else?"

Somewhere beneath the layers of misery Annabelle was startled by the endearment, not to mention the fact that a gentleman should never, ever have referred to one of a lady's internal parts. However, at the moment she was too ill to do anything but cling to his coat lapels. Concentrating on his question, she pondered the chaos inside her inhospitable body. "I hurt everywhere," she whispered. "My head, my stomach, my back . . . but most of all my ankle."

As she spoke, she noticed that her lips felt numb. She licked at them experimentally, alarmed by the lack of sensation. Had she been just a bit less disoriented, she would have noticed that Hunt was staring at her in a way that he never had before. Later, Daisy would describe in detail how protective Simon Hunt had seemed as he had stood with his arms around her. For now, however, Annabelle was too wretched to perceive anything outside her own swamping illness.

Lillian spoke briskly, moving forward to extricate Annabelle from Hunt's grasp. "Thank you for the use of your handkerchief, sir. You may leave now, as my sister and I are fully capable of taking care of Miss Peyton."

Ignoring the American girl, Hunt kept his arm around Annabelle as he stared into her blanched face. "How did you hurt your ankle?" he asked.

"The Rounders game, I think . . ."

"I didn't see you drink anything at dinner." Hunt laid his hand across her forehead, searching for signs of fever. The gesture was astonishingly intimate and familiar. "Did you have something earlier?"

"If you mean spirits or wine, no." Annabelle's body seemed to be collapsing slowly, as if her mind had released all control over the movement of her limbs. "I drank some willow-bark tea in my room."

Hunt's warm hand moved to the side of her face, conforming gently to the curve of her cheek. She was so cold, shivering inside her sweat-dampened gown, her skin covered with gooseflesh. Perceiving the inviting heat that radiated from his body, she was nearly overcome with the urge to delve into his coat like a small burrowing animal. "I'm f-freezing," she whispered, and his arm tightened reflexively around her.

"Hold on to me," he murmured, adroitly

managing to shed his coat while supporting her trembling form at the same time. He wrapped her in the garment, which retained the warmth of his skin, and she responded with an inarticulate sound of gratitude.

Nettled by the sight of her friend being held by a detested adversary, Lillian spoke impatiently. "See here, Mr. Hunt, my sister and I—"

"Go find Mrs. Peyton," Hunt interrupted, in a tone that was no less authoritative for its softness. "And tell Lord Westcliff that Miss Peyton needs a doctor. He'll know whom to send for."

"What are *you* going to do?" Lillian demanded, clearly unaccustomed to being given orders in such a fashion.

Hunt's eyes narrowed as he replied. "I'm going to carry Miss Peyton through the servants' entrance at the side of the house. Your sister will go with us to avoid any appearance of impropriety."

"That shows how little you know about propriety!" Lillian snapped.

"I'm not going to debate the matter. Try to be of some use, will you? *Go.*"

After a furious, tension-fraught pause, Lillian turned and strode toward the ballroom doors.

Daisy was clearly awestruck. "I don't think anyone has ever dared to speak to my sister that way. You're the bravest man I've ever met, Mr. Hunt."

Hunt bent carefully to hook his arm beneath Annabelle's knees. He lifted her with ease, clasping a mass of shivering limbs and rustling silk skirts in his arms. Annabelle had never been carried anywhere by a man—she could not conceive that it was really happening. "I think . . . I could walk part of the way," she managed to say.

"You wouldn't make it down the terrace steps," Hunt said flatly. "Indulge me while I demonstrate the chivalrous side of my nature. Can you put your arms around my neck?"

Annabelle obeyed, grateful to have the weight taken off her burning ankle. Surrendering to the temptation to put her head on his shoulder, she curled her left arm around his neck. As he carried her down the flagstone steps of the back terrace, she could feel the facile play of muscle beneath the layers of his shirt.

"I didn't think you had a chivalrous side," she said, her teeth clicking as another chill shook her. "I th-thought you were a complete scoundrel."

"I don't know how people get such ideas about me," he replied, glancing down at her with a teasing gleam in his eyes. "I've always been tragically misunderstood."

"I still think you're a scoundrel."

Hunt grinned and shifted her more comfortably in his arms. "Obviously illness hasn't impaired your judgment."

"Why are you helping me after I just told you to go to the devil?" she whispered.

"I have a vested interest in preserving your health. I want you to be in top form when I collect on my debt."

As Hunt descended the steps with surefooted

swiftness, she felt the smooth grace with which
he moved—not like a dancer, but like a cat
on the prowl. With their faces so close, Annabelle saw that a ruthlessly close shave had not
been able to disguise the dark grain of whis-
kers beneath his skin. Seeking a more secure
hold on him, Annabelle reached farther around
his neck, until her fingertips brushed the ends
of hair that curled slightly against his nape.
What a pity I'm so sick, she thought. *If I wasn't
so cold and dizzy and weak, I might actually
enjoy being carried like this.*

Reaching the path that extended along the
side of the manor, Hunt paused to allow Daisy
to skirt around them and lead the way. "The
servants' door," he reminded her, and the girl
nodded.

"Yes, I know which one it is." Daisy glanced
over her shoulder as she preceded them on the
path. Her small face was tense with worry. "I've
never heard of a sprained ankle making anyone
sick to her stomach," she commented.

"I suspect this is more than a sprained
ankle," Hunt replied.

"Do you think it was the willowbark tea?"
Daisy asked.

"No, willowbark wouldn't cause such a reaction. I have an idea about what the problem
might be, but I won't be able to confirm it until
we reach Miss Peyton's room."

"How do you intend to 'confirm' your idea?"
Annabelle asked warily.

"All I want to do is look at your ankle."

Hunt smiled down at her. "Surely I deserve that much, after I take you up three flights of stairs."

As it turned out, the stairs were no effort for him at all. When they reached the top of the third flight, his breathing hadn't even altered. Annabelle suspected that he could have carried her ten times as far without breaking a sweat. When she said as much to him, he replied in a matter-of-fact tone. "I spent most of my youth hauling sides of beef and pork to my father's shop. Carrying you is far more enjoyable."

"How sweet," Annabelle mumbled sickly, her eyes closed. "Every woman dreams of being told that she's preferable to a dead cow."

Laughter rumbled in his chest, and he turned to avoid bumping her foot against the doorframe. Daisy opened the door for them, and stood watching anxiously as Hunt brought Annabelle to the brocade-covered bed.

"Here we are," he said, laying her down and reaching for an extra pillow to prop her to a half-sitting position.

"Thank you," she whispered, staring into the thick-lashed sable eyes above her own.

"I want to see your leg."

Her heart seemed to stop at the outrageous statement. When her pulse resumed, it was weak and far too brisk. "I would rather wait until the doctor arrives."

"I'm not asking for permission." Ignoring her protests, Hunt reached for the hem of her skirts.

"Mr. Hunt," Daisy exclaimed in outrage,

hurrying over to him. "Don't you dare! Miss Peyton is ill, and if you don't remove your hands at once—"

"Settle your feathers," Hunt replied sardonically. "I'm not going to abuse Miss Peyton's maidenly virtue. Not yet, at any rate." His gaze switched to Annabelle's pale face. "Don't move. Charming as your legs undoubtedly are, they're not going to incite me to a frenzy of—" He broke off with a sharp intake of breath as he lifted her skirts and saw her swollen ankle. "Damn. Until now I've always thought of you as a reasonably intelligent woman. Why the hell did you go downstairs in this condition?"

"Oh, Annabelle," Daisy murmured. "Your ankle looks terrible!"

"It wasn't that bad earlier," Annabelle said defensively. "It's gotten much worse in the past half hour, and—" She yelped in a mixture of pain and alarm as she felt Hunt reach farther beneath her skirts. "What are you doing? Daisy, don't let him—"

"I'm removing your stocking," Hunt said. "And I would advise Miss Bowman not to interfere."

Frowning at him, Daisy came to Annabelle's side. "I would advise *you* to proceed with caution, Mr. Hunt," she said smartly. "I am not going to stand by passively while you molest my friend."

Hunt sent her a glance of scalding mockery, while he found the ridge of Annabelle's garter and unfastened it deftly. "Miss Bowman, in a few minutes we're going to be overrun with visitors, including Mrs. Peyton, Lord Westcliff, and your hardheaded sister, followed soon thereafter by the doctor. Even I, seasoned ravisher that I am, require more time than that to molest someone." His expression changed as Annabelle gasped in pain at his gentle touch. Deftly he unrolled her stocking, his fingertips feather-light, but her skin was so sensitive that even the softest stroke caused an unbearable sting. "Hold still, sweetheart," he murmured, drawing the length of silk from her flinching leg.

Biting her lip, Annabelle watched as his dark head bent over her ankle. He turned it carefully, taking care not to touch her more than necessary. Then he went still, his dark head bent over her leg. "Just as I thought."

Leaning forward, Daisy looked at the place on her ankle that Hunt indicated. "What are those little marks?"

"Adder bite," Hunt said tersely. He rolled up his shirtsleeves, exposing muscular forearms covered with dark hair.

The two girls glanced at him in shock. "I've been bitten by a *snake*?" Annabelle asked dazedly. "But how? When? That can't be true. I would have felt something . . . wouldn't I?"

Hunt reached inside the pocket of the coat that was still wrapped around her, searching for something. "Sometimes people don't notice the moment they're bitten. The Hampshire woods are full of adders at this time of year. It probably happened during your outing this afternoon." Finding what he sought, he extracted a small folding knife and flipped it open.

Annabelle's eyes widened with alarm. "What are you doing?"

Picking up her stocking, Hunt severed it neatly in two. "Making a tourniquet."

"D-do you always carry one of those with you?" She had always thought of him as somewhat piratical, and now seeing him in his shirtsleeves with a knife in hand, the image was strongly reinforced.

Sitting beside her outstretched leg, Hunt smoothed her skirts up to her knee and fastened a length of silk above her ankle. "Nearly always," he said wryly, concentrating on his handiwork. "Being a butcher's son consigns me to a lifelong fascination with knives."

"I never thought—" Annabelle stopped and gasped in pain at the soft cinch of silk.

Hunt's gaze shot to hers, and there was a new tautness in his face. "I'm sorry," he said, carefully looping the other half of the stocking beneath her injury. He talked to distract her while he tightened the second tourniquet. "This is what comes of wearing those damned flimsy slippers outside. You must have walked right over an adder who was sunning himself . . . and when he saw one of those pretty little ankles, he decided to take a nibble." He paused, and said something beneath his breath that sounded like, "I can't say that I blame him."

Her leg pulsed and burned, causing a watery sting of response in her eyes. Fighting the mortifying threat of tears, Annabelle dug her fingers into the thick, brocaded counterpane beneath her. "Why has my ankle only started to hurt this badly now if I was bitten earlier in the day?"

"It can take several hours for the effects to set in." Hunt glanced at Daisy. "Miss Bowman, ring the servants' bell—tell them that we need some clivers steeped in boiling water. Immediately."

"What are clivers?" Daisy asked suspiciously.

"A hedgerow weed. The housekeeper has kept a dried bundle of them in her closet ever since the master gardener was bitten last year."

Daisy rushed to comply, leaving the two of them temporarily alone.

"What happened to the gardener?" Annabelle asked through chattering teeth. She was overcome with continuous shivers, as if she had been immersed in ice water. "Did he die?"

Hunt's expression did not change, but she sensed that her question had startled him. "No," he said gently, drawing closer. "No, sweetheart . . ." Taking her trembling hand in his, he warmed her fingers in a gentle grip. "Hampshire adders don't produce enough venom to kill anything larger than a cat, or a very small dog." His gaze was caressing as he continued. "You'll be fine. Uncomfortable as hell for the next few days, but after that you'll be back to normal."

"You're not trying to be kind, are you?" she asked anxiously.

Bending over her, Hunt stroked back a few

tendrils of hair that had stuck to her sweat-shimmered forehead. Despite the size of his hand, his touch was light and tender. "I never lie for the sake of kindness," he murmured, smiling. "One of my many flaws."

Having given instructions to a footman, Daisy hastened back to the bedside. Although she raised her slender dark brows at the sight of Hunt leaning over Annabelle, she forbore to comment. Instead, she asked, "Shouldn't we cut across the puncture wounds to let the poison out?"

Annabelle sent her a warning glance and croaked, "Don't give him ideas, Daisy!"

Hunt looked up briefly as he replied. "Not for an adder bite." His eyes narrowed as he returned his attention to Annabelle, noting that her breathing was rapid and shallow. "Is it difficult to breathe?"

Annabelle nodded, struggling to pull air into lungs that seemed to have shrunk to a third of their usual size. It felt as if bands were drawing more tightly around her chest with every breath she took, until her ribs threatened to crack from the pressure.

Hunt touched her face softly, his thumb passing over the dry surface of her lips. "Open your mouth." Looking beyond her parted lips, he observed, "Your tongue isn't swelling—you'll be fine. Your corset has to come off, however. Turn over."

Before Annabelle could form a reply, Daisy protested indignantly. "*I'll* help Annabelle with her corset. Leave the room, please."

"I've seen a woman's corset before," he informed her sarcastically.

Daisy rolled her eyes. "Don't be deliberately obtuse, Mr. Hunt. Obviously *you're* not the one I'm worried about. Men don't remove young ladies' corsets for any reason, unless the circumstances are life-threatening—which you have just assured us that they are not."

Hunt regarded her with a long-suffering expression. "Dammit, woman—"

"Swear all you like," Daisy said implacably. "My older sister could outcurse you ten times over." She drew herself up to her full height, though at five feet and one debatable inch, the effect was hardly impressive. "Miss Peyton's corset stays on until you leave the room."

Hunt glanced down at Annabelle, who suddenly craved air too badly to care who removed her corset, so long as it was done. "For God's sake," he said impatiently, and strode to the window, turning his back to them. "I'm not looking. *Do it*."

Seeming to realize that it was the only concession he was prepared to make, Daisy obeyed hurriedly. She eased the coat away from Annabelle's stiff body. "I'll untie the laces in the back and slip it off beneath your gown," she murmured to Annabelle. "That way you'll remain decently covered."

Annabelle couldn't summon sufficient breath to tell her that any concerns she might have had about modesty had paled in comparison to the far more immediate problem of not being able to breathe. Wheezing harshly, she turned to her side and felt Daisy's fingers plucking at the slippery back of her ball gown. Her lungs spasmed in their frustrated attempts to pull in precious air. Letting out an anxious moan, she began to pant desperately.

Daisy let out a few choice curses. "Mr. Hunt, I'm afraid I must borrow your knife—the corset strings are knotted, and I can't—*oof!*" The last exclamation came as Hunt strode to the bed, shoved her unceremoniously aside, and set to work on the corset himself. A few judicious applications of his knife, and suddenly the obstinate garment released its punishing clasp around Annabelle's ribs.

She felt him tug the boned garment away from her body, leaving only the thin veil of her chemise between his gaze and her bare skin. In Annabelle's current condition, the exposure was of little concern. However, she knew in the back of her mind that she would later die of embarrassment.

Turning Annabelle to her back as easily if she were a rag doll, Hunt bent over her. "Don't try so hard, sweetheart." His hand flattened over the upper reach of her chest. Holding her frightened gaze intently, he rubbed in a soothing circle. "Slowly. Just relax."

Staring into the compelling dark glitter of his eyes, Annabelle tried to obey, but her throat clenched around every wheezing breath. She was going to die of suffocation, right there and then.

He wouldn't let her look away from him. "You'll be all right. Let your breath ease in and out. Slowly. That's it. Yes." Somehow the gentle weight of his hand on her chest seemed to help her, as if he had the power to will her lungs back to their normal rhythm. "You're going through the worst of it right now," he said.

"Oh, lovely," she tried to say in acerbic response, but the effort made her choke and hiccup.

"Don't try to talk—just breathe. Another long, slow one . . . another. Good girl."

As Annabelle gradually recovered her breath, the panic began to fade. He was right . . . it was easier if she didn't struggle. The sound of her fitful gasping was underlaid by the mesmerizing softness of his voice. "That's right," he murmured. "That's the way of it." His hand continued to move in a slow, easy rotation over her chest. There was nothing sexual in his touch— in fact, she might have been a child he was trying to soothe. Annabelle was amazed. Who would have ever dreamed that Simon Hunt could be so kind?

Filled with equal parts of confusion and gratitude, Annabelle fumbled for the large hand that moved so gently on her chest. She was so feeble that the gesture required all her strength. Assuming that she was trying to push him away, Hunt began to withdraw, but as he felt her fingers curl around two of his, he went very still.

"Thank you," she whispered.

The touch made Hunt tense visibly, as if the contact had sent a shock through his body. He stared not at her face but at the delicate fingers entwined with his, in the manner of a man who was trying to solve a complex puzzle. Remaining motionless, he prolonged the moment, his lashes lowering to conceal his expression.

Annabelle used her tongue to moisten her dry lips, discovering that she still couldn't feel them. "My face is numb," she said scratchily, letting go of his hand.

Hunt looked up with the wry smile of a man who had just discovered something unexpected about himself. "The clivers will help." He touched the side of her throat, his thumb gliding along the edge of her jaw in a gesture that could only be characterized as a caress. "Which reminds me—" He glanced over his shoulder as if just remembering that Daisy was in the room. "Miss Bowman, has that damned footman brought—"

"It's here," the dark-haired girl said, coming from the doorway with a tray that had just been brought up. Apparently they had both been too absorbed in each other to notice the servant's knock. "The housekeeper sent up the clivers tea, which smells ghastly, and there's also a little bottle that the footman said was 'tincture of nettle.' And it seems the doctor has just arrived and will be coming upstairs any minute— which means that you must leave, Mr. Hunt."

His jaw hardened. "Not yet."

"*Now*," Daisy said urgently. "At least wait outside the door. For Annabelle's sake. She'll be ruined if you're seen in here."

Scowling, Hunt looked down at Annabelle. "Do you want me to go?"

She didn't, actually. In fact, she had an irrational desire to beg him to stay. Oh, what a bewildering turn of events, that she should so desire the company of a man she detested! But the past few minutes had somehow wrought a fragile connection between them, and she found herself in the odd predicament of being unable to say "yes" or "no." "I'll keep breathing," she finally whispered. "You probably should leave."

Hunt nodded. "I'll wait in the hallway," he said gruffly, standing from the bed. Motioning Daisy forward with the tray, he continued to stare at Annabelle. "Drink the clivers, no matter how it tastes. Or I'll come back in here and pour it down your throat." Retrieving his coat, he left the room.

Sighing with relief, Daisy set the tray at the bedside table. "Thank God," she said. "I wasn't certain how I was going to make him go, if he refused. Here . . . let me lift you a bit higher, and I'll push another pillow behind you." The girl elevated her deftly, demonstrating surprising competence. Taking up a huge earthenware mug filled with steaming contents, Daisy pressed the edge against her lips. "Have some of this, dear."

Annabelle swallowed the bitter brown liquid and recoiled. "*Ugh*—"

"More," Daisy said inexorably, lifting it to her mouth.

Annabelle drank again. Her face was so numb that she wasn't aware that some of the medicine had dribbled from her lips until Daisy picked up a napkin from the tray and blotted

her chin. Cautiously Annabelle lifted explor-
atory fingertips to the frozen skin of her face.
"Feels so odd," she said, her voice slurred. "No
sensation in my mouth. Daisy . . . don't say that
I was drooling while Mr. Hunt was here?"

"Of course not," Daisy said immediately. "I
would have done something about it if you had
been. A true friend doesn't let another friend
drool when a man is present. Even if it's a man
that one doesn't wish to attract."

Relieved, Annabelle applied herself to downing more of the clivers, which tasted rather like
burned coffee. Perhaps it was wishful thinking, but she was beginning to feel the tiniest bit
better.

"Lillian must have had a devil of a time finding your mother," Daisy commented. "I can't
imagine what has taken them so long." She
drew back a little to look at Annabelle, her
brown eyes sparkling richly. "I'm actually glad,
though. If they had come quickly, I would have
missed seeing Mr. Hunt's transformation from
a big bad wolf into . . . well . . . a somewhat
nicer wolf."

A reluctant laugh gurgled in Annabelle's
throat. "Quite something, isn't he?"

"Yes, indeed. Arrogant and oh-so-masterful.
Like a figure from one of those torrid novels
that Mama is forever ripping from my hands.
It's a good thing that I was here, or he probably
would have stripped you right down to your un-
mentionables." She continued to chatter as she
helped Annabelle to drink more of the clivers,
and blotted her chin once more. "You know, I

never thought I would say this, but Mr. Hunt isn't quite as terrible as I thought."

Annabelle twisted her lips experimentally as a modicum of sensation returned, making them prickle. "He has his uses, it seems. But . . . don't expect that the transformation is permanent."

Chapter 13

*B*arely two minutes had passed before Simon saw the group he had earlier predicted, consisting of the doctor, Lord Westcliff, Mrs. Peyton, and Lillian Bowman. Leaning his shoulders back against the wall, Simon gave them a speculative stare. Privately, he was amused by the palpable dislike between Westcliff and Miss Bowman, whose obvious mutual animosity betrayed the fact that words had been exchanged.

The doctor was a venerable old man who had attended Westcliff and his relatives, the Marsdens, for nearly three decades. Glancing at Simon with keen eyes set deeply in an age-furrowed face, he spoke with unflappable calmness. "Mr. Hunt, I am told that you assisted the young lady to her room?"

Simon brusquely described Annabelle's condition and symptoms to the doctor, choosing to omit that he, and not Daisy, had been the one to discover the puncture marks on Annabelle's

ankle. Mrs. Peyton listened in white-faced distress. Frowning, Lord Westcliff bent to murmur
to Mrs. Peyton, who nodded and thanked him
distractedly. Simon guessed that Westcliff had
promised that the best care possible would be
provided until her daughter had recovered fully.

"Of course I won't be able to confirm
Mr. Hunt's opinion until I examine the young
lady," the doctor remarked. "However, it may
be advisable to begin brewing some clivers right
away, in the event that the illness was indeed
caused by adder bite—"

"She's already drinking some," Simon interrupted. "I sent for it about a quarter hour ago."

The doctor regarded him with the special
vexation reserved for those who undertook to
make a diagnosis without benefit of a medical
degree. "Clivers is a potent drug, Mr. Hunt,
and possibly injurious in the event that a patient is *not* suffering from snake venom. You
should have waited for a doctor's opinion before administering it."

"The symptoms of adder bite are unmistakable," Simon replied impatiently, wishing the
man would cease tarrying in the hallway and go
do his job. "And I wanted to alleviate Miss Peyton's discomfort as quickly as possible."

The old man's wiry gray brows descended
low over his eyes. "You're quite certain of your
own judgment," came the peppery observation.

"Yes," Simon replied, without blinking.

Suddenly the earl let out a muffled chuckle
and settled a hand on the doctor's shoulder.

"I'm afraid that we'll be forced to stand out here indefinitely, sir, if you attempt to convince my friend that he's wrong about anything. 'Opinionated' is the mildest of adjectives one could apply to Mr. Hunt. I assure you, your energies are far better directed toward caring for Miss Peyton."

"Perhaps so," the doctor returned testily. "Although one suspects that my presence is superfluous in light of Mr. Hunt's expert diagnosis." With that sarcastic comment, the old man entered the room, followed by Mrs. Peyton and Lillian Bowman.

Left alone in the hallway with Westcliff, Simon rolled his eyes. "Bilious old bastard," he muttered. "Could you have sent for someone a bit more decrepit, Westcliff? I doubt he can see or hear well enough to make his own damned diagnosis."

The earl arched one black brow as he regarded Simon with amused condescension. "He's the best doctor in Hampshire. Come downstairs, Hunt. We'll have a brandy."

Simon glanced at the closed door. "Later."

Westcliff replied in a light, far-too-pleasant tone. "Ah, forgive me. Of course you'll want to wait by the door like a stray dog hoping for kitchen scraps. I'll be in my study—do be a good lad and run down to tell me if there's any news."

Rankled, Simon flashed him a cold glare and pushed away from the wall. "All right," he growled, "I'll come."

The earl responded with a satisfied nod. "The doctor will deliver a report to me after he's finished with Miss Peyton."

As Simon accompanied Westcliff to the great staircase, he reflected moodily on his own behavior of the past few minutes. It was a new experience, being driven by his emotions rather than his intellect, and he didn't like it. That didn't seem to matter, however. At the first realization that Annabelle was ill, he had felt his chest turn painfully hollow, as if his heart had been seized for ransom. There had been no question in his mind that he would do whatever was necessary to make her safe and comfortable. And in the moments when Annabelle had struggled to breathe, staring at him with eyes bright with pain and fear, he would have done anything for her. Anything.

God help him if Annabelle ever came to realize the power she had over him . . . a power that posed a perilous threat to pride and self-control. He wanted to possess every part of her body and soul, in every imaginable cast of intimacy. The ever-increasing depth of his passion for her shocked him. And no one of his acquaintance, least of all Westcliff, would understand.

Forcing his features into a blank mask, Simon followed Westcliff into his study.

It was a small, austere room, fitted with gleaming oak paneling and ornamented only by a row of stained-glass windows on one side. With its hard angles and unforgiving furniture, the study was not a comfortable room.

However, it was a thoroughly masculine place, where one could smoke, drink, and talk frankly. Lowering himself to one of the hard chairs positioned by the desk, Simon accepted a brandy from Westcliff and downed it without tasting it. He held out the snifter and nodded in wordless thanks as the earl replenished it.

Before Westcliff could launch into an unwanted diatribe regarding Annabelle, Simon sought to distract him. "You don't seem to rub on well with Miss Bowman," he remarked.

As a diversionary tactic, the mention of Lillian Bowman was supremely effective. Westcliff responded with a surly grunt. "The ill-mannered brat dared to imply that Miss Peyton's mishap was my fault," he said, pouring a brandy for himself.

Simon raised his brows. "How could it be your fault?"

"Miss Bowman seems to think that, as their host, it was my responsibility to ensure that my estate wasn't 'overrun with a plague of poisonous vipers,' as she put it."

"How did you reply?"

"I pointed out to Miss Bowman that the guests who choose to remain clothed when they venture out of doors don't usually seem to get bitten by adders."

Simon couldn't help grinning at that. "Miss Bowman is merely concerned for her friend."

Westcliff nodded in grim agreement. "She can't afford to lose one of them, as she undoubtedly has so few."

Smiling, Simon stared into the depths of his

brandy. "What a difficult evening you've had," he heard Westcliff remark sardonically. "First you were compelled to carry Miss Peyton's nubile young body all the way to her bedroom . . . then you had to examine her injured leg. How terribly inconvenient for you."

Simon's smile faded. "I didn't say that I had examined her leg."

The earl regarded him shrewdly. "You didn't have to. I know you too well to presume that you would overlook such an opportunity."

"I'll admit that I looked at her ankle. And I also cut her corset strings when it became apparent that she couldn't breathe." Simon's gaze dared the earl to object.

"Helpful lad," Westcliff murmured.

Simon scowled. "Difficult as it may be for you to believe, I receive no lascivious pleasure from the sight of a woman in pain."

Leaning back in his chair, Westcliff regarded him with a cool speculation that raised Simon's hackles. "I hope you're not fool enough to fall in love with such a creature. You know my opinion of Miss Peyton—"

"Yes, you've aired it repeatedly."

"And furthermore," the earl continued, "I would hate to see one of the few men of good sense I know to turn into one of those prattling fools who run about pollenating the atmosphere with maudlin sentiment—"

"I'm not in love."

"You're in *something*," Westcliff insisted. "In all the years I've known you, I've never seen you look so mawkish as you did outside her bedroom door."

"I was displaying simple compassion for a fellow human being."

The earl snorted. "Whose drawers you're itching to get into."

The blunt accuracy of the observation caused Simon to smile reluctantly. "It was an itch two years ago," he admitted. "Now it's a full-scale pandemic."

Letting out a sighing groan, Westcliff rubbed the narrow bridge of his nose with his thumb and forefinger. "There is nothing I hate worse than watching a friend charge blindly into disaster. Your weakness, Hunt, is your inability to resist a challenge. Even when the challenge is unworthy of you."

"I like a challenge." Simon swirled the brandy in his snifter. "But that has nothing to do with my interest in her."

"Good God," the earl muttered, "either drink the brandy or stop playing with it. You'll bruise the liquor by swishing it around like that."

Simon sent him a darkly amused glance. "How, exactly, does one 'bruise' a glass of brandy? No, don't tell me—my provincial brain couldn't begin to grasp the concept." Obediently, he took a swallow and set the glass aside. "Now, what were we talking about . . . ? Oh yes, my weakness. Before we discuss that any more, I want you to admit that, at one time in your life or another, you've given greater shrift to desire than to common sense. Because if you haven't, there's no use in talking to you any further about this."

"Of course I have. Every man over the age of twelve has. But the purpose of the higher intellect is to prevent us from repeatedly making such mistakes—"

"Well, there's my problem," Simon said reasonably. "I don't bother with a higher intellect. I've done quite well with just my lower one."

The earl's jaw hardened. "There's a reason that Miss Peyton and her carnivorous friends are all unwed, Hunt. *They're trouble.* If the events of today haven't made that clear, then there's no hope for you."

As Simon Hunt had predicted, Annabelle was in considerable discomfort for the next few days. She had become wretchedly familiar with the flavor of clivers tea, which the doctor had prescribed to be taken every four hours for the first day, and every six hours for the next. Although she could tell that the medicine was helping to reduce the symptoms of the adder venom, it set her stomach in constant revolt. She was exhausted, and yet she couldn't seem to sleep well, and although she longed for something to alleviate her boredom, she couldn't seem to focus on anything for more than a few minutes at a time.

Her friends did their best to cheer and entertain her, for which Annabelle was acutely grateful. Evie sat at her bedside and read aloud from a lurid novel purloined from the estate library.

Daisy and Lillian came to deliver the latest gossip, and made her laugh with their mischievous imitations of various guests. At her insistence, they dutifully reported who seemed to be winning the race for Kendall's attentions. One in particular, a tall, slender, fair-haired girl named Lady Constance Darrowby, had captured his interest.

"She looks to be a very cold sort, if you ask me," Daisy said frankly. "She has a mouth that reminds one of a drawstring purse, and a terribly annoying habit of giggling behind her palm, as if it's unladylike to be caught laughing in public."

"She must have bad teeth," Lillian said hopefully.

"I think she's quite dull," Daisy continued. "I can't imagine what she has to say that Kendall would find of such interest."

"Daisy," Lillian said, "we're talking about a man whose idea of high entertainment is to look at *plants*. His threshold of boredom is obviously limitless."

"At the picnic after the water party today," Daisy told Annabelle, "I thought for a supremely satisfying moment that I had caught Lady Constance in a compromising position with one of the guests. She disappeared for a few minutes with a gentleman who was *not* Lord Kendall."

"Who was it?" Annabelle asked.

"Mr. Benjamin Muxlow—a local gentleman farmer. You know, the salt-of-the-earth sort who's got some decent acreage and a handful of servants and is looking for a wife who will bear him eight or nine children and mend his shirt cuffs and make him pig's-blood-pudding at slaughtertime—"

"Daisy," Lillian interrupted, noticing that Annabelle had suddenly turned green, "try to be a bit less revolting, will you?" She smiled at Annabelle apologetically. "Sorry, dear. But you must admit that the English are willing to eat things that make Americans flee the table with screams of horror."

"Anyway," Daisy continued with exaggerated patience, "Lady Constance vanished after having been seen in the company of Mr. Muxlow, and naturally I went looking for them in the hopes of seeing something that would discredit her, thereby causing Lord Kendall to lose all interest. You can imagine my pleasure at discovering the two of them behind a tree with their heads close together."

"Were they kissing?" Annabelle asked.

"No, drat it. Muxlow was helping Lady Constance to replace a baby robin that had fallen from its nest."

"Oh." Annabelle felt her shoulders slump as she added grumpily, "How sweet of her." She knew that part of her despondency was caused by the effects of the snake venom, not to mention its unpalatable antidote. However, knowing the cause of her low spirits did nothing to improve them.

Seeing her dejection, Lillian picked up a tarnished silver-backed hairbrush. "Forget about

Lady Constance and Lord Kendall for now," she said. "Let me braid your hair—you'll feel much better when it's off your face."

"Where is my looking glass?" Annabelle asked, moving forward to allow Lillian to sit behind her.

"Can't find it," came the girl's calm reply.

It had not escaped Annabelle's notice that the looking glass had conveniently disappeared. She knew that her illness had ravaged her looks, leaving her hair dull and her skin drained of its usual healthy color. In addition, her ever-present nausea had kept her from eating, and her arms looked far too thin as they rested limply on the counterpane.

In the evening, as she lay in her sickbed, the sounds of music and dancing floated through her open bedroom window from the ballroom below. Envisioning Lady Constance waltzing in Lord Kendall's arms, Annabelle shifted restlessly amid the bedclothes, concluding morosely that her chances of marrying had all but vanished. "I hate adders," she grumbled, watching her mother straighten the collection of articles on the beside table . . . medicine-sticky spoons, bottles, handkerchiefs, a hairbrush, and hairpins. "I hate being sick, and I hate walking through the forest, and most of all I hate Rounders-in-knickers!"

"What did you say, dearest?" Philippa asked, pausing in the act of setting a few empty glasses on a tray.

Annabelle shook her head, suddenly overcome

with melancholy. "I . . . oh, nothing, Mama. I've been thinking—I want to go back to London in a day or two, when I'm fit to travel. There's no use in staying here. Lady Constance is as good as Lady Kendall now, and I don't look or feel well enough to attract anyone else, and besides—"

"I wouldn't give up all hope just yet," Philippa said, setting down the tray. She leaned over Annabelle and stroked her brow with a soft, motherly hand. "No betrothal has been announced—and Lord Kendall has been asking after you quite often. And don't forget that enormous bouquet of bluebells that he brought for you. Picked by his own hands, he told me."

Wearily Annabelle glanced at the huge arrangement in the corner, its perfume hanging thickly in the air. "Mama, I've been meaning to ask . . . could you get rid of it? It's lovely, and I did appreciate the gesture . . . but the smell . . ."

"Oh, I didn't think of that," Philippa said immediately. Hurrying to the corner, she picked up the vase of nodding blue flowers and carried them to the door. "I'll set them out in the hall, and I'll ask a housemaid to take them away . . ." Her voice trailed away as she busied herself for a few moments.

Picking up a stray hairpin, Annabelle toyed with the crimped wire and frowned. Kendall's bouquet had been one of many, actually. The news of her illness had prompted a great deal of friendly sympathy from the guests at Stony Cross Manor. Even Lord Westcliff had sent up an arrangement of hothouse roses on behalf of himself and the Marsdens. The proliferation of flowers in vases had given the room a funereal appearance. Oddly, there had been nothing from Simon Hunt . . . not a single note or flower stem. After his solicitous behavior two nights ago, she would have expected *something*. Some small indication of concern . . . but the thought occurred to her that perhaps Hunt had decided that she was an absurd and troublesome creature, no longer worthy of his attention. If so, she should be grateful that she would never again be plagued by him.

Instead, Annabelle felt a stinging pressure behind her nose and the threat of unwanted tears in her eyes. She didn't understand herself. She could not identify the emotion that moved beneath the mass of hopelessness. But she seemed to be filled with a craving for an indescribable something . . . if only she knew what it was. If only—

"Well, this is odd." Philippa sounded thoroughly perplexed as she reentered the room. "I found these just inside the door. Someone has set them there without a note, and no word to anyone. And they're completely new, by the looks of them. Do you think that they are from one of your friends? It must be. Such an eccentric gift could only have come from the American girls."

Raising herself up on a pillow, Annabelle found a pair of objects deposited in her lap, and she regarded the offering with blank surprise. It was a pair of ankle boots, tied together with a dapper red bow. The leather was buttery-soft, dyed a fashionable bronze, and polished until it shone like glass. With low stacked-leather heels and tightly stitched soles, the ankle boots were sensible but stylish. They were ornamented with a delicate embroidered design of leaves that extended across the toes. Staring at the boots, Annabelle felt a sudden laugh rise in her throat.

"They must be from the Bowmans," she said . . . but she knew better.

The boots were a gift from Simon Hunt, who was fully aware that a gentleman should never give an article of clothing to a lady. She should return them at once, she thought, even as she found herself clutching the boots tightly. Only Simon Hunt could manage to give her something so pragmatic and yet so inappropriately personal.

Smiling, she untied the red bow and held one of the boots up. It was surprisingly light, and she knew at a glance that it would fit her perfectly. But how had Hunt known what size to request, and where had he gotten the boots? Slowly she traced a finger across the tiny, exquisite stitches that joined the sole to the gleaming bronze upper.

"How attractive they are," Philippa remarked. "Almost too nice for walking through the muddy countryside."

Annabelle lifted the boot to her nose, inhaling the clean, earthy scent of polished leather. She ran a fingertip around the softly buffed edge of the upper, then held it back to examine it as if it were a priceless sculpture. "I've had quite enough of walking through the country-side," she said with a smile. "These boots will stay on nicely graveled garden paths."

Regarding her fondly, Philippa reached down to smooth Annabelle's hair. "I wouldn't have thought that a new pair of shoes would animate your spirits like this—but I'm awfully glad of it. Shall I send for a tray of soup and toast, dear? You must try to eat something before your next dose of clivers."

Annabelle made a face. "Yes, I'll have soup."

Nodding in satisfaction, Philippa reached for the ankle boots. "I'll just remove these from your lap and set them in the armoire—"

"Not yet," Annabelle murmured, clasping one of the boots possessively.

Philippa smiled as she went to ring the servants' bell.

As Annabelle leaned back and ran her fingertips over the silky leather, she felt a weight from her chest seem to ease. No doubt it was a sign that the venom's effects were fading . . . but that didn't explain why she suddenly felt so relieved and peaceful.

She would have to thank Simon Hunt, of course, and tell him that his gift was unseemly. And if he acknowledged that he had indeed been the one who had bestowed the boots, then Annabelle would have to return them. Something like a book of verse, or a tin of toffee, or a bouquet of flowers would have been far more appropriate. But no gift had ever touched her as this one had.

Annabelle kept the ankle boots with her all

evening, despite her mother's warning that it was bad luck to set footwear on the bed. As she eventually dropped off to sleep, with the orchestra music still washing lightly through the window, she consented to set the boots on the bedside table. When she awoke in the morning, the sight of them made her smile.

Chapter 14

On the third morning after the adder bite, Annabelle finally felt well enough to get out of bed. To her relief, the majority of the guests had gone to a party that was being held at a neighboring estate, which left Stony Cross Manor quiet and largely empty. After consulting with the housekeeper, Philippa settled Annabelle in a private upstairs parlor that overlooked the garden. It was a lovely room, with walls that had been covered with flowered blue paper and hung with cheerful portraits of children and animals. According to the housekeeper, the parlor was usually reserved only for the Marsdens' use, but Lord Westcliff himself had offered the room for Annabelle's comfort.

After tucking a lap blanket around Annabelle's knees, Philippa set a cup of clivers tea on a table beside her. "You must drink this," she said firmly, in response to Annabelle's grimace. "It's for your own good."

"There's no need for you to stay in the parlor

and watch over me, Mama," Annabelle said. "I will be quite happy to relax here, while you go have a stroll or chat with one of your friends."

"Are you certain?" Philippa asked.

"Absolutely certain." Annabelle picked up the clivers tea and took a sip. "I'm drinking my medicine . . . see? Do go, Mama, and don't give me another thought."

"Very well," Philippa said reluctantly. "Just for a little while. The housekeeper said for you to ring the bell on the table, if you want a servant. And remember to drink every drop of that tea."

"I will," Annabelle promised, pasting a wide smile on her face. She retained the smile until Philippa had left the room. The moment that her mother was out of sight, Annabelle leaned over the back of the settee and carefully poured the contents of the cup out the open window.

Sighing with satisfaction, Annabelle curled into the corner of the settee. Now and then a household noise would interrupt the placid silence: the clatter of a dish, the murmur of the housekeeper's voice, the sound of a broom being employed to sweep the hallway carpet. Resting her arm on the windowsill, Annabelle leaned forward into a shaft of sunlight, letting the brilliance bathe her face. She closed her eyes and listened to the drone of bees as they moved lazily among the flowering bursts of deep pink hydrangea and delicate tendrils of sweet pea that wound through the basket-bed borders. Although she was still very weak, it was pleasant to sit in warm lethargy, half-drowsing like a cat.

She was slow to respond when she heard a sound from the doorway . . . a single light rap, as if the visitor was reluctant to disrupt her reverie with a loud knock. Blinking her sun-dazzled eyes, Annabelle remained sitting with her legs tucked beneath her. The mass of light speckles gradually faded from her vision, and she found herself staring at Simon Hunt's dark, lean form. He had leaned part of his weight on the doorjamb, bracing a shoulder against it in an unself-consciously rakish pose. His head was slightly tilted as he considered her with an unfathomable expression.

Annabelle's pulse escalated to a mad clatter. She recalled the hardness of his arms and chest as he had carried her, the touch of his hands on her body . . . oh, she would never be able to look at him again without remembering!

"You look like a butterfly that's just flown in from the garden," Hunt said softly.

He must be mocking her, Annabelle thought, perfectly aware of her own sickroom pallor. Self-consciously she raised a hand to her hair, pushing back the untidy locks. "What are you doing here?" she asked. "Shouldn't you be at the neighbor's party?"

She had not meant to sound so abrupt and unwelcoming, but her usual facility with words had deserted her. As she stared at him, she couldn't help thinking of how he had rubbed her chest with his hand. The recollection caused the stinging heat of embarrassment to cover her skin.

Hunt replied in a gently caustic tone. "I have business to conduct with one of my managers, who is due to arrive from London later this morning. Unlike the silk-stockinged gentlemen whose pedigrees you so admire, I have things to consider other than where I should settle my picnic blanket today." Pushing away from the doorframe, Hunt ventured farther into the room, his gaze frankly assessing. "Still weak? That will improve soon. How is your ankle? Lift your skirts—I think I should take another look."

Annabelle regarded him with alarm for a fraction of a second, then began to laugh as she saw the glint in his eyes. The audacious remark somehow eased her embarrassment and caused her to relax. "That is very kind," she said dryly. "But there's no need. My ankle is much better, thank you."

Hunt smiled as he approached her. "I'll have you know that my offer was made in a spirit of purest altruism. I would had taken no illicit pleasure at the sight of your exposed leg. Well, perhaps a small thrill, but I would have concealed it fairly well." Grasping the back of a side chair with one hand, he moved it easily to the settee and sat close to her. Annabelle was impressed by the way he had lifted the sturdy piece of carved mahogany furniture as if it were feather-light. She threw a quick glance at the empty doorway. As long as the door wasn't closed, it was acceptable for her to sit in the parlor with Hunt. And her mother would eventually come to look in on her. Before that happened, however, Annabelle decided to bring up the subject of the boots.

"Mr. Hunt," she said carefully, "there is something I must ask you . . ."

"Yes?"

His eyes were definitely his most attractive feature, Annabelle thought distractedly. Vibrant and full of life, they made her wonder why people generally preferred blue eyes to dark ones. No shade of blue could ever convey the simmering intelligence that lurked in the depths of Simon Hunt's sable eyes.

Try as she might, Annabelle could think of no subtle way to ask him. After grappling silently with a variety of phrases, she finally settled for a blunt question. "Were you responsible for the boots?"

His expression gave nothing away. "Boots? I'm afraid I don't take your meaning, Miss Peyton. Are you speaking in metaphor, or are we talking about actual footwear?"

"Ankle boots," Annabelle said, staring at him with open suspicion. "A new pair that was left inside the door of my room yesterday."

"Delighted as I am to discuss any part of your wardrobe, Miss Peyton, I'm afraid I know nothing about a pair of boots. However, I am relieved that you have managed to acquire some. Unless, of course, you wished to continue acting as a strolling buffet to the wildlife of Hampshire."

Annabelle regarded him for a long moment.

Despite his denial, there was something lurking behind his neutral facade . . . some playful spark in his eyes . . . "Then you deny having given the boots to me?"

"Most emphatically I deny it."

"But I wonder . . . if someone wished to have a pair of boots made up for a lady without her knowledge . . . how would he be able to learn the precise size of her feet?"

"That would be a relatively simple task . . ." he mused. "I imagine that some enterprising person would simply ask a housemaid to trace the soles of the lady's discarded slippers. Then he could take the pattern to the local cobbler. And make it worth the cobbler's while to delay his other work in favor of crafting the new shoes immediately."

"That is quite a lot of trouble for someone to go through," Annabelle murmured.

Hunt's gaze was lit with sudden mischief. "Rather less trouble than having to haul an injured woman up three flights of stairs every time she goes out walking in her slippers."

Annabelle realized that he would never admit to giving her the boots—which would allow her to keep them, but would also ensure that she would never be able to thank him. And she knew he had—she could see it in his face.

"Mr. Hunt," she said earnestly, "I . . . I wish . . ." She paused, unable to find words, and stared helplessly at him.

Taking pity on her, Hunt stood and went to the side of the room, picking up a small circular game table. It was only about two feet in diameter, constructed with a clever mechanism to allow a player to flip the top from a chessboard to a draughtsboard. "Do you play?" he asked casually, setting the table in front of her.

"Draughts? Yes, occasionally—"

"No, not draughts. Chess."

Annabelle shook her head, shrinking back into the corner of the settee. "No, I've never played chess. And I don't wish to sound uncooperative, but . . . the way I feel at present, I have no desire to try something as difficult as—"

"It's time for you to learn, then," Hunt said, heading to a niche of shelves to retrieve a polished burlwood box. "It's been said that you can never really know someone until you play chess with him."

Annabelle watched him cautiously, feeling nervous at the prospect of being alone with him . . . and yet she was thoroughly beguiled by his deliberate gentleness. It seemed almost as if he were trying to coax her to trust him. There was a softness in his manner that seemed utterly at odds with the cynical rake she had always known him to be.

"Do you believe that?" she asked.

"Of course not." Hunt brought the box to the table and opened it to reveal a set of onyx and ivory chessmen, carved in scrupulous detail. He slid her a provocative glance. "The truth is, you can never really know a man until you've loaned him money."

Half-standing over her as Hunt was, Annabelle became aware of the intriguing scent of him, the whisper of starch and shaving soap overlaying the fragrance of clean male skin . . . and there was something more elusive . . . some sweet tang to his breath, as if he had recently eaten pears, or perhaps a slice of pineapple. As she looked up at him, she realized that with very little effort he could have bent down and kissed her. The thought caused her to tremble. She actually wanted to feel his mouth on hers. She wanted him to hold her again.

The realization caused her eyes to widen. Her sudden stillness communicated swiftly to Hunt. His attention swerved from the chessboard to her upturned face, and whatever he saw in her expression caused his breath to catch. Neither of them moved. Annabelle could only wait in silence, her fingertips curling into the upholstery of the settee as she wondered what he might do next.

Hunt broke the tension with a long breath, and spoke in a softly abraded voice. "No . . . you're not well enough yet."

It was difficult to hear the words above the thunder of her heartbeat. "Wh-what?" she asked faintly.

Seeming unable to help himself, Hunt brushed a little curling wisp of hair back from her temple. The stroking fingertip burned her silken skin, leaving a glow of sensation in its wake. "I know what you're thinking. And believe me, I'm tempted. But you're still too weak—and my self-control is in short supply today."

"If you're implying that I—"

"I never waste time with implications," he murmured, resuming his careful placement of the chess pieces. "Obviously, you want me to kiss you. And I'll be happy to oblige, when the time is right. But not yet."

"Mr. Hunt, you are the most—"

"Yes, I know," he said with a grin. Lowering himself to the chair, Hunt pressed a chess piece into her palm. The carved onyx was heavy and cool, its slick surface warming slowly to the touch.

"That is the queen—the most powerful piece on the board. She can move in any direction, and go as far as she wishes."

There was nothing overtly suggestive in his manner of speaking . . . but when he spoke softly, as he was doing at that moment, there was a husky depth in his voice that made her toes curl inside her slippers.

"More powerful than the king?" she asked.

"Yes. The king can only move one square at a time. But the king is the most important piece."

"Why is he more important than the queen if he's not the most powerful?"

"Because once he's captured, the game is over." Reaching for the piece he had given her, Hunt exchanged it for another. His fingers brushed over hers, lingering in a brief but unmistakable caress. "This is the pawn, which moves one square at a time. It can't move backward or sideways, unless it is taking another piece. Most novice players like to move a lot of their pawns in the beginning, to control a larger area on the chessboard. But it's a better strategy to make good use of your other pieces . . ."

As Hunt continued to explain each chess piece and its uses, he pressed them into her palm one at a time. Annabelle was mesmerized by the hypnotic brushes of his hands. Her usual defenses seemed to have been pulverized like grain beneath a mill wheel. Something had happened to her, or Hunt, or perhaps to both of them, allowing them to interact with an ease that had not existed before. She did not want to invite him closer . . . nothing good could possibly come of it . . . and yet she couldn't help but enjoy his nearness.

Hunt coaxed her into a game, waiting patiently as she considered each possible move, readily offering advice when she asked for it. His manner was so charming and playfully distracting that she almost didn't care who won. Almost. When she slid her piece into a position that attacked not one but two of his pieces, Hunt glanced at her with an approving grin. "That's called a pin-and-fork strategy. As I suspected, you have a natural instinct for chess."

"Now you have no choice, other than to retreat," Annabelle said triumphantly.

"Not yet." He moved another piece in another area on the board, instantly threatening her queen.

Puzzling over the strategy, Annabelle realized that he had just put *her* in the position of having to retreat.

"That's not fair," she protested, and he chuckled.

Lacing her fingers together, Annabelle leaned

her chin on her hands and contemplated the board. A full minute passed as she debated various strategies, but nothing seemed appropriate. "I don't know what to do," she finally admitted. Raising her eyes to his, she found that he was staring at her in an odd way, his gaze caressing and concerned. It unraveled her, that look, and she swallowed hard against a sensation of thick sweetness, like honey coating her throat.

"I've tired you," Hunt murmured.

"No, I'm fine—"

"We'll continue the game later. You'll see your next move more clearly when you've rested."

"I don't want to stop," she said, annoyed by his refusal. "Besides, neither of us will remember how the pieces are arranged."

"I will." Ignoring her protests, Hunt stood and moved the table aside, out of her reach. "You need a nap. Do you require some help to return upstairs, or—"

"Mr. Hunt, I'm *not* going back to my room," she said stubbornly. "I'm sick of it. In fact, I would rather sleep in the hallway than—"

"All right," Hunt murmured with a smile, resuming his seat. "Calm yourself. Far be it from me to make you do something that you don't want to do." He laced his fingers together and leaned back in a deceptively casual pose, his gaze narrowing on her. "Tomorrow the guests will be back at the manor in full force," he remarked. "I suppose you'll resume your pursuit of Kendall soon?"

"Probably," Annabelle admitted, covering

her mouth as an insistent yawn stretched her lips.

"You don't want him," Hunt said softly.

"Oh, yes I do." Annabelle paused dreamily, half propping her head on her curled arm. "And . . . although you have been very kind to me, Mr. Hunt . . . I'm afraid that I can't let that change my plans."

He stared at her in the same relaxed but engrossed way he had regarded the chessboard. "I'm not going to change my plans, either, sweetheart."

If Annabelle hadn't been so tired, she would have objected to the endearment. Instead she pondered his words sleepily. His plans . . . "Which are to try and stop me from catching Lord Kendall," she said.

"They go somewhat beyond that," he replied, amusement lurking in one corner of his mouth.

"What do you mean?"

"I'm hardly going to reveal my strategy. Clearly I need every advantage I can get. The next move is yours, Miss Peyton. Just remember that I'll be watching you."

Annabelle knew that the warning should have alarmed her. But she was filled with overwhelming weariness, and she closed her eyes.

She napped lightly, awakening long enough to ascertain that she was alone in the private parlor, then dozing off again in the gentle sunshine. As her body relaxed into deeper slumber, she found herself in a brilliantly colored dream. *She wandered across a parquet floor made* of huge white-and-black squares that looked like a chessboard, with life-sized stone statues poised on some of the squares.

Wishing for someone to talk to, some warm human hand to cling to, she walked across the giant chessboard, searching blindly through the crowd of immobile figures . . . until she saw a dark form leaning indolently against a white marble column. Her heart began to hammer, and her steps slowed as she was filled with a rush of excitement that heated her skin and made her pulse beat in urgent rhythm.

It was Simon Hunt, walking toward her with a slight smile on his face. He caught her before she could retreat, and bent to whisper in her ear.

"Will you dance with me now?"

"I can't," she said breathlessly, struggling in his tightening embrace.

"Yes, you can," he urged gently, his mouth hot and tender as it moved across her face. "Put your arms around me . . . Annabelle . . ."

She awakened, her eyes widening in her sleep-flushed face as she sensed that someone was with her.

"Annabelle," she heard again . . . but it was not the husky, caressing baritone of her dream.

Chapter 15

As Annabelle looked up, she saw Lord Hodgeham standing over her. She struggled to a sitting position and inched backward, comprehending that this was not an imaginary figure, but an all-too-real one. Rendered speechless with surprise, she shrank from him as he reached out with a heavy hand and flicked the lace trim at the front of her day gown.

"I heard about your illness," Hodgeham said, his gaze heavy-lidded as he glanced over her half-reclining form. "How sorry I was to learn that you had suffered such an affliction. But it appears there was no permanent harm done. You seem . . ." He paused and moistened his plump lips, ". . . as exquisite as ever . . . though perhaps a bit pale."

"How . . . how did you find me here?" Annabelle asked. "This is the Marsdens' private parlor. Surely no one gave you leave—"

"I made a servant tell me," came Hodgeham's smug reply.

"Get out," Annabelle snapped. "Or I'll scream that you're assaulting me."

Hodgeham chortled richly. "You can't afford a scandal, my dear. Your interest in Lord Kendall is obvious to everyone. And we both know that one hint of disgrace attached to your name would completely ruin your chances with him." He grinned at her silence, revealing a mouthful of crooked yellow teeth. "That's better. My poor, pretty Annabelle . . . I know what will restore a blush to those pale cheeks." Reaching into his coat pocket, he extracted a large gold coin and waved it in front of her tantalizingly. "A token to express my sympathy for your ordeal."

Annabelle's breath came in an outraged hiss as Hodgeham leaned very close, the coin clutched between his fat fingers as he attempted to tuck it into the bodice of her dress. She knocked his hand away with a stiff, jerking movement. Although she was still feeble, the gesture was enough to send the coin flying from his hand. It fell to the carpeted floor with a solid thud.

"Leave me alone," she said fiercely.

"Haughty bitch. You needn't try to pretend that you're any better than your mother."

"You swine—" Cursing her own lack of strength, Annabelle struck out at him feebly as he bent over her, her body racked with chills of horror. "No," she said through gritted teeth, covering her face with her arms. She resisted fiercely as he grasped her wrists. "No—"

A clatter from the doorway caused Hodgeham to straighten in surprise. Shaking from head to toe, Annabelle looked in the direction of the noise and saw her mother standing there with a lunch tray. Silverware had tumbled from the edge of the tray as Philippa realized what was happening.

Philippa shook her head as if finding it impossible to believe that Hodgeham was there. "You dare to approach my daughter . . ." she began in a thick voice. Scarlet with rage, she went to settle the tray on a nearby table, then spoke to Hodgeham with quiet wrath. "My daughter is ill, my lord. I will not allow her health to be compromised—you will come with me *now,* and we will discuss this in some other place."

"Discussion isn't what I want," Hodgeham said.

Annabelle saw a quick succession of emotions cross her mother's face: disgust, resentment, hatred, fear. And finally . . . resignation. "Come away from my daughter, then," she said coldly.

"No," Annabelle croaked in protest, realizing that Philippa intended to go somewhere alone with him. "Mama, stay with me."

"Everything will be fine." Philippa didn't look at her, but kept her emotionless gaze on Hodgeham's ruddy countenance. "I've brought you a lunch tray, dearest. Try to eat something—"

"*No.*" Disbelieving, despairing, Annabelle watched her mother calmly precede Hodgeham from the room. "Mama, don't go with him!" But Philippa left as if she had not heard.

Annabelle was not aware of how many minutes passed as she stared blankly at the empty doorway. There was no thought in her mind of touching the lunch tray. The tang of vegetable broth that flavored the air made her feel nauseous. Bleakly, Annabelle wondered how this hellish affair had ever started, if Hodgeham had forced himself on her mother, or if it had initially been a matter of mutual consent. No matter how it had begun, it had now turned into a travesty. Hodgeham was a monster, and Philippa was trying to pacify him to keep him from ruining them.

Weary and miserable, trying not to think of what might be occurring between her mother and Hodgeham at that very moment, Annabelle levered herself off the settee. She winced at the protesting ache of her muscles. Her head hurt, and she was dizzy, and she wanted to go to her room. Walking like an old woman, she made her way to the bellpull and tugged. After what seemed an interminable length of time, there was still no response. With the guests gone, most the staff had been allowed their day off, and maids were in short supply.

Scrubbing her fingers distractedly through the limp locks of her hair, Annabelle assessed the situation. Although her legs were weak, they felt serviceable. That morning her mother had helped her to walk the length of two hallways from their room to the Marsdens' upstairs parlor. Now, however, she was fairly certain that she could manage the short journey on her own.

Ignoring the brilliant sparks that danced across her vision like fireflies, Annabelle left the room with short, careful steps. She stayed close to the wall in case she needed to avail herself of its support. How odd it was, she thought grimly, that even this minor exertion should cause her to pant as if she had just run for miles. Infuriated with her own weakness, she wondered ruefully if she shouldn't have drunk that last cup of clivers after all. Concentrating on setting one foot in front of the other, she made slow progress along the first hallway, until she was nearly at the corner that led to the east wing of the estate, where her room was located. She stopped as she heard quiet voices coming from another direction.

Hell's bells. It would be mortifying to be seen by anyone while she was in this condition. Praying that the voices belonged to a pair of servants, Annabelle leaned her weight against the wall and stood without moving. A few strands of hair stuck to her clammy forehead and cheeks.

Two men crossed the passageway before her, so involved in their conversation that it seemed they wouldn't notice her. Relieved, Annabelle thought that she managed to escape detection.

But she was not that fortunate. One of the men happened to glance in her direction, and his attention was immediately riveted. As he approached her, Annabelle recognized the masculine grace of his long strides even before she saw his face clearly.

It seemed that she was destined to be forever making herself an exhibition in front of Simon Hunt. Sighing, Annabelle pushed away from the wall and tried to appear composed, even with her legs trembling beneath her. "Good afternoon, Mr. Hunt—"

"What are you doing?" Hunt interrupted as he reached her. He sounded annoyed, but as Annabelle looked up at his face, she saw the concern in his gaze. "Why are you standing alone in the hallway?"

"I'm going to my room." Annabelle started a little as he slid his arms around her, one at her shoulders, the other at her waist. "Mr. Hunt, there's no need—"

"You're as weak as a kitten," he said flatly. "You know better than to go anywhere by yourself in this condition."

"There wasn't anyone to help me," Annabelle replied irritably. Her head swam, and she found herself against him, letting him support some of her weight. His chest was wonderfully solid and hard, the fabric of his coat silky-cool against her cheek.

"Where is your mother?" Hunt persisted, smoothing back a tangled lock of her hair. "Tell me, and I'll—"

"No!" Annabelle glanced up at him with instant alarm, her slender fingers biting into his coat sleeves. Dear God, the last thing she needed was for Hunt to instigate a search for Philippa when she was probably in some damnably compromising situation with Hodgeham at that very moment. "Don't look for her," she said sharply. "I . . . I don't need anyone. I can reach my room by myself, if you'll just let go of me. I don't want—"

"All right," Hunt murmured, his arm remaining firmly around her. "Hush, I won't look for her. Hush." His hand continued to smooth her hair in gentle, repeated motions.

She wilted against him, trying to catch her breath. "Simon," she whispered, vaguely surprised she had just used his first name, for she had never used it even in the privacy of her thoughts. Moistening her dry lips, she tried once more, and to her astonishment, she did it again. "Simon . . ."

"Yes?" A new tension had entered his long, hard body, and at the same time, his hand moved over the shape of her skull in the softest caress possible.

"Please . . . take me to my room."

Hunt tilted her head back gently and regarded her with a sudden faint smile playing on his lips. "Sweetheart, I would take you to the ends of the earth if you asked."

By that time, the other man in the hallway had reached them, and Annabelle was dismayed, though not surprised, to see that it was Lord Westcliff.

The earl glanced at her with cold disapproval, as if he suspected she had somehow arranged this situation as an intentional inconvenience.

"Miss Peyton," he said crisply, "I assure you,

there was no need for you to make your way through the hall unescorted. If there was no one available to help you, you had only to ring for a servant."

"I did, my lord," Annabelle said defensively, trying to push away from Hunt, who wouldn't let her. "I rang the bellpull and waited for at least a quarter hour, and no one came."

Westcliff regarded her with obvious skepticism. "Impossible. My servants always come when they're summoned."

"Well, today seems to be an exception," Annabelle snapped. "Perhaps the bellpull is broken. Or perhaps your servants—"

"Easy," Hunt murmured, pressing her head back to his chest. Although Annabelle couldn't see his face, she heard the note of quiet warning in his voice as he spoke to Westcliff. "We'll continue our discussion later. Right now I intend to escort Miss Peyton to her room."

"That is not a wise idea, in my opinion," the earl said.

"I'm glad I didn't ask for it, then," Simon returned pleasantly.

There was the sound of the earl's taut sigh, and Annabelle was vaguely aware of his carpet-muffled footsteps as he walked away from them.

Hunt bent his head, his breath warming the tip of her ear, as he inquired, "Now . . . would you care to explain what is going on?"

All her veins seemed to dilate, bringing a flush of pleasure to her cool skin. Hunt's nearness filled her with equal amounts of delight and yearning. As he held her, she couldn't help remembering her dream, the erotic illusion of his body pressing over hers. This was all so terribly wrong, that she should revel silently in being held by him . . . even knowing that she would get nothing from him but temporary pleasure followed by everlasting dishonor. She managed to shake her head in answer to his question, her cheek rubbing against the lapel of his coat.

"I didn't think so," Hunt said wryly. He released her experimentally, assessed her unsteady balance with a narrow-eyed glance, and bent to lift her in his arms. Annabelle surrendered with an inarticulate murmur and linked her arms around his neck. As Hunt carried her along the hallway, he spoke in a quiet voice. "I might be able to help, if you would tell me the problem."

Annabelle considered that for a moment. The only thing that would come from confiding her woes to Simon Hunt was an almost certain offer to support her as his mistress. And she hated the part of herself that was tempted by the idea. "Why should you wish to involve yourself in my problems?" she asked.

"Do I have to have an ulterior motive for wanting to help you?"

"Yes," she replied darkly, causing him to chuckle.

He set her carefully down at the threshold of her room. "Can you reach the bed by yourself, or shall I tuck you in?"

Though his voice was lightly teasing, Annabelle suspected that with very little encouragement, he would do just that. She shook her head hastily. "No. I'm fine, please don't come in." She put a palm to his chest to keep him from entering the room. Frail though her hand was, it was enough to stop him.

"All right." Hunt looked down at her, his gaze searching. "I'll see that a maid is sent up to attend you. Though I suspect that Westcliff is already making inquiries."

"I did ring for a maid," Annabelle insisted, embarrassed by the peevish note in her own voice. "Obviously, the earl doesn't believe me, but—"

"I believe you." With great care, Hunt removed her hand from his chest, briefly holding her slender fingers in his before letting go. "Westcliff isn't quite the ogre he seems. You have to be acquainted with him for some time before you appreciate his finer qualities."

"If you say so," Annabelle said doubtfully, and heaved a sigh as she stepped back into the stale, darkened sickroom. "Thank you, Mr. Hunt." Wondering anxiously when Philippa would return, she glanced at the empty room, then turned back to Hunt.

His penetrating gaze seemed to unearth every emotion beneath her strained facade, and she sensed the multitude of questions that hovered on his lips. However, all he said was, "You need to rest."

"I've done nothing *but* rest. I'm going mad from boredom . . . but the thought of actually doing anything makes me exhausted." Lowering her head, Annabelle stared at the few inches of floor between their feet with morose concentration, before asking cautiously, "I suppose you have no interest in continuing the chess game later this evening?"

A short silence, and then Hunt replied in a softly mocking drawl. "Why, Miss Peyton . . . I'm overwhelmed by the thought that you might have a desire for my company."

Annabelle couldn't bring herself to look at him, her face covered with an awkward blush, as she muttered, "I'd keep company with the devil himself, if only to have something to do besides stay in bed."

Laughing quietly, he reached out to tuck a lock of hair behind her ear. "We'll see," he murmured.

And with that, he gave her a deft, shallow bow and left, walking down the hallway with his usual self-assured stride.

Too late, Annabelle recalled something about a musical evening that had been planned for the guests while they enjoyed a buffet supper. Certainly Simon Hunt would prefer to keep company with the guests downstairs rather than play a rudimentary game of chess with a sickly, unkempt, cross-tempered girl. She cringed, wishing that she could withdraw the spontaneous invitation . . . oh, how pitifully desperate she must have appeared! Clapping a hand to her forehead, Annabelle trudged into her room and let herself collapse stiffly onto the unmade bed like a tree that had just been chopped down.

Within five minutes, there was a knock at the

door, and a pair of chastened-looking maids entered the room. "We came to tidy up, miss,"
one of them ventured. "The master sent us—
'e said we must 'elp you with anyfing you need."

"Thank you," Annabelle said, hoping that
Lord Westcliff had not been too severe on the
girls. Retreating to a chair, she watched the
whirlwind of activity that ensued. With almost
magical speed, the young housemaids changed
the bed linens, opened the window to admit
fresh air, cleaned and dusted the furniture,
and brought in a portable bath that they proceeded to fill with hot water. One of the girls
helped Annabelle to remove her clothes, while
the other brought in a length of folded toweling
and a bucket of warm rinse water for her hair.
Shivering in comfort, Annabelle stepped into
the mahogany-rimmed folding tub.

"Take my arm, please, miss," the younger of
the two said, extending her forearm for Annabelle to take hold of. "Yer not quite steady on
yer feet, looks like."

Annabelle obeyed and sank down into the
water, and let go of the girl's muscular arm.
"What is your name?" she asked, lowering her
shoulders until they were submerged beneath
the steaming surface of the water.

"Meggie, miss."

"Meggie, I believe I dropped a gold sovereign
on the floor of the family's private parlor—will
you try to find it for me?"

The girl gave her a perplexed glance, clearly
wondering why Annabelle had left a valuable
coin on the floor and what would transpire if

she couldn't find it. "Yes, miss." She bobbed an uneasy curtsey and rushed from the room. Dunking her head beneath the water, Annabelle sat up with a streaming face and hair and wiped her eyes as the other maid bent to rub a cake of soap over her head. "It feels nice to be clean," Annabelle murmured, sitting still beneath the girl's ministrations.

"Me ma allus says 'tisn't good to bathe when yer ill," the maid told her dubiously.

"I'll take my chances," Annabelle replied, gratefully tilting her head back as the maid poured the rinse water over her soapy hair. Wiping her eyes once more, Annabelle saw that Meggie had returned.

"I found it, miss," Meggie exclaimed breathlessly, extending the coin in her hand. It was possible that she had never held a sovereign before, since the average housemaid earned approximately eight shillings a month. "Where shall I put it?"

"You may divide it between the two of you," Annabelle said.

The housemaids stared at her, dumbfounded. "Oh, thank you, miss!" they both exclaimed, eyes wide and mouths open in amazement.

Grimly aware of the hypocrisy of giving away money from Lord Hodgeham, when the Peyton household had benefited from his questionable patronage for more than a year, Annabelle lowered her head, embarrassed by their gratitude. Seeing her discomfort, the two hastened to help her from the tub, drying her hair and shivering body, and helping her to don a fresh gown.

Refreshed but tired after the bath, Annabelle got into bed and lay between the soft, smooth bed linens. She dozed while the maids removed the bath, only hazily aware when they tiptoed from the room. It was early evening when she awoke, blinking as her mother lit a lamp on the table.

"Mama," she said groggily, dazed with sleepiness. Remembering the earlier encounter with Hodgeham, she shook herself awake. "Are you all right? Did he—"

"I don't wish to discuss it," Philippa said softly, her delicate profile gilded by the lamplight. She wore a numb, blank look, her forehead lightly scored with tense furrows. "Yes, I am quite all right, dearest."

Annabelle nodded briefly, abashed and despondent, and aware of a pervasive feeling of shame. She sat up, her back feeling as if her spine had been replaced by an iron poker. Aside from the stiffness of her unused muscles, however, she felt much stronger, and for the first time in two days her stomach was aching with real hunger. Slipping from the bed, she went to the vanity table and picked up a hairbrush, dragging it through her hair. "Mama," she said hesitantly, "I need a change of scene. Perhaps I will go back to the Marsden parlor and ring for a supper tray, and dine in there."

Philippa appeared to have only half heard the words. "Yes," she said absently, "that seems a fine idea. Shall I go with you?"

"No, thank you . . . I'm feeling quite well, and it isn't far. I'll go by myself. You probably want some privacy after . . ." Annabelle paused uncomfortably and set down the brush. "I'll be back in a little while."

With a low murmur, Philippa sat in the chair by the hearth, and Annabelle sensed that she was relieved by the prospect of being alone. After braiding her hair into a long rope that lay over her shoulder, Annabelle left the room, quietly closing the door behind her.

As she went out into the hall, she heard the subtle rumble of the guests who were enjoying the supper buffet in the drawing room. Music overlaid the blend of conversation and laughter—a string quartet with an accompanying piano. Pausing to listen, Annabelle was astonished to realize that it was the same sad, beautiful melody that she had heard in her dream. She closed her eyes and listened intently, while her throat tightened with a wistful ache. The music filled her with the kind of longing that she should not have allowed herself to feel. *Good God*, she thought, *I'm becoming maudlin in my illness—I have to get some control over myself.* Opening her eyes, she started to walk again, only to narrowly miss plowing into someone who had approached from the opposite direction.

Her heart seemed to expand painfully as she looked up at Simon Hunt, who was dressed in a formal scheme of black and white, a lazy smile curving his wide mouth. His deep voice sent a shiver down her spine. "Where do you think you're going?"

So he had come for her, in spite of the elegant crowd that he should have been mingling with downstairs. Aware that the sudden weakness in her knees had nothing to do with her illness, Annabelle toyed nervously with the end of her braid. "To have a supper tray in the parlor."

Taking her elbow, Hunt turned and guided her along the hallway, keeping his steps slow to accommodate hers. "You don't want a supper tray in the parlor," he informed her.

"I don't?"

He shook his head. "I have a surprise for you. Come, it's not far." As she went with him willingly, Hunt slid an assessing gaze over her. "Your balance has improved since this afternoon. How are you feeling?"

"Much better," Annabelle replied, and flushed as her stomach growled audibly. "A bit hungry, actually."

Hunt grinned and brought her to a partially opened door. Leading her over the threshold, he brought her into a small, lovely room with rosewood-paneled walls hung with tapestries, and furniture upholstered in amber velvet. The room's most distinctive feature, however, was the window on the inside wall, which opened out onto the drawing room two stories below. This place was perfectly concealed from the view of the guests below, while music floated clearly through the wide opening. Annabelle's round-eyed gaze moved to a small table that was covered with silver-domed plates.

"I had the devil of a time trying to decide what would tempt your appetite," Hunt said.

"So I told the kitchen staff to include some of everything."

Overwhelmed, and unable to think of a time that any man had gone to such lengths for her enjoyment, Annabelle suddenly found it difficult to speak. She swallowed hard and looked everywhere but at his face. "This is lovely. I . . . I didn't know this room was here."

"Few people do. The countess sometimes sits here when she is too infirm to go downstairs." Hunt moved closer to her and slid his long fingers beneath her chin, coaxing her to meet his gaze. "Will you have dinner with me?"

Annabelle's pulse throbbed so rapidly that she was certain he could feel it against his fingers. "I have no chaperone," she half whispered.

Hunt smiled at that, his hand dropping from her chin. "You couldn't be safer. I'm hardly going to seduce you while you're obviously too weak to defend yourself."

"That's very gentlemanly of you."

"I'll seduce you when you're feeling better."

Biting back a smile, Annabelle raised a fine brow, and said, "You're very sure of yourself. Should you have said you're going to *try* to seduce me?"

" 'Never anticipate failure'—that's what my father always tells me." Sliding a strong arm around her back, Hunt guided her to one of the chairs. "This is probably the last time I'll see you for a while," he remarked as he seated her. "I'm traveling to London in the morning."

Annabelle frowned. "Why?"

"I'm overseeing the development of a locomotive works Westcliff and I have invested in."

"Really? I've never been on a train before. What is it like?"

"Fast. Exciting. The average speed of a passenger locomotive is about fifty miles an hour, but Consolidated is building a six-coupled express engine design that should go up to seventy."

"Seventy miles an hour?" Annabelle was unable to imagine traveling at such speed. "Wouldn't that be uncomfortable for the passengers?"

The question made him smile. "Once the train reaches its traveling speed, you don't feel the momentum."

"What are the passenger cars like on the inside?"

"Not especially luxurious," Hunt admitted, pouring more wine into his own glass. "I wouldn't recommend traveling in anything other than a private car—especially for someone like you."

"Someone like me? If you're implying that I'm spoiled, I assure you that I'm not."

"You should be." His warm gaze slid over her pink-tinted face and slender upper body. "You could do with a bit of spoiling."

Annabelle blushed and tried to steer the conversation into safer channels. "Consolidated is the name of your company?"

Hunt nodded. "It's the British partner of Shaw Foundries."

"Which belongs to Lady Olivia's fiancé, Mr. Shaw?"

"Exactly. Shaw is helping us to adapt to the American system of engine building, which is far more efficient and productive than the British method."

"I've always heard that British-made machinery is the best in the world," Annabelle commented.

"Arguable. But even so, it's seldom standardized. No two locomotives built in Britain are exactly alike, which slows production considerably and makes repairs difficult. However, if we could follow the American example and produce uniform cast-molded parts, using standard gauges and templates, we can build an engine in a matter of weeks rather than months, and perform repairs with lightning speed."

As they talked and shared a meal, Simon was charming, amusing, and far nicer than Annabelle had ever thought he could be. To her surprise, he was wonderful company.

Annabelle did not look at him. Rather, she lapsed into a restless silence and turned her unseeing gaze to the window aperture, through which the luxuriant melody of Schubert's *Rosamunde* poured.

Eventually there came a discreet rap at the door, and a footman came in to remove the plates. Keeping her face averted, Annabelle wondered if the news that she had dined in private with Simon Hunt would soon be spread through the servants' hall. However, after the footman left, Simon spoke reassuringly, seeming to have read her thoughts. "He won't say a word to anyone. Westcliff recommended him for his ability to keep his mouth shut about confidential matters."

Annabelle gave him a worried glance. "Then . . . the earl knows that you and I are . . . but I am certain that he must not approve!"

"I've done many things Westcliff doesn't approve of," Simon returned evenly. "And I don't always approve of his decisions. However, in the interest of maintaining a profitable friendship, we don't generally cross each other." Standing, he rested his palms on the table and leaned forward. "What about a game of chess? I had a board brought up . . . just in case."

Annabelle nodded. As she stared into his warm black eyes, she reflected that this was perhaps the first evening of her adult life in which she was wholly happy to be exactly where she was. With this man.

"Where did you learn to play chess?" she asked as he set the pieces in their previous formations.

"From my father."

"Your *father?*"

One corner of his mouth lifted in mocking half smile. "Can't a butcher play chess?"

"Of course, I . . ." Annabelle felt a hot blush sweep over her face. She was mortified by her tactlessness. "I'm sorry."

Hunt's slight smile lingered as he studied her. "You seem to have a mistaken impression of my family. The Hunts are solidly middle-class. My brothers and sisters and I all attended school. Now my father employs my brothers, who also live over the shop. And in the evenings they often play chess."

Relaxing at the absence of censure in his voice, Annabelle picked up a pawn and rolled it between her fingers. "Why didn't you choose to work for your father, as your brothers did?"

"I was a hellion in my youth," Hunt admitted with a grin. "Whenever my father told me to do something, I always tried to prove him wrong."

"And what was his response?" Annabelle asked, her eyes twinkling.

"At first he tried to be patient with me. When that didn't work, he took the opposite tack." Hunt winced in reminiscence, smiling ruefully. "Trust me, you never want to be thrashed by a butcher—their arms are like tree trunks."

"I can imagine," Annabelle murmured, stealing a circumspect glance at the wide expanse of his shoulders and remembering the hardness of his muscles. "Your family must be very proud of your success."

Simon shrugged, his mouth twisting. "Unfortunately, it seems to have put a distance between us. My family doesn't approve of my profession or understand why I wanted a different life than theirs. For that matter, neither do my old friends."

Annabelle had already known Simon wasn't fully accepted by upper-class circles he often moved in. But until this moment, it hadn't occured to her that he was similarly out of place in the world he'd come from. It must be lonely, she thought.

With a compassionate glance, Annabelle impulsively reached out and touched his hand. "They should be proud of you and what you've made of yourself."

Gently his fingers closed around hers while their gazes met and held. Annabelle was shocked by the feelings that rushed over her, pleasure and vulnerability and warmth. Dangerous feelings. She jerked her hand away. "I'm sorry," she said with an unsteady laugh, suddenly afraid of what might happen if she stayed alone with him any longer. She stood clumsily and moved away from the table. "I-I've just realized that I'm very tired . . . the wine seems to have affected me after all. I should go back to my room. I think there is still ample time for you to socialize with everyone downstairs, so your evening hasn't been entirely wasted. Thank you for the dinner, and the music, and—"

"Annabelle." He stood with her, frowning. "You're not afraid of me, are you?"

She shook her head.

"Then why the rush to leave?"

"I . . . don't want this."

"This?"

"I'm not going to become your mistress."

Simon's eyes narrowed. "If you can stand to be Hodgeham's mistress, God knows you can stand to become mine. Don't claim you're not attracted to me—we both know you'd be lying. Name any sum, Annabelle. Do you want a house of your own? Done. A carriage and matched team? A yacht? Done. Tell me your price—I'm tired of waiting for you."

Annabelle felt herself turn scarlet, then bleach-white. So that's what he thought of her, she thought with a mixture of hurt and rage. There was no use trying to defend herself—he'd already made up his mind. "My God, how romantic," she said acidly. "You're wrong to assume my only option is to be someone's mistress. Lord Kendall is going to propose, and I intend to marry him and make him very happy."

"He wouldn't make you happy. Marriage to him would be a living hell. He'll never even know you."

"Neither will you! You don't understand the first thing about me, or you'd never have insulted me with such a proposition."

"I fail to see how it's an insult to offer you something better than what you have."

"It's not better."

"I just told you—"

"I don't care how much you're willing to pay, you arrogant lout! The answer is no. The answer is never. As far as I'm concerned, you're no different than Hodgeham." She let out a shaking breath. "I'm going back to my room. I don't want you to accompany me. As a matter of fact . . . I don't want you to speak to me ever again."

"Wait, Annabelle . . ." His face changed, his eyes softening with regret and concern. "I'm sorry, I'm—"

He broke off and reached for her, and then she was in his arms.

Chapter 16

His mouth was on hers, gentle but sure as he coaxed a response from her. She was filled with instant fever, burning everywhere, helpless against the onslaught of a desire like nothing she had ever known before. The pressure of his lips floated lightly over hers, straying briefly to her chin, her cheek, leaving trails of soft fire wherever they ventured, before he returned to her mouth with more explicit pressure. She felt the tip of his tongue against hers, the silken touch so unexpected that she would have recoiled had he not been holding her so tightly.

He slid one hand up to the side of her face, cradling her cheek as he pulled back just enough to nibble and tease, catching gently at her upper lip, then the lower one, lavishing her with feathery brushes of warmth. Compulsively, she exerted shaky pressure behind his neck, urging him back down to her, and when his mouth took hers in another penetrating kiss, she nearly moaned aloud. Before the sound could escape

her dilated throat, she tore her mouth away and
buried her face against his shoulder.

She felt the quick rise and fall of his deep-
vaulted chest, and the hot rush of his breath
against her hair. Grasping the mass of pinned-up
curls at the back of her head, he pulled her head
back to expose her throat. The burning path of
his lips began at the tiny hollow just beneath
her right ear, awakening exquisitely sensitive
nerves as he traced the line of a delicate vein
with his tongue. His fingers slid over the top of
her shoulder, his thumb finding the wing of her
collarbone, his open hand exploring the fragile architecture of her body. Nuzzling the side
of her throat, he found a place that made her
shiver, and he lingered there until she felt another moan threatening to break from her kiss-
dampened lips.

Pushing at him frantically, she managed to
divert him for all of three seconds, after which
he sought her mouth with another hungering
kiss. His palm brushed over the silk that covered her breast, once, twice, thrice. With each
slow pass, the heat of his skin sank through the
veil of fabric. As her nipple tingled and budded,
he stroked it tenderly with the backs of his fingers until it tightened even more. The increasing pressure of his kiss forced her head back in
a position of surrender, opening her to the lazy
caress of his tongue, the artful investigation of
his hands. This wasn't supposed to happen, her
nerves shattering with pleasure, her body consumed with sensual heat.

He made her forget everything in those silent moments—she lost awareness of time, of where they were, and even who she was. All she knew was that she needed him closer, deeper, tighter . . . his skin, his hard flesh, his mouth wandering in heated trails over her body. She gripped at his shirt until it loosened from his trousers, clutching handfuls of the starched white linen in desperate need of the warm skin beneath. He seemed to understand that she had no experience at controlling this level of desire—his kisses became soothing, his hands beginning to move over her back in calming strokes. However, the more he tried to ease her craving, the worse it became, her mouth moving frantically beneath his, her body twisting in an anxious rhythm.

He finally resorted to taking his mouth away and holding her in a crushing embrace, his lips buried against the flushed curve of her neck and shoulder. As the desire ebbed, Annabelle was left with only sickening shame. "Leave me alone," she managed to say, and fled.

Chapter 17

After Annabelle had fled the room, Simon remained there for at least a half hour, letting his blood cool. The fact that he had been brought to this state by a woman was infuriating. He, who was known as a crafty and disciplined negotiator, had made the clumsiest possible offer for her, and he had been roundly rejected. Deservedly so. He should never have tried to force her to name a price before she had even admitted that she wanted him. But the knowledge that she was sleeping with Hodgeham . . . *Hodgeham*, of all men, had nearly driven Simon mad with jealousy, and all his usual skills had deserted him.

Brooding, he went down to the ballroom. The prospect of another social evening was nearly maddening. His tolerance for extended parties had never been high—he was not a man who enjoyed hours of indolent chatter and idle amusements. He would have been long gone, had it not been for Annabelle's presence at Stony Cross.

Catching sight of Westcliff, Simon approached him, and the earl turned to him with slightly raised brows. "Enjoying yourself?"

"Not particularly." Simon shoved his hands into his coat pockets and glanced around the ballroom with simmering impatience. "I've stayed long enough in Hampshire—I need to return to London, to see what is happening at the foundry."

"What of Miss Peyton?" came the soft-voiced question.

Simon considered that for a moment. "I think," he said slowly, "I'm going to wait and see what comes of her pursuit of Kendall." He looked at Westcliff with a questioning arch of his brow.

The earl responded with a brief nod. "When will you depart?"

"Early in the morning." Simon could not repress a long, taut sigh.

Westcliff smiled wryly. "The situation will untangle itself," he said in a prosaic manner. "Go to London, and come back when your head is clear."

Annabelle could not seem to shake the melancholy that clung to her like a mantle of ice. Sleep had been elusive, and she had hardly been able to eat a bite of the sumptuous breakfast that had been served downstairs. Lord Kendall had regarded her wan countenance and her quietness as lingering effects of her recent illness, and he had plied her with sympathy and solace until she had wanted to shove him away in irritation. Her friends, too, were being similarly annoying in their niceness, and for the first time Annabelle took no enjoyment in their cheerful banter.

As the rest of the week unfolded, Annabelle had the sense of standing outside herself, watching a mechanical doll move stiffly through each day.

Despite the wallflowers' promise to tell each other everything about their romantic adventures, Annabelle could not bring herself to confide in any of them. What had happened with Simon had been too private and too personal. It was not something to be scrutinized by eager friends who knew no more about men than she did. And had she tried to explain the experience to them, she knew they would not have understood. There were no words to describe such soul-stealing intimacy and the devastating confusion that had followed.

How in God's name could she feel this way about a man she had always despised? For two years she had dreaded seeing him at social events—she had considered him to be the most unpleasant companion imaginable. And now . . . and now . . .

Shoving aside the unwanted thoughts, Annabelle retreated to the Marsden parlor one day, hoping to divert her churning mind with some reading material. Under her arm, she carried a heavy tome inscribed with gilded letters on the front: *Royal Horticultural Society—Findings and Conclusions of Reports Submitted by Our Respected Members in the Year 1843.*

The book was as heavy as an anvil, and Annabelle wondered wryly how anyone could find so much to say about plants. Setting the book on a small table, Annabelle began to lower herself to the settee by the window, when something about the chessboard in the corner caught her attention. Was it her imagination, or . . .

Eyes narrowing in curiosity, Annabelle strode to the table and stared at the configuration of chessmen, which had remained undisturbed all week long. Yes . . . something was different. She had used her queen to capture Simon's pawn. Now her queen had been taken from the board, and set precisely to the side.

He's come back, she thought with a sudden blaze of feeling that went all through her body. She felt certain that Simon Hunt was the only one who would have touched the chessboard. He was there, at Stony Cross. Her face turned paper white except for the flags of heat that scorched the crests of her cheeks. Realizing that her reaction was all out of proportion, she struggled to calm herself. His return meant nothing—she did not want him, could not have him, and must avoid him at all cost.

She looked down at the chessboard, trying to understand his last move. How had he taken her queen? Rapidly she calculated the previous locations of the pieces. Then she realized . . . he had lured her forward with the defensive pawn, positioning her perfectly for capture by his rook. And with her queen having been eliminated, her king was threatened and . . .

He had put her in check.

He had tricked her with that humble pawn, and she was in jeopardy. Letting out an incredulous laugh, Annabelle turned from the chess table and paced around the room. Defense strategies filled her head, and she tried to decide on the one he wouldn't expect. As her hand hovered over the board, however, the flood of warm excitement died away completely, and her face turned to stone. What was she doing? Continuing this game, maintaining even this fragile communication with him, was pointless. No . . . it was dangerous. There was no choice to be made between safety and disaster.

Annabelle's hand trembled a little as she reached for one chess piece after another, arranging them neatly in the box, methodically packing the game away. She wasn't fool enough to allow herself to want something . . . someone . . . who was so obviously wrong for her. When the chess box was closed, she backed away from the table and stood looking at it for a moment. She felt faded and abruptly weary, but resolute.

Tonight. Her ambiguous courtship with Lord Kendall would have to be resolved this evening. The party was almost over, and now that Simon Hunt had returned, she couldn't afford to risk having everything ruined by another complication with him. Squaring her shoulder, she went to tell Lillian, and together they would come up with a plan. The evening would end with her betrothal to Lord Kendall.

Chapter 18

"The trick is all in the timing," Lillian said, her brown eyes gleaming with enjoyment. Surely no military officer had ever conducted a campaign with more determination than Lillian Bowman currently displayed. The four wallflowers sat together on the back terrace with glasses of cool, pulpy lemonade, giving every appearance of indolence, while in reality they were carefully plotting the evening to come.

"I'll suggest a nice before-supper walk through the garden to awaken our appetites," Lillian said to Annabelle, "and Daisy and Evie will agree, and we'll bring our mother and Aunt Florence and anyone else we happen to be talking with—and hopefully by the time we reach the clearing on the other side of the pear orchard, you will be seen *in flagrante delicto* with Lord Kendall."

"What is *flagrante delicto?*" Daisy asked. "It sounds illegal."

"I don't know, precisely," Lillian admitted. "I read it in a novel . . . but I'm sure it's just the thing to get a girl compromised."

Annabelle responded with a halfhearted laugh, wishing that she could feel even a modicum of the Bowmans' enjoyment of the situation. A fortnight ago, she would have been beside herself with glee. But somehow it felt all wrong. There was no pleasurable anticipation in the prospect of *finally* prying a proposal out of a peer. No sense of excitement or relief, or anything remotely positive. It felt like an unpleasant duty that had to be done. She concealed her apprehensiveness while the Bowman sisters plotted and calculated with the expertise of seasoned conspirators.

However, it seemed that Evie, who was more observant than the rest of them put together, perceived the true emotions behind Annabelle's facade. "Is this what you w-want, Annabelle?" she asked softly, her blue eyes filled with concern. "You don't have to do this, you know. We'll find another suitor for you, if you don't want Kendall."

"There's no time to find another one," Annabelle whispered back. "No . . . it must be Kendall, and it has to be tonight, before . . ."

"Before?" Evie repeated, tilting her head as she regarded Annabelle with soft perplexity. The sun illuminated her scattered freckles, making them glint like gold dust on her velvety skin. "Before what?"

As Annabelle kept silent, Evie lowered her head and drew a fingertip along the edge of her glass, collecting fragments of sweetened pulp that had clung to the rim. The Bowman sisters were talking animatedly, debating the question of whether or not the pear orchard was the best place to waylay Kendall. Just as Annabelle thought that Evie would abandon the side conversation, the girl murmured softly, "Have you heard, Annabelle, that Mr. Hunt returned to Stony Cross late last night?"

"How do you know that?"

"Someone told my aunt."

Meeting Evie's perceptive gaze, Annabelle couldn't help thinking that woe befall anyone who ever made the mistake of underestimating Evangeline Jenner. "No, I hadn't heard," she murmured.

Tilting the glass of lemonade slightly, Evie stared into the depths of sugar-clouded liquid.

"Annabelle," she said slowly, "would you mind awfully if I didn't come along with the others to catch you with Lord Kendall tonight? There will be m-more than enough people to witness it. No doubt Lillian will bring an entire crowd of unsuspecting witnesses. I would be s-superfluous."

"Of course I wouldn't mind," Annabelle said, and asked with a sheepish smile, "Ethical reservations, Evie?"

"Oh, no, I'm not being hypocritical. I'm quite ready to admit guilt by association . . . and wh-whether or not I come to the garden tonight, I'm part of the group. It's just that . . ." She paused and continued quite softly. "I don't th-think you want Lord Kendall. Not as a man—not for what he truly is. And now after having come to know you a little better, I . . . I don't believe that marriage to him will make you happy."

"But it will," Annabelle argued, her tone sharpening until it had caught the Bowmans' attention. They stopped chattering and stared at her curiously. "No one could possibly come closer to my ideal than Lord Kendall."

"He's perfect for you," Lillian agreed firmly. "I hope you're not trying to sow seeds of doubt, Evie—it's far too late for that. We're hardly going to jettison a perfectly good plan now, when we've almost achieved victory."

Evie shook her head instantly, seeming to shrink in her chair. "No, no . . . I wasn't tr-trying to . . ." Her voice faded to a mumble, and she threw Annabelle an apologetic glance.

"Of course she wasn't," Annabelle said in Evie's defense, summoning a reckless smile. "Let's go over the plan once more, Lillian."

Lord Kendall reacted with amused complacency when Annabelle Peyton urged him to slip away with her for an early-evening walk through the garden. The air was soft with twilight, settling damply over the estate with no breeze to stir the thick atmosphere. With most of the guests dressing for dinner, or idling and fanning themselves in the card room and parlor, the outside grounds were mostly unoccupied. No man could be unaware of what a girl wanted when she suggested an unchaperoned walk in such circumstances. Apparently not adverse to the prospect of a stolen kiss or two, Kendall allowed Annabelle to coax him along the side of the terraced gardens and behind the drystone wall covered with climbing roses.

"I rather think we should have enlisted a chaperone," he said with a slight smile. "This is decidedly improper, Miss Peyton."

Annabelle flashed him a smile. "Steal away with me just for a moment," she urged. "No one will notice."

As he went with her willingly, Annabelle became aware of the growing weight of guilt that seemed to press on her from all sides. She felt as if she were leading a lamb to the slaughter. Kendall was a nice man—he didn't deserve to be tricked into a forced marriage. If only she had more time, she might have been able to let things progress naturally and pry a genuine proposal out of him. But this was the last weekend of the party, and it was imperative that she bring him up to scratch now. If she could just get this part of her plan over with, things would be so much easier from then on. *Annabelle, Lady Kendall* she reminded herself grimly. Annabelle, Lady Kendall . . . she could see herself as a respectable young matron who lived in the peaceful world of Hampshire society, taking occasional trips to London, welcoming her brother home from school on the holidays. Annabelle, Lady Kendall would have a half dozen fair-haired children, some of them endearingly fitted with spectacles like their father. And Annabelle, Lady Kendall would be a devoted wife who would spend the rest of her days trying to atone for the way she had deceived her husband into marrying her.

They reached the clearing beyond the pear orchard, where a stone table had been set in a graveled circle. Coming to a stop, Kendal looked down at Annabelle, who had leaned back against the edge of the stone table in a studied pose. He dared to touch a stray curl that had fallen to her shoulder, admiring the glints of gold in the pale brown strands. "Miss Peyton," he murmured, "by now it must be evident to you that I've developed a decided preference for your company."

Annabelle's heart had begun to hammer high in her throat, until she thought she might choke on it. "I . . . I have found great pleasure in our conversations and walks together," she managed to say.

"How lovely you are," Kendall whispered, drawing closer to her. "I've never seen eyes so blue."

A month ago, Annabelle would have been overjoyed for this to happen. Kendall was a nice man, not to mention attractive, young, and wealthy, and *titled* . . . oh, what the devil was wrong with her? Her entire being was suffused with reluctance as he bent over her. She tried to hold still for him. Before their lips could meet, however, she wrenched away with a muffled gasp and turned away from him.

Silence descended in the clearing.

"Have I frightened you?" came Kendall's inquiry. His manner was gentle and quiet . . . so different from Simon Hunt's arrogance.

"No . . . it's not that. It's just . . . I can't do this." Annabelle rubbed her suddenly aching forehead, her shoulders stiff amid the florid puffs of her peach silk gown. When she spoke again, her voice was heavy with defeat and self-disgust. "Forgive me, my lord. You are one of the nicest gentlemen I've ever had the privilege of knowing. Which is exactly why I must leave you now. It's not right for me to encourage your interest when nothing could come of it."

"Why do you think that?" he asked, openly confused.

"You don't really know me," Annabelle said with a bitter smile. "Take my word for it, we're an ill-matched pair. No matter how I tried, I wouldn't be able to keep from trampling you eventually—and you would be too much of a gentleman to object, and we would both be miserable."

"Miss Peyton," he murmured, trying to make sense of her outburst, "I can't begin to understand—"

"I'm not certain that I understand it, either. But I am sorry. I wish the best for you, my lord. And I wish . . ." Her breath came in irregular spurts, and she laughed suddenly. "Wishes are dangerous things, aren't they," she murmured, and left the clearing quickly.

Chapter 19

Railing at herself, Annabelle strode along the path that led back to the house. She couldn't believe it. Right when everything she wanted had been within her grasp, she had thrown it all away. "Stupid," she muttered to herself beneath her breath. "Stupid, stupid . . ." She couldn't begin to imagine what she should tell her friends after they arrived at the clearing only to find it empty. Perhaps Lord Kendall would remain where she had left him, looking like a horse whose feed bag had been yanked from his jaws before he had the chance to eat.

Annabelle vowed that she would not ask the other wallflowers to help her find another potential husband—not when she had just thrown away the opportunity that had been handed to her. She deserved whatever happened to her now. Her pace increased to a near run as she headed to her room. She was so intent on her frantic retreat that she nearly plowed into a man who was walking slowly along the path behind the drystone wall. Stopping suddenly, she murmured "I beg your pardon," and would have rushed around him. However, his distinctive height and the sight of the large, tanned hands withdrawing from his coat pockets immediately betrayed his identity. Stunned, she staggered backward as Simon Hunt looked at her.

They regarded each other with identical blank stares.

Simon's gaze turned hard. "You put away the chess game."

"I . . ." She looked away from him, biting her lip. "I couldn't afford distractions."

"No one's distracting you now. You want Kendall?—Have at him."

"Oh, thank you," she said sarcastically. "It's so kind of you to step aside gracefully, now that you've ruined everything."

He glanced at her alertly. "Why do you say that?"

Annabelle felt absurdly cold in the swaddling of summer-warm evening air. A fine trembling began in her bones and rose upward through her skin. "The ankle boots I received when I was ill," she said recklessly, "the ones I'm wearing right now—they were from you, weren't they?"

"Does it matter?"

"*Admit it*," she insisted.

"Yes, they were from me," he said curtly. "What of it?"

"I was with Lord Kendall just a minute or two ago, and everything was going according to plan, and he was just about to . . . but

I *couldn't*. I couldn't let him kiss me while I was wearing these blasted boots. No doubt he thinks that I'm deranged, after the way I left him. But you were right after all . . . he's far too nice for me. And it would have been a terrible match." She paused to inhale raggedly as she saw the sudden blaze in Hunt's eyes.

"So," he said softly, "now that you've thrown Kendall aside, what are your plans? Going back to Hodgeham?"

Goaded by the jeering question, Annabelle scowled. "If I do, it's no business of yours." She spun on her heel and began to walk away from him.

Hunt reached her in two strides. He whirled her around to face him, his hands closing around her upper arms. "Tell me what you want. Now, before I lose what's left of my mind."

The smell of him, soapy and fresh and wonderfully male, made Annabelle dizzy. She wanted to crawl inside his clothes . . . she wanted him to kiss her until she fainted. She wanted the despicable, arrogant, mesmerizing, devilishly handsome Simon Hunt. But oh, he would be merciless. Her threatened pride asserted itself, clotting in her throat until she could hardly speak. "I can't," she said gruffly.

Drawing his head back, Hunt gazed down at her, his eyes glinting with wicked amusement. "You can have whatever you want, Annabelle . . . but only if you can bring yourself to ask for it."

"You're determined to humble me completely, aren't you? You won't allow me to retain one particle of dignity—"

"I, humble *you?*" He raised one brow in a sardonic slant. "After two years of receiving cuts and slights every time I asked you to dance—"

"Oh, all right," she said balefully, beginning to shake all over. "I'll admit it—I want you. There, are you satisfied? I want *you.*"

"In what capacity? Lover, or husband?"

Annabelle stared at him in shock. "What?"

His arms slid around her, holding her quivering frame securely against his. He said nothing, only watched her intently as she tried to grasp the implications of the question.

"But you're not the marrying kind," she managed to say weakly.

He touched her ear, his fingertip tracing the fragile outer curve. "I've discovered that I am when it comes to you."

The subtle caress set fire to her blood, making it difficult to think. "We would probably kill each other within the first month."

"Probably," Hunt conceded, his smiling mouth brushing over her temple. The warmth of his lips sent a rush of dizzying pleasure through her. "But marry me anyway, Annabelle. As I see things, it would solve most of your problems . . . and more than a few of mine." His big hand slid gently down her spine, calming her tremors. "Let me spoil you," he whispered. "Let me take care of you. You've never had anyone to lean on, have you? I've got strong shoulders, Annabelle." A deep laugh rumbled in his chest. "And I may possibly be the only man of your acquaintance who'll be able to afford you."

She was too stunned to respond to the gibe. "But why?" she asked, as his hand traveled up to her unprotected nape. She gasped as his fingertip dipped softly into the shallow depression at the base of her skull. "Why offer to marry me when you might have me as your mistress?"

He nuzzled her throat gently. "Because I realized during the past few days that I can't leave doubt in anyone's mind about to whom you belong. Especially not yours."

Annabelle closed her eyes, her senses flooded with euphoria as his mouth wandered slowly up to her dry, parted lips. His hands and arms compressed her willing flesh into his demanding hardness. If there was mastery in the way he held her, there was also reverence, his fingertips discovering the most sensitive places on her exposed skin and teasing in whisper-light strokes. She let him coax her lips open, and she moaned at the gentle probe of his tongue. He ravished her with tender kisses that assuaged her need, yet made her desperately aware of empty places that longed to be filled. As Hunt felt the urgent quiver of her flesh against his, he soothed her with a long caress of his mouth, while his arms supported her body. Cradling her blood-hot cheek in his hand, he drew his thumb across the satin veneer of her lips. "Give me your answer," he whispered.

The warmth of his hand sent fine shivers across her skin, and she nestled her cheek deeper into his palm. "Yes," she said breathlessly.

Hunt's eyes gleamed with triumph. He tilted her head back and kissed her again, stealing deeper and deeper tastes. His palms clamped gently on either side of her head, altering the angle between them until their mouths fit together perfectly. The rhythm of her breath became capricious, and she was suddenly light-headed from the inrush of too much oxygen. Reaching for him, she clutched at the support of his hard-muscled body, her fingers digging into the broadcloth of his coat. Without breaking the kiss, Hunt helped her to hold on to him, reaching for her hand to draw it around his neck. When he was satisfied that her balance had been secured, he moved his hand to her corseted waist and applied light pressure to bring her body closer to his. He kissed her with rising urgency, until the potent influence of his mouth had reduced her to sensual delirium.

Eventually he took his mouth away and hushed her as she moaned in protest, telling her in a low murmur that they had company. Sleepy-eyed and bewildered, Annabelle peered out from the circle of his arms. They were confronted by a group of witnesses who could hardly avoid the sight of a couple embracing in the middle of the path by the drystone wall. Lillian . . . Daisy . . . their mother . . . Lady Olivia and her handsome American fiancé, Mr. Shaw . . . and, finally, none other than Lord Westcliff. "Oh, God," Annabelle said feelingly, and turned her face against Hunt's shoulder, as if closing her eyes would make them all disappear.

Her ear tingled as Hunt bent to murmur to her, his voice threaded with amusement. "Checkmate."

Lillian was the first to speak. "What in the world is going on, Annabelle?"

Cringing, Annabelle forced herself to meet her friend's gaze. "I couldn't go through with it," she said sheepishly. "I'm so sorry—the plan was such a good one, and you did your part beautifully—"

"And it would have been a great success if you hadn't been *kissing the wrong man*," Lillian exclaimed. "What in God's name happened? Why aren't you in the pear orchard with Lord Kendall?"

It was hardly the sort of thing that one wanted to articulate in front of a crowd. Annabelle hesitated and looked up at Hunt, who was watching her with a mocking smile, seeming fascinated to hear what explanation she might offer.

In the lengthening silence, Lord Westcliff appeared to have put two and two together, and he looked from Annabelle to Lillian with obvious disgust. "So this is why you were so insistent upon a walk. You two made an arrangement to trap Kendall!"

"I was part of it, too," Daisy asserted, determined to share in the blame.

Westcliff didn't appear to hear the comment, his gaze locked on Lillian's unrepentant face. "Good God—is there *nothing* you won't stoop to?"

"If there is," Lillian replied smartly, "I haven't discovered it yet."

Had her own circumstances not been quite so mortifying, Annabelle would have dissolved into laughter at the earl's expression.

Frowning, Lillian returned her attention to Annabelle. "It may not be too late to salvage things," she said. "We'll make everyone here promise to hold their tongues about having seen you and Mr. Hunt together. Without any witnesses, it hasn't happened."

Lord Westcliff considered the words with a scowl. "Much as I despise the prospect of agreeing with Miss Bowman," he said darkly, "I have to concur. The best thing for all concerned is for us to ignore this incident. Miss Peyton and Mr. Hunt have not been seen, and, therefore, no one has been compromised, which means that there will be no consequences to this unfortunate situation."

"Oh, yes, she *has* been compromised," Hunt said in sudden grim determination. "By me. And I don't want to avoid the consequences, Westcliff. I—"

"Yes, you do," the earl assured him authoritatively. "I'll be damned if I'll allow you to ruin your life over this creature, Hunt."

"*Ruin his life?*" Lillian repeated indignantly. "Mr. Hunt couldn't do better than to marry a girl like Annabelle! How dare you insinuate that she isn't good enough for him, when obviously he's the one who—"

"No," Annabelle interrupted anxiously. "Please, Lillian—"

"Excuse us," Mr. Shaw murmured with impeccable politeness, doing a poor job of concealing a grin. He pulled Lady Olivia's hand through the crook of his arm and executed a graceful bow in no particular direction. "I believe that my fiancée and I will excuse ourselves from the proceedings, being somewhat *de trop.*" His blue eyes sparkled with good-natured humor. "We'll leave the rest of you to decide just what has been seen and heard tonight . . . or not. Come, darling." Drawing Lady Olivia away with him, he escorted her back toward the manor.

The earl turned to the Bowmans' mother, a tall woman with a narrow, foxlike face. She had worked her expression into one of righteous indignation, but had held her tongue out of a desire not to miss anything. As Daisy later explained ruefully, Mrs. Bowman never had her conniptions in the middle of an act, preferring to save them for intermission.

"Mrs. Bowman," Westcliff asked, "may I prevail on you to maintain your silence regarding this matter?"

Had the earl, or any other titled man within reach, asked the ambitious Mrs. Bowman to jump headfirst into the flower bed for his amusement, she would have done so with a perfect somersault. "Oh, of course, my lord—I would *never* spread such distasteful gossip. My daughters are such sheltered innocents—it grieves me to see what their association with this . . . this unscrupulous girl has brought them to. I'm certain that a gentleman of your discernment can see that my two angels are completely blameless in this situation, having been led astray by the scheming young woman they sought to befriend."

Casting a skeptical glance at the two "angels," Westcliff replied coldly. "Quite."

Hunt, who had retained a possessive arm around Annabelle's waist, surveyed the lot of them coolly. "Do as you please. Miss Peyton is going to be compromised tonight, one way or another." He began to pull her along the path with him. "Come."

"Where are we going?" Annabelle asked, resisting his hold on her wrist.

"To the house. If they're not willing to be witnesses, then it seems I'll have to debauch you in front of someone else."

"Wait!" Annabelle squeaked. "I've already agreed to marry you! Why must I be compromised again?"

Hunt ignored the combined protests of Westcliff and the Bowmans as he replied succinctly. "Insurance."

Annabelle braced her heels, refusing to budge as he pulled at her arm. "You have no need of insurance! Do you think I would break my promise to you?"

"In a word, yes." Calmly, Hunt began to drag her along the path. "Now, where should we go? The entrance hall, I think. Plenty of people to witness you being ravished there. Or maybe the card room—"

"Simon," Annabelle protested, as she was hauled unceremoniously in his wake. "*Simon*—"

Her use of his name caused Hunt to stop suddenly, turning to look down at her with a curious half smile. "Yes, sweet?"

"For God's sake," Westcliff muttered, "let's save this for amateur theatrical night, shall we? If you're so bloody bent on having her, Hunt, then you may as well spare us all any further exhibitions. I'll gladly bear witness from here to London about your fiancée's besmirched honor, if only to have some peace around here. Just don't ask me to stand up with you at the wedding, as I have no desire to be a hypocrite."

"No, just an ass," came Lillian's murmur.

Low-spoken as the words were, it appeared that Westcliff had heard. His dark head whipped around, and he met Lillian's deliberately innocent expression with a threatening scowl. "As for you—"

"We're all agreed, then," Simon interrupted, preventing what surely would have evolved into a prolonged argument. He glanced at Annabelle with purely male satisfaction. "You've been compromised. Now let's go find your mother."

The earl shook his head, exhibiting a degree of frosty offense that could only be achieved by an aristocrat whose wishes had just been gainsaid. "I've never heard of a man being so eager to confess to the parent of a girl he's just ruined," he said sourly.

Chapter 20

$\mathcal{P}$hilippa's reaction to the news was one of astonishing calmness. As the three of them sat in the Marsdens' private parlor, and Simon relayed the news of their betrothal, and the reason for it, Philippa's face turned white, but she made no sound. In the brief silence that followed Simon's spare recitation, Philippa regarded Simon with an unblinking stare, and spoke carefully. "As Annabelle has no father to protect her, Mr. Hunt, it falls to me to ask for certain reassurances from you. Every mother wishes for her daughter to be treated with respect and kindness . . . and you must agree that the circumstances . . ."

"I understand," Simon said. Struck by his soberness, Annabelle watched him intently, while he focused his attention completely on Philippa. "I give you my word that your daughter will have no cause for complaint."

A flicker of wariness crossed Philippa's face, and Annabelle chewed her inner lip, knowing what was coming next. "I suspect you are already aware, Mr. Hunt," her mother murmured, "that Annabelle has no dowry."

"Yes," Simon replied matter-of-factly.

"And it makes no difference to you," Philippa said with a questioning lilt in her voice.

"None whatsoever. I am fortunate in being able to set aside financial considerations in the matter of choosing a wife. I don't give a damn if Annabelle comes to me without a shilling to her name. Moreover, I intend to make things easier for your family—assuming debts, taking care of bills and creditors, school tuition and the like—whatever is required to see that you're comfortably settled."

Annabelle saw Philippa's hands tighten in her lap until her fingers were white, and an unfathomable tremor of what could have been excitement, relief, embarrassment, or some combination of the three, shook her voice. "Thank you, Mr. Hunt. You understand, if Mr. Peyton was still with us, things would be much different—"

"Yes, of course."

There was a contemplative silence before Philippa murmured, "Of course, without a dowry, Annabelle will have no source of pin money . . ."

"I'll open an account for her at Barings," Hunt said equably. "We'll start it at, say, five thousand pounds? . . . and I'll refresh the balance from time to time as necessary. Of course, I'll be responsible for the maintenance of a carriage and horses . . . clothes . . . jewelry . . . and Annabelle may have credit at every shop in London."

Philippa's reaction to the news was lost on Annabelle, whose mind spun like a top. The thought of having five thousand pounds at her disposal . . . a fortune . . . it scarcely seemed real. Her amazement was tinged with a tingle of anticipation. After years of deprivation, she would be able to go to the best modistes, and buy a horse for Jeremy, and refurbish her family's home with the most luxurious furniture and fittings. However, this blunt discussion of money coming on the heels of a marriage proposal gave Annabelle the disquieting feeling of having sold herself for profit. Glancing cautiously at Simon, she saw that a familiar taunting gleam had entered his eyes. He understood her far too well, she thought, while unwanted heat climbed up her cheeks.

Annabelle kept silent as the conversation touched upon lawyers, contracts, and stipulations, discovering that her mother had the persistence of a bull terrier when it came to marriage negotiations. The businesslike discussion was hardly the stuff of high romance. Furthermore, it did not escape Annabelle that Philippa had not asked Hunt if he loved Annabelle, nor had he claimed to.

After Simon Hunt had left, Annabelle followed her mother to their room, where they would undoubtedly talk some more. Worried by Philippa's unnatural quietness, Annabelle closed the door and considered what to say to her, wondering if she had reservations about the prospect of Simon Hunt as a son-in-law.

As soon as they were alone, Philippa went to the window and looked outside at the evening sky, then covered her eyes with one hand. Alarmed, Annabelle heard the sound of a muffled sob. "Mama . . ." she said hesitantly as she stared at her mother's rigid back, "I'm sorry, I—"

"Thank God," Philippa murmured unsteadily, not seeming to hear her. "Thank God."

Despite Lord Westcliff's vow that he would not stand up with Simon at the wedding, he came to London in a fortnight to attend the ceremony. Grim-faced but polite, he even offered to give Annabelle away, assuming the place of her deceased father. She was strongly tempted to turn him down, but the offer had made Philippa so happy that Annabelle was forced to accept. And she even took a certain spiteful pleasure in obliging the earl to take a significant part in a ceremony that he so obviously opposed. Only Westcliff's loyalty to Hunt had brought him to London, revealing a bond of friendship between the two men that was far stronger than Annabelle would have guessed.

Lillian, Daisy, and their mother were also present at the private church ceremony, their presence made possible only by Lord Westcliff's presence. Mrs. Bowman would never have allowed her daughters to attend the wedding of a girl who was marrying outside the peerage and was a bad influence to boot. However, any opportunity to be in the proximity of the most eligible bachelor in England was to be seized on. The fact that Westcliff was completely indifferent to her younger daughter, and actively disdainful of the elder, was a minor hindrance that Mrs. Bowman was certain could be overcome.

Evie, unfortunately, had been forbidden to attend by her aunt Florence and the rest of her mother's family. Instead, she had sent Annabelle a long, affectionate letter, and a Sèvres china tea service painted with pink-and-gold flowers as a wedding gift. The rest of the small congregation consisted of Hunt's parents and siblings.

If only Jeremy could have attended the wedding . . . but he was still at school, and she and Philippa had decided that it would be best for him to finish the term and come to London when Hunt and Annabelle had returned from their honeymoon. Annabelle wasn't quite certain what Jeremy's reaction would be to the prospect of having Simon Hunt as a brother-in-law. Although Jeremy had seemed to like him, Jeremy had long been accustomed to being the only male in the family. There was every chance that he would chafe at any restrictions that Hunt might impose on him. For that matter, Annabelle herself wasn't terribly fond of the prospect of kowtowing to the wishes of a man whom, in all honesty, she didn't know that well.

That fact was forcibly brought home to Annabelle on her wedding night, as she waited

for her new husband in a room at the Rutledge
Hotel. The next day, they would leave for a
two-week honeymoon in Paris. First, however,
Annabelle would have to go through the wedding night, and she couldn't help being nervous.

Dressed in a nightgown trimmed with lavish
falls of white lace from the bodice and sleeves,
Annabelle sat and began to draw a brush
through her loose hair. Her heart stopped as Simon's dark, lean form entered the private suite.

She forced herself to continue brushing her
hair with calm strokes, though her grip was too
tight on the handle, and her fingers were shaking. Simon's gaze wandered over the drifts of
lace and muslin that covered her body. Still
dressed in his formal black wedding suit, he
approached her slowly and came to stand before her as she remained sitting in the chair. To
her surprise, he lowered to his knees to bring
their faces level, his thighs bracketing her slender calves. A large hand lifted to the shim-
mering fall of her hair, and he combed his
fingers through it, watching with fascination
as the golden brown strands slipped across his
knuckles.

Although Simon was immaculately dressed,
there were signs of dishevelment that lured her
attention . . . the short forelocks of his hair fall-
ing over his forehead, the loosened knot of his
ice gray silk cravat. Dropping the brush to the
floor, Annabelle used her fingers to smooth his
hair in a tentative stroke. The sable filaments
were thick and gleaming, springing willfully
against her fingertips. Simon held still for her as

she untied the cravat, the heavy silk saturated with the warmth of his skin. His eyes contained an expression that caused a ticklish sensation in the pit of her stomach.

"Every time I see you," he murmured, "I think you couldn't possibly become any more beautiful—and you always prove me wrong."

Letting the cravat hang on either side of his neck, Annabelle smiled at the compliment. She jumped a little in her seat as she felt his hand close around hers. His mouth curved slightly as he gave her a quizzical glance. "You're nervous?"

Annabelle nodded, her fingers unresisting in his as he held and chafed them gently. Simon spoke quietly, seeming to choose his words with unusual care. "Sweetheart . . . I assume that your experiences with Lord Hodgeham were not pleasant. But I hope you'll trust me when I say that it doesn't have to be like that. Whatever your fears are—"

"Simon," she interrupted with an apprehensive croak, and cleared her throat. "That is very kind of you. A-And the fact that you are prepared to be so understanding about it . . . well . . . I appreciate that. But . . . I'm afraid I wasn't entirely forthcoming about my relationship with Hodgeham." Seeing his sudden curious stillness, and the way his expression had been wiped clean of emotion, Annabelle took a deep, steadying breath. "The truth is, Hodgeham did indeed come to our house some evenings, and he did pay some of our bills in return for . . . for . . ." Pausing, she felt her throat contract until it was hard to force the words through. "But . . . I wasn't actually the one that he was visiting."

Simon's dark eyes widened slightly. "What?"

"I never slept with him," she admitted. "His arrangement was with my mother."

He stared at her, dumbfounded. "Holy hell," he breathed.

"It started a year ago," she said, her voice edged with defensiveness. "Our circumstances were desperate. We had endless bills and no means to pay them. The income from my mother's jointure had dwindled because it had been invested badly. Lord Hodgeham had been sniffing at my mother's heels for some time . . . I don't know precisely when his evening visits began . . . but I saw his hat and cane in the entrance hall at odd hours, and the debts eased a little. I realized what was happening, but I never said anything about it. And I should have."

"Why did you let me think that *you* were sleeping with him?"

Annabelle shrugged uncomfortably. "You just assumed so . . . and there didn't seem to be any reason to correct you, as I certainly never thought that we would end up like this. And then you proposed to me anyway, which led me to conclude that it wasn't especially important to you whether or not I was a virgin."

"It wasn't," Simon murmured, his voice sounding strange. "I wanted you regardless. But now that I . . ." He broke off and shook his head in amazement. "Annabelle—just to be clear—are you saying that you've never been to bed with a man before?"

She tugged at her hands, for his grip had become crushingly tight. "Well . . . yes."

"Yes, you have, or no, you haven't?"

"I have never slept with anyone," Annabelle said precisely, and gave him a questioning glance. "Are you annoyed because I didn't tell you earlier? I'm sorry. But it's not the sort of thing one can just blurt out over tea, or in the entrance hall . . . 'Here's your hat, and by the way, I'm a virgin'—"

"I'm not annoyed." Simon's gaze traveled over her pensively. "I'm just wondering what to do with you now."

"The same thing you were going to do before I told you?" she asked hopefully.

Simon stood and pulled her to her feet and embraced her, as if he feared she might shatter with too much pressure. He pressed his face into the shining fall of her hair and breathed deeply. "First it seems there are a few things I need to ask you."

Annabelle pushed her arms inside the front of his coat and slid them around his hard, sleek torso. "Yes?" she prompted.

"Do you know what to expect? Do you have all the . . . er, necessary information?"

"I think so," Annabelle replied, smiling at the interesting discovery that his heart was beating very fast against her cheek. "My mother and I had a talk just a little while ago—after which I was strongly tempted to ask for an annulment."

He grinned. "I'd better claim my husbandly rights without delay, then." Taking her fingers in his hot, light grip, he lifted them to his mouth. The touch of his breath was like steam. "What did she tell you?" he murmured against her fingertips.

"After imparting the basic facts, she said that I should let you do as you wished and try not to complain if I didn't like something. And she suggested that if it becomes too unpleasant, I should turn my mind to thoughts of that enormous bank account you opened for me."

Annabelle regretted the words as soon as they left her lips, expecting that Simon might be offended.

"Shall I woo you with whispers of balance transfers and rates of interest, then?"

Turning her hand in his, Annabelle let her fingertips graze the surface of his lips, lingering at the velvety edge, then drifting down to the masculine scrape of his chin. "That won't be necessary. Just say the usual things."

"No . . . the usual things won't do for you." Simon tucked a loose lock of hair behind her ear and cupped her cheek in his palm as he leaned forward. His mouth teased hers into yielding openness, while his hands found the outline of her body within the ample billows of lace. With no corset to constrict her ribs, she could feel his touch through the thin veil of her gown. The stroke of his hands along her unbound sides caused her to quiver, the tips of her breasts turning exquisitely sensitive. His palm traveled slowly over her front, finding the pliant weight of one breast, and he made a gentle cup of his fingers, lifting the vulnerable flesh. Her breath halted momentarily as his thumb nudged her nipple into delicately aching distension.

"It's usually painful for a woman, the first time," he murmured.

"Yes, I know."

"I don't want to hurt you."

The admission touched and surprised her. "My mother says it doesn't last for long," she said.

"The pain?"

"No, the rest of it," she said, and for some reason that made him laugh.

He looked into her eyes, their faces so close that their noses were nearly touching. "Come to bed with me," he whispered. "Trust me to take care of you."

She nodded with a shaky sigh and let him lead her to the large four-poster bed, covered with a counterpane made of heavy quilted burgundy silk. Drawing back the covers, Simon lifted Annabelle onto the slick-pressed linens, and she slid over to make room for him. He stood by the bed, watching her face as he removed the rest of his formal clothes. Annabelle doubted that a healthier, more vigorous-looking man could be found anywhere. Perhaps he didn't match the fashionable ideal of a pale, slender-framed aristocrat . . . but she thought he was altogether splendid.

Pangs of excited apprehension went through her stomach as he joined her on the bed.

"Simon," she said, breathing fast as he took her into her arms, "my mother didn't tell me if . . . if tonight there was something that I should do for you . . ."

His hand began to play in her hair, his fingers drifting over her scalp in a way that sent hot tingles down her spine. "You don't have to do anything tonight. Just let me hold you . . . touch you . . . discover some of the things that please you . . ."

His hand found the placket of mother-of-pearl buttons at the back of her gown. Annabelle closed her eyes as she felt the frothy mass of ruffled lace loosening over her shoulders. "Do you remember that night you kissed me?" she whispered, gasping as she felt him ease the gown from her breasts.

"Every blistering second," he whispered back, pulling her arms from the billowing sleeves. "Why?"

"I couldn't stop thinking about it," she confessed. She wriggled to help him strip the gown away from her body, a blush covering every inch of exposed skin.

"Neither could I," he admitted. His hand slid over her breast, cupping the cool roundness until the peak was rosy and hard in his palm.

He bent to kiss the tip of her breast. She gasped at the tender tugs of his mouth, his tongue flicking her sensitive flesh until she could no longer remain still beneath him. Her legs parted involuntarily, and immediately he filled the space with his own hair-roughened thigh. As his hands and mouth wandered slowly over her body, Annabelle lifted her hands to his head, letting the thick waves slip through her fingers as she had so often longed to do. He kissed the fragile skin of her wrists, and the insides of her elbows, and the shallow depressions between her ribs, leaving no part of her unexplored. She let him do as he wished, quivering as she felt the prickle of his night beard contrasting with the silky wet heat of his mouth. But when he reached her navel, and she felt the slick point of his tongue enter the little hollow, she rolled away from him with a shocked inhalation. "No . . . Simon, I . . . *please* . . ."

Immediately he levered upward to gather her in his arms, smiling into her scarlet face. "Too much?" he asked tenderly. "I'm sorry—let me hold you. You're not frightened, are you?"

Before she could answer, his mouth had settled on hers, dragging gently back and forth. The hair on his chest abraded her breasts like coarse velvet, her nipples rubbing against him with each breath she took. Her throat vibrated with low sounds, evincing the pleasure that had escaped her crumbling restraint. She gasped sharply as his fingers drifted over her stomach and his knee intruded more deeply between hers. Widening the angle between her thighs, he slipped his fingers into the soft feminine curls, exploring her swollen flesh. He parted her, found the silken peak that throbbed at his touch, and stroked just above it with sweet, dancing lightness.

She gasped against his mouth, her flesh heating into melting pliancy. Simon sought the opening of her body, his gentle fingertip insinuating carefully into the fluid-drenched suppleness. Her heart pounded, and all her limbs stiffened against the heightening pleasure. Rolling away from him with a muffled exclamation, she stared at Simon with wide eyes.

He lay on his side, raised on one elbow, his dark hair disheveled and his gaze bright with passion and subtle amusement. It seemed as if he understood what had begun to happen inside her and was fascinated by her innocent consternation. "Don't go anywhere," he murmured, smiling. "You don't want to miss the best part." Slowly, he pulled her back beneath him, arranging her body with caressing hands. "Sweetheart, I won't hurt you," he whispered against her cheek. "Let me pleasure you . . . let me inside you . . ."

He continued to murmur to her, while he kissed and caressed his way stealthily down her body. His mouth slid gently between her thighs. She shrank from him bashfully, but he gripped . her hips in his hands and explored her mercilessly, the tip of his tongue gliding over every tender fold and crevice. The room around them blurred, and she felt as if she was floating amid layers of shadow and candlelight, conscious of nothing but exquisite, twisting rapture. She could hide nothing from him, could do nothing except surrender to the demanding mouth that solicited unholy delight from her awakening flesh. He centered on the peak of her sex, licking softly, steadily, until it finally became too much to endure, and she felt her hips rise of their own accord, quivering against his mouth, heat jetting through her pleasure-racked limbs.

Giving her sated flesh a last savoring lick, Simon worked his way back up her body. Her thighs were limp as he pushed them wide apart, the head of his shaft nudging against her. Looking down into her dazed face, Simon smoothed her hair back from her forehead.

Her lips curved in a wobbly smile as she glanced up at him. "I forgot all about my bank account," she said, and he laughed softly.

His thumb brushed over the edge of her forehead, where fine skin blended into flossy hair. "Poor Annabelle . . ." The pressure between her legs increased, delivering the first intimation of pain. "I'm afraid the next part won't be nearly as enjoyable. For you, at any rate."

"I don't mind . . . I . . . I'm just so glad it's you."

No doubt it was an odd thing for a bride to say on her wedding night, but it brought a smile to his lips. He lowered his head and began to whisper in her ear, even as he tightened his hips to breach her untried flesh. She forced herself to hold still despite the instinct to writhe away from the intrusion. "Sweetheart . . ." His breath became ragged, and as he paused inside her, he seemed to struggle for self-control. He deepened his entry in lingering degrees, carefully courting her body into accepting him.

Gradually it became easier, the pain fading into a mild, prolonged burn. A long sigh escaped her as she felt her body yielding. Holding himself deep inside her, Simon groaned, while a shiver ran across his shoulders. "You're so tight," he said hoarsely.

"I-I'm sorry—"

"No, no," he managed. "Don't be sorry. My God." His voice was slurred, as if he was drunk on pleasure.

They studied each other, one gaze sated, the other brilliant with yearning. A sense of wonder crept over Annabelle as she realized how thoroughly he had controverted her expectations. She had been so certain that Simon would use this opportunity to prove himself her master . . . and instead he had come to her with infinite patience. Filled with gratitude, she wrapped her arms around his neck. She kissed him and let her tongue enter his mouth, and she drew her hands down his back, until her palms reached the hard contours of his buttocks. She stroked him in shy encouragement, urging him to sink deeper inside her. The caress seemed to eradicate the remainder of his self-control. With a growl of hunger, he pushed rhythmically inside her, shaking with the effort to be gentle. The force of his release caused him to shiver hard, his teeth gritting as sensation culminated in blinding rapture. Burying his face in the filtering strands of her hair, he soaked in her honey-slick warmth. A long time passed before the iron-hard tension left his muscles, and he let out a slow breath. As he withdrew carefully from Annabelle's body, she winced at the intimate soreness. Perceiving her discomfort, he caressed her hip in gentle consolation.

"I may never leave this bed again," he muttered, cuddling her in the crook of his arm.

"Oh, yes you will," Annabelle said, half-drowsing. "You're going to take me to Paris tomorrow. I won't be deprived of the honeymoon you promised."

Nuzzling into her tangled curls, Simon replied with the trace of a smile in his voice. "No, sweet wife . . . you won't be deprived in any way."

Chapter 21

During the two weeks of their honeymoon, Annabelle fell in love with Paris, which was so stylish and modern, it made London look like a dowdy country cousin.

Their hotel, the *Coeur de Paris*, was located on the left bank of the Seine, between a dazzling array of shops on rue de Montparnasse and the covered markets of Saint-Germain-des-Pres, where exotic produce and fabrics and laces and art and perfume were displayed in bewildering varieties. The *Coeur de Paris* was a palace, with suites of rooms that had been designed for sensual pleasure. The bathing room, for example—the *salle de bain*, it was called—had been fitted with a rosy marble floor and Italian tiled walls, and a gilded rococo settee where the bather rested after the exertions of washing. There was not one but two porcelain tubs, each with its own boiler and cold water tank. The tubs were surmounted with a painted oval landscape on the ceiling, designed to entertain the bather as

he or she relaxed. Having been brought up with
the British view of a bath as a matter of hygiene
to be conducted with expediency, Annabelle was
amused by the notion that the act of bathing
should be a decadent entertainment.

To Annabelle's delight, a man and a woman
could share a table in a public restaurant without having to request a private dining room.
She had never had such delicious food . . .
tender cockerel that had been simmered with
tiny onions in red wine . . . duck confit expertly
roasted until it was melting-soft beneath crisp
oiled skin . . . rascasse fish served in truffled
sauce.

One night Simon took her to a ballet with
scandalously underdressed dancers, and the
next, a performance by a symphony orchestra.
They also attended balls and soirées given by
acquaintances of Simon's. Some were French
citizens, while others were tourists and émi-
grés from Britain, America, and Italy. A few
were stockholders or board members of companies that he had part ownership in, while others
had been involved with his shipping or railway
enterprises. "How do you know so many people?" Annabelle had asked Simon in bewilderment, when he was hailed by several strangers
at the first party they attended.

Simon had laughed and gently mocked that
one would think that she had never realized
that there was a world outside of the British
peerage. And the truth was, she hadn't. She had
never thought to look outside the narrow con-
fines of that rarefied society until now.

Annabelle realized that when her husband spoke, the other men paid keen attention to his opinions. Perhaps Simon was someone of little consequence in the view of the British aristocracy, but he wielded considerable influence outside of it.

At the first ball they attended, Simon asked Annabelle to dance as a beautiful melody began to play. Annabelle recognized the waltz, which was so haunting and sweet, the wallflowers had agreed it was literally torture to sit still in a chair while it was being played.

As she took Simon's arm, she thought of the countless times in the past she had spurned his invitations to dance. Reflecting that Simon had finally gotten his way, Annabelle smiled. "Do you always succeed at getting what you want?" she asked.

"Sometimes it takes longer than I would prefer," he said. As they entered the ballroom, he put his hand on Annabelle's waist and guided her to the edge of the swirling mass of dancers.

She experienced a pang of giddy nervousness, as if they were about to share something far more significant than a mere dance. "This is my favorite waltz," she told him, moving into his arms.

"I know. That's why I requested it."

"How did you know?" she asked with an incredulous laugh. "I suppose one of the Bowman sisters told you?"

Simon shook his head, while his gloved fingers curved around hers. "On more than one occasion, I saw your face when they played it. You always looked ready to fly out of your chair."

Annabelle's lips parted in surprise, and she stared up at him with a wondering gaze. How could he have noticed something so subtle? She had always been so dismissive of him, and yet he had noticed her reaction to a particular piece of music and remembered it. The realization brought the sting of tears to her eyes, and she looked away immediately, fighting to bring the baffling swell of emotion under control.

Simon drew her into the current of waltzing couples, his arms strong, the hand at her back offering firm pressure and guidance. It was so easy to follow him, to let her body relax into the rhythm he established while her skirts swept across the gleaming floor and whipped lightly around his legs.

Simon, for his part, was not above a sense of triumph as he guided Annabelle across the floor. Finally, after two years of pursuit, he was having his long-sought waltz with her. And more satisfying still, Annabelle would still be his after the waltz . . . he would take her back to the hotel, and undress her, and make love to her until dawn.

She followed his lead so gracefully as if she knew what direction he would take her in before he even knew it himself. The result was a physical harmony that enabled them to move swiftly across the room like a bird in flight.

Simon had not been surprised by the reactions from his acquaintances upon meeting his new bride—the congratulatory words and subtly covetous gazes, and the sly murmurs of a few men who said they did not envy him the burden of having such a beautiful wife. Lately Annabelle had become even lovelier, if possible, the strain leaving her face after many nights of dreamless slumber. In bed she was affectionate and even frolicsome—the previous night she had climbed over him with the grace of a sportive seal, scattering kisses over his chest and shoulders. He had not expected that of her, having known beautiful women in the past who invariably lay back passively to be worshiped. Instead, Annabelle had teased and caressed him until he'd finally had enough. He had rolled on top of her while she giggled and protested that she wasn't yet finished with him. "I'll finish you," he had growled in mock-threat, and thrust inside her until she was moaning with pleasure.

Simon had no illusions that their relationship would be continually harmonious—they were both too independent and strong by nature to avoid the occasional clashes. Having relinquished her chance to marry a peer, Annabelle had closed the door on the kind of life she had always dreamed of, and instead would have to adjust to a far different existence. With the exception of Westcliff and two or three other wellborn friends, Simon had relatively little interaction with the aristocracy. His world consisted mainly of professional men like him, unrefined and happily driven to the endeavor of making money. This crowd of industrialists could not have been more different than the cultivated class Annabelle had always been familiar with. Simon was not entirely certain how Annabelle would accommodate such people, but she seemed game to try. He understood and appreciated her efforts more than she could have known.

"Are you sorry now that you never danced with me?"

"No. If I hadn't been a challenge, you would have lost interest."

Letting out a low laugh, Simon hooked his arm around her waist and led her to the side of the room. "That would never happen. Everything you do or say interests me."

"Really," she said skeptically. "What about Lord Westcliff's claim that I'm shallow and self-absorbed?"

As she faced him, Simon braced one hand on the wall near her head and leaned over her protectively. His voice was very soft. "He doesn't know you."

"And you do?"

"Yes, I know you." He reached out to finger a tendril of damp hair that clung to her neck. "You guard yourself carefully. You don't like to depend on anyone. You're determined and strong-willed, and you're decided in your opinions. Not to mention stubborn. But never self-absorbed. And anyone with your intelligence could never be called shallow." He let his finger stray into the wisps of hair behind her ear. A teasing glint entered his eyes as he added, "You're also delightfully easy to seduce."

With an outraged laugh, Annabelle lifted a fist as if to pummel him. "Only for you."

Chuckling, he grasped her fist in his large hand, and kissed the points of her knuckles. "Now that you're my wife, Westcliff knows better than ever to utter another word of objection to you or the marriage. If he did, I would end the friendship without a second thought."

"Oh, but I would never want that, I . . ." She looked at him in sudden bemusement. "You would do that for me?"

Simon traced a vein of golden hair that ran through the honey brown locks. "There is nothing I wouldn't do for you." The vow was sincere. Simon was not a man given to half measures. In return for Annabelle's commitment to him, she would have his unequivocal loyalty and support.

Annabelle was unaccountably quiet after that, leading Simon to conclude that she was tired. But when they returned to their room at the *Coeur de Paris* that evening, she gave herself to him with a new fervor, trying to express with her body what she could not say in words.

Chapter 22

Near the end of the honeymoon, Annabelle spent a day with some other women staying at the hotel. They went to the Palais Royal, a fashionable tourist attraction with covered shopping arcades, gardens, and a promenade.

Simon, meanwhile, had gone out riding with friends, and then lounged at a cafe to discuss business and politics. He returned to the hotel and found Annabelle amid a group playing cards in one of the public rooms.

Annabelle started as she felt someone come up behind her chair and rest his hand on her shoulder, then relaxed as she recognized her husband's touch.

"I missed you today," Simon murmured near her ear.

She twisted in her chair to smile into his dark eyes. "I missed you, too," she whispered.

"Come up to the suite with me."

Her lips twitched with amusement. "I have to finish my game."

"You'd better do it quickly," he advised.

Her brows lifted. "Why?"

"Because I'm going to make love to you in precisely five minutes," he whispered. "Wherever we happen to be ... here ... in our suite ... or on the stairs. So if you'd like me to do it in privacy, you'd better lose the game. Fast."

He wouldn't, Annabelle thought, her heartbeat quickening with alarm. On the other hand, knowing Simon ...

Anxiously, Annabelle considered ways to bow out of the game. The voice of reason said that no matter how audacious Simon was, he wouldn't actually ravish his wife on the hotel staircase. However, the voice of reason was abruptly strangled as Simon leisurely consulted his watch.

"You have three minutes," came his soft murmur in her ear.

The players conversed lazily, fanning themselves and sending a waiter for another pitcher of iced lemonade. At last it was Annabelle's turn, and she threw out her highest face card and drew another. Relief stabbed through her as she saw that her new card was worthless, and she cast down her hand. "I'm afraid I'm out," she said, making an effort to keep from sounding breathless. "What a lovely day it was—thank you, I must go—"

"Do stay for the next round," one of the ladies urged, and the others added their own entreaties.

"Yes, do!"

"At least have a glass of wine while we finish this round—"

"Thank you, but—" Annabelle stood and gasped slightly as she felt the gentle pressure of Simon's hand on her back. "I'm simply exhausted from all the dancing last night," she improvised. "I must have some rest before we attend the theater this evening."

Followed by a chorus of farewells, and a few knowing glances, Annabelle attempted a dignified exit from the salon. As soon as they reached the winding staircase that led to the upper floors, she heaved a sigh of relief, and cast her husband a reproving glance. "If you were trying to embarrass me, you—what are you doing?" Her gown had become loose across her shoulders, and she realized with a little shock of amazement that he had unfastened some of her buttons. "Simon," she hissed, "don't you dare!" She hurried from him, but he kept pace with her easily.

"You have one minute left."

"Don't be silly," she said shortly. "We can't possibly reach the suite in less than a minute, and you wouldn't—" She broke off with a squeak as she felt him pluck at another button, and turned to swat at his marauding hands. Her gaze caught his, and she realized incredulously that he had every intention of carrying out his threat. "Simon, *no*."

"Yes." His eyes were filled with tigerish playfulness, and the look on his face was one that she had become entirely familiar with by now.

Hiking up her skirts, Annabelle turned to

rush up the stairs, her breath coming in pants of panicked laughter. "You're impossible! Leave me alone. You're—oh, if anyone sees us, I'll never forgive you!"

Simon followed without apparent hurry—but then, he didn't have masses of skirts and binding underclothes to hamper him. She reached the top landing and rounded the corner, her knees aching as her legs pumped in a desperate ascent, stair after stair. Her skirts felt weighted, and her lungs were close to bursting. Oh, damn him for doing this to her—and damn herself for the airless giggles that kept slipping from her throat.

"Thirty seconds," she heard behind her, and she wheezed as she arrived at the top of the second flight. Three long hallways before she reached their suite—and not nearly enough time. Clutching at the sagging front of her dress, she looked up and down the hallways that extended from the landing. She rushed toward the first door she could find, which opened into a small, unlit closet. The scent of starched linen billowed outward, and shelves of neatly stacked bed linens and toweling were just visible in the light from the hallway.

"Keep going," Simon murmured, crowding her into the closet and closing the door.

Annabelle was immediately engulfed in darkness. Laughter swelled in her chest, and she shoved ineffectually at the hands that reached for her. It seemed that her husband had suddenly developed more arms than an octopus, unfastening her clothes and peeling them away much faster than she could move to defend herself. "What if you've locked us in here?" she asked, as her dress dropped to the floor.

"I'll break the door down," he replied, tugging at the tapes of her drawers. "Afterward."

"If one of the maids finds us, we'll be thrown out of the hotel."

"Believe me, the maids have seen far worse than this." Her dress was crushed beneath Simon's feet as he shoved Annabelle's drawers to her ankles.

She made a few more halfhearted protests, until Simon reached between her thighs and discovered the evidence of her arousal, after which further remonstrations seemed rather pointless. Her mouth opened to his kiss, eagerly returning the rough, stroking pressure of his lips. The plush entrance of her body stretched easily to take him, and a whimper slipped from her throat as she felt his fingers there, spreading her so that every rolling thrust of his hips gently abraded the sensitive peak of her sex.

They struggled to press closer, their bodies flexing, fusing, each kiss a searching invasion that aroused her further. Her corset was too tight, but there was unexpected delight in the constriction, as if extra sensation had been detoured to the lower half of her body. Her fingers clawed uselessly at his clothes as her desire escalated to near madness. Simon invaded her in deep lunges, his rhythm insistent, until rapture shot and echoed through both of them, and their lungs pulled in drafts of air laden with the scent of clean, pressed linen, and their entwined limbs tightened as if to trap the sensation between them.

"Damn," Simon muttered a few minutes later, when he was able to catch his breath.

"What?" Annabelle whispered, her head resting heavily against his coat lapel.

"For the rest of my life, the smell of starch is going to make me hard."

"That's your problem," she replied with a languid smile, and inhaled as she felt his body, still joined with hers, nudge upward.

"Yours, too," he told her, just before his mouth found hers in the darkness.

Chapter 23

Soon after Simon and Annabelle's return to England, they were confronted with the inevitable interaction of two families that could not have been more different. Simon's mother, Bertha, demanded that they come to dinner so that they all could become better acquainted, as they had not been able to do before the wedding. Although Simon had warned Annabelle what to expect, and she in turn had endeavored to prepare her mother and brother, she suspected that the encounter would produce, at best, mixed results.

Thankfully Jeremy was happily reconciled to the fact that Simon Hunt was now his brother-in-law. Having grown tall and lanky in the past few months, he stood over Annabelle as he embraced her in the parlor of their home. His golden brown hair had lightened considerably from all the time he had spent out of doors, and his blue eyes were bright and smiling in his sun-browned face. "I couldn't believe my eyes when I read Mama's letter saying that you were going to marry Simon Hunt," he told her. "After all the things you've said about him during the past two years—"

"Jeremy," Annabelle scolded. "Don't you dare repeat any of that!"

Laughing, Jeremy continued to keep an arm around her while he extended his hand to Simon. "Congratulations, sir." As they shook hands, he continued mischievously, "Actually, I wasn't a bit surprised. My sister complained about you so often and for so long that I knew she entertained a strong feeling for you."

Simon's warm gaze fell on his scowling wife. "I can't imagine what she found to complain about," he said blandly.

"I believe she said—" Jeremy began, and gave an exaggerated wince as Annabelle shoved her elbow against his ribs. "All right, I'll be quiet," he said, holding up his hands defensively and laughing as he staggered back from her. "I was just having a little polite parlor conversation with my new brother-in-law."

"'Polite parlor conversation' entails talking about the weather, or asking after someone's health," Annabelle informed him. "Not revealing potentially embarrassing remarks that one's sister made in confidence."

Sliding an arm around Annabelle's waist, Simon pulled her back against his chest and lowered his head to murmur in her ear, "I have a fair idea of what you said. After all, you were willing enough to tell me face-to-face."

Hearing the note of amusement in his voice, Annabelle relaxed against him.

Having never seen his sister interact so comfortably with a man, and noticing the changes in her, Jeremy smiled. "I would say that marriage seems to agree with you, Annabelle."

Just then Philippa entered the room, and she rushed to her daughter with a glad cry. "Darling, I have missed you so!" She embraced her daughter tightly, then turned to Simon with a brilliant smile. "Dear Mr. Hunt, welcome home. Did you enjoy Paris?"

"Beyond telling," Simon replied pleasantly, bending to kiss her proffered cheek. He did not look at Annabelle as he added, "I especially enjoyed the champagne."

"Why, of course," Philippa replied, "I'm certain that anyone who . . . Annabelle, dear, what are you doing?"

"Just opening the window," Annabelle said in a strangled voice, her face having turned the color of pickled beets at Simon's remark, as she remembered the evening when he had put a glass of champagne to especially creative use. "It's terribly warm in here—why on earth are the windows closed at this time of year?" Keeping her face averted, she struggled with the latch until Jeremy came to help her.

While Simon and Philippa conversed, Jeremy pushed the paned glass open and grinned as Annabelle turned her overheated cheeks toward the cooling breeze. "It must have been quite a honeymoon," he murmured with a swift grin.

Simon squeezed her hand affectionately. "I

can see that your brother and I would do well to share our manly confidences outside, while you go tell your mother all about Paris. Jeremy— would you care for a ride in my phaeton?"

Her brother needed no further urging. "Let me find my hat and coat—"

"Don't bother with a hat," Simon advised laconically. "You wouldn't be able to keep it on your head for more than a minute."

"Mr. Hunt," Annabelle called after them, "if you maim or kill my brother, you won't get any supper."

Simon called out something indistinct over his shoulder, and the pair of them disappeared into the entrance hall.

Later, as Annabelle sat talking to her mother in the parlor, Jeremy burst in looking disheveled and wild-eyed.

"Jeremy?" Annabelle exclaimed in worry, jumping to her feet. "What happened? Where is Mr. Hunt?"

"Walking the horses around the square to cool them." He shook his head and spoke breathlessly. "The man is a lunatic. We nearly overturned at least three times, we came close to killing a half dozen people, and I was jolted until the entire lower half of my body is black-and-blue. If I'd had the breath to spare, I would have started praying, as we were clearly going to die. Hunt has the meanest horses I've ever set eyes on, and he let out curses so foul that just one of them would have gotten me expelled from school for good—"

"Jeremy," Annabelle began apologetically,

aghast that Simon would have treated her brother so terribly. "I'm so—"

"It was without doubt the *best* afternoon of *my entire life!*" Jeremy continued jubilantly. "I begged Hunt to take me out again tomorrow, and he said that he would if he had the time— Oh, what a *ripper* he is, Annabelle! I'm off to get some water—I've got a half inch of dust lining my throat." He rushed off with adolescent glee, while his mother and sister stared after him, openmouthed.

In the evening Simon took Annabelle, Jeremy, and their mother to the residence over the butcher shop, where his parents still lived. Consisting of three main rooms and a narrow staircase leading to a third-floor loft, the place was small but well-appointed. Even so, Annabelle could read the perplexed disapproval on her mother's face, for Philippa could not understand why the Hunts did not choose to live in a handsome town house or terrace. The more Annabelle had tried to explain that the Hunts felt no shame about their profession, and had no wish to escape the stigma of belonging to the working class, the more confused Philippa had become. Suspecting with annoyance that her mother was being deliberately obtuse, Annabelle had abandoned all attempts to discuss Simon's family and had privately enjoined Jeremy to keep Philippa from saying anything disdainful in front of them.

"I'll try," Jeremy had said doubtfully. "But you know that Mama has never rubbed on well with people who are different from us."

Annabelle had sighed in exasperation. "Heaven forbid that we should spend an evening with people who are not exactly the same as ourselves. We might learn something. Or worse, we might even enjoy it . . . oh, the shame!"

A curious smile touched her brother's lips. "Don't be too severe on her, Annabelle. It wasn't so long ago that you had the same disdain for those on the lower rungs."

"I did not! I . . ." Annabelle had paused with a scowl, then sighed. "You're right, I did. Though now I can't see why. There's no dishonor in work, is there? Certainly it's more admirable than idleness."

Jeremy had continued to smile. "You've changed," was his only comment, and Annabelle had replied ruefully.

"Perhaps that's not a bad thing."

As they ascended the narrow stairs that led up from the butcher shop to the Hunts' private rooms, they heard a cacophony of adult voices, childrens' squeals, and thumps that sounded like furniture being overturned.

"Dear me," Philippa exclaimed. "That sounds like . . . like . . ."

"A brawl?" Simon supplied helpfully. "It could be."

As they entered the main room, Annabelle tried to sort through the mass of faces . . . there was Simon's older sister, Sally, the married mother of a half dozen children who were currently stampeding like Pamplona bulls through the little circuit of rooms . . . Sally's husband

and Simon's parents and three younger brothers, and a younger sister named Meredith, whose dark serenity was oddly jarring in all the tumult. From what Simon had told Annabelle, he had a special fondness for Meredith, who was quite different from her rough-and-tumble siblings, being shy and bookish.

The children crowded around Simon, who displayed a surprising facility with them, tossing them easily into the air and managing to simultaneously inspect a newly lost tooth and apply a handkerchief to a runny nose. The first few minutes of welcome were confusing ones, with rounds of shouted introductions, and children scattering back and forth, and the yowling indignation of a hearthside cat who had just been nipped by an inquisitive puppy. Annabelle had every expectation that things would calm down after that, but in truth, the general upheaval continued all through the evening. She had brief glimpses of her mother's frozen smile, and Jeremy's relaxed enjoyment, and Simon's amused exasperation as his efforts to settle the bedlam met with poor results.

Simon's father, Thomas, was a huge, imposing man with features that could easily have lent themselves to intimidating austerity. Occasionally his face and eyes were softened with a smile that was not quite as charismatic as Simon's but possessed its own quiet appeal. Annabelle managed to have a friendly exchange with him as she was seated beside him at dinner. Unfortunately, it appeared that the two mothers found it nearly impossible to relate to one another.

Their lives, the accumulation of experiences that had formed them and shaped their views, could not have been more opposed.

Dinner consisted of thick cuts of well-cooked beefsteak, sided by pudding and the barest spoonful of vegetables. Suppressing a wistful sigh as she thought of the cuisine they had enjoyed in France, Annabelle worked diligently on the heavy slab of beef.

Before long, Meredith engaged her with a friendly comment. "Annabelle, you must tell us more about Paris. My mother and I will soon be touring the Continent for the very first time."

"How wonderful," Annabelle exclaimed. "When will you depart?"

"In a week, actually. We'll be gone for at least a month and a half, starting at Calais and finishing with Rome . . ."

The conversation about travel continued until the meal was concluded, and a cook-maid came to clear the plates while the family retired to the parlor for tea and sweets. To the children's delight, Jeremy sat with them on the floor near the hearth, playing jackstraws and helping to restrain the puppy. Annabelle sat nearby, watching their antics while she conversed with Simon's older sister.

"Oh, blast," came Jeremy's exclamation. "The puppy's made a puddle on the hearth."

"Someone please find the maid and tell her," Sally said, while the children laughed uproariously at the ill-mannered puppy.

Since Annabelle was sitting closest to the

door, she jumped up at once. Entering the next room, Annabelle discovered the cook-maid still clearing away the remnants of dinner. After Annabelle informed her of the small mishap, the girl swiftly went to the parlor with a handful of rags. Annabelle would have followed her, but she heard the sounds of conversation coming from the nearby kitchen, and she paused as she heard Bertha's low, disapproving voice.

". . . and does she love you, Simon?"

Annabelle froze where she stood, listening intently to Simon's reply. "People marry for many reasons."

"She doesn't, then," came Bertha's flat statement. "I can't say as I'm surprised. Women like that never—"

"Have a care," Simon murmured. "You're speaking of my wife."

"She makes a pretty ornament for your arm," Bertha persisted, "when you go among higher-ups. But would she have married you without your money? Would she stay by you in times of trouble or want? If only you had given a second glance to one of the girls I tried to match you with . . ."

Annabelle could bear to hear no more. Controlling her expression, she slipped back into the noise and light of the parlor.

Troubled, she wondered if she should say anything to Simon about what she had overheard and immediately decided against it. Broaching the subject would only force him to offer reassurance, or perhaps apologize for his mother, neither of which was necessary. She knew that it would take time for her to prove her worth to Simon, and his family . . . and perhaps even to herself.

Much later in the evening, when Annabelle and Simon had returned to the Rutledge Hotel, Simon took her shoulders in his hands and regarded her with a slight smile. "Thank you," he said.

"For what?"

"For being so agreeable to my family." Pulling her forward, he pressed his mouth to the top of her head. "And for choosing to overlook the fact that they're so different from you."

Annabelle flushed with pleasure at his praise, suddenly feeling much better. "I enjoyed the evening," she lied, and Simon grinned.

"You don't have to go that far."

"Oh, perhaps there was a moment or two, when your father was discussing animal entrails . . . or when your sister talked about what the baby did in his bathwater . . . but on the whole, they were very, very . . ."

"Noisy?" Simon suggested, his eyes glinting with sudden laughter.

"I was going to say 'nice.' "

Simon slid his hands over her back, massaging the tense places beneath her shoulder blades. "You're taking to this wife-of-a-commoner business fairly well, all things considered."

"It's not so bad, really," Annabelle mused. She ran a light, flirtatious hand along the front of his body, and gave him a teasing glance. "I

can overlook quite a lot, in return for this . . .
impressive . . . well-endowed . . ."

"Bank account?"

Annabelle smiled and slipped her fingers
into the waist of his trousers. "Not the bank
account," she whispered, just before his mouth
closed over hers.

The following day, Annabelle was thrilled to
be reunited with Lillian and Daisy, whose suite
was in the same wing of the Rutledge as her
own. Squealing and laughing as they embraced,
the three of them made far too much noise,
until Mrs. Bowman sent a maid to tell them to
be quiet.

"I want to see Evie," Annabelle complained,
locking arms with Daisy as they went to the
suite's receiving room. "How is she faring?"

"She landed in dreadful trouble a fortnight
ago for trying to see her father," Daisy replied
with a sigh. "His condition has worsened, and
he's bedridden now. But Evie was caught sneak-
ing out of the house, and now she's being kept
in seclusion by Aunt Florence and the rest of the
family."

"For how long?"

"Indefinitely," came the discouraging reply.

"Oh, those odious people," Annabelle muttered. "I wish we could go and rescue Evie."

"Wouldn't that be fun?" Daisy mused, instantly taken with the idea. "We should kidnap
her. We'll bring a ladder and set it beneath her
window, and—"

"Aunt Florence would set the dogs on us," Lillian said darkly. "They have two huge mastiffs that wander the grounds at night."

"We'll toss them some drugged meat," Daisy countered. "And then while they're sleeping—"

"Oh, plague take your harebrained plans," Lillian exclaimed. "I want to hear about Annabelle's honeymoon."

Two pairs of dark brown eyes regarded Annabelle with unmaidenly interest. "Well?" Lillian asked. "What was it like? Was it as painful as they say?"

"Out with it, Annabelle," Daisy urged. "Remember, we promised to tell each other everything!"

Annabelle grinned, rather enjoying the position of being knowledgeable about something that was still so much a mystery to them. "Well, at certain moments it was rather uncomfortable," she admitted. "But Simon was very kind, and . . . attentive . . . and although I have no prior experience for comparison, I can't imagine that any man could be a more wonderful lover."

"What do you mean?" Lillian asked.

A warm shade of pink stained Annabelle's cheeks. Hesitating, she searched for the words to explain something that suddenly seemed impossible to describe. One might detail the mechanics of it, but that would hardly convey the tenderness of such a private experience. "The intimacy of it is far beyond what you could ever imagine . . . at first you want to die of embarrassment, but then there are moments when it feels so wonderful that you forget to be self-conscious, and the only thing that matters is being close to him."

There was a short silence as the sisters contemplated her words.

"How long does it take?" Daisy ventured.

Annabelle's blush deepened. "Sometimes only a few minutes . . . sometimes a few hours."

"*A few hours?*" both of them repeated at once, looking amazed.

Lillian wrinkled her nose in distaste. "My God, that sounds horrid."

Annabelle laughed at her expression. "It's not at all horrid. It's lovely, actually."

Lillian shook her head. "I'm going to figure out a way to make my husband get it over with quickly. There are far better things to do than spend hours in bed doing *that*."

Annabelle grinned. "Speaking of the mysterious gentleman who will someday be your husband . . . we should begin planning the strategy for our next campaign. The season won't begin until January, which leaves us several months to prepare."

"Daisy and I need an aristocratic sponsor," Lillian said with a sigh. "Not to mention some etiquette lessons. And unfortunately, Annabelle, since you've married a commoner, you've got no real social influence, and we're no farther along than when we started." Hastily she added, "No offense meant, dear."

"None taken," Annabelle replied mildly. "However, Simon does have some friends in the peerage—Lord Westcliff in particular."

"Oh, no," Lillian said firmly. "I want nothing to do with him."

"Why not?"

Lillian raised her brows as if surprised by the need to explain. "Because he's the most insufferable man I've ever encountered?"

"But Westcliff is very highly placed," Annabelle wheedled. "And he is Simon's best friend. I have no great liking for him myself, but he could be a useful ally. They say that Westcliff's title is the oldest one in England. Blood doesn't get any bluer than his."

"And well he knows it," Lillian said sourly.

"I wonder why Westcliff hasn't married yet," Daisy mused. "Despite his flaws, one has to admit that he is a whale-sized catch."

"I'll be thrilled when someone harpoons him," Lillian muttered, making the other two laugh.

Chapter 24

One evening Simon came home at an unusually late hour, having spent all day at the Consolidated Locomotive works. Strongly scented of coal smoke, oil, and metal after spending a day at the site, he returned to the Rutledge with his clothes decidedly the worse for wear.

"What have you been doing?" Annabelle asked.

"Walking through the foundry," Simon replied, stripping off his waistcoat and shirt as soon as he crossed the threshold of their bedroom.

Annabelle threw him a skeptical glance. "You did more than merely 'walk.' What are those stains on your clothes? You look as if you were trying to build the locomotive by yourself."

"There was a moment when some extra help was required." An expanse of well-honed muscle was revealed as Simon dropped his shirt to the floor.

Frowning, Annabelle went to draw a bath for him, and returned to find her husband clad in his linens. There was a fist-sized bruise on his leg, and a red scorch mark on his wrist, causing her to exclaim anxiously, "You've been hurt! What happened?"

Simon looked momentarily puzzled by her concern, and by the way she flew to him. "It's nothing," he said, reaching out to catch her waist.

Pushing his hands away, Annabelle sank to her knees to inspect the bruise on his leg. "What caused this?" she demanded, skimming the edge of it with her fingertip. "It happened in the foundry, didn't it? Simon Hunt, I want you to stay away from that place! All those boilers and cranes and vats . . . the next time you'll probably be crushed or boiled or punched full of holes—"

"Annabelle . . ." Simon's voice was edged with amusement. Bending to grasp her elbows, he pulled her to her feet. "I can't talk to you when you're kneeling in front of me like that. Not coherently, at any rate. I can explain exactly what—" He broke off, his dark eyes flickering strangely as he saw her expression. "You're upset, aren't you?"

"Any wife would be, if her husband came home in this condition!"

Simon slid his hand behind her neck and squeezed lightly. "You're reacting a bit strongly to a bruise and a slight burn, aren't you?"

Annabelle scowled. "First tell me what happened, then I'll decide how to react."

"Four men were trying to pull a metal plate out of a furnace with long-handled pincers. They had to carry it to a frame where it could be rolled and pressed. The metal plate turned out to be a bit heavier than they expected, and when it became clear that they were about to drop the damned thing, I picked up another pair of pincers and went to help."

"Why couldn't one of the other foundrymen do it?"

"I happened to be standing closest to the furnace." Simon shrugged in an effort to make light of the episode. "I got the bruise when I knocked my knee against the frame before we managed to lower the plate—and the burn happened when someone else's pincers brushed against my arm. But no harm done. I heal quickly."

"Oh, that was all?" she asked. "You were only lifting hundreds of pounds of red-hot iron in your shirtsleeves?—how silly of me to be concerned."

Simon lowered his head until his lips brushed her cheek. "You don't have to worry about me."

"Someone needs to." Annabelle was keenly aware of the strength and solidity of his body, standing so close to hers. His big-boned frame was formed with power and masculine grace. But Simon wasn't invulnerable, or indestructible. He was only human, and the dawning realization of how important his safety had become to her was nothing short of alarming. Twisting away from him, Annabelle went to check the accumulating bathwater, saying over her shoulder, "You smell like a train."

"With an extended smokestack," he rejoined, following at her heels.

Annabelle snorted derisively. "If you're trying to be amusing, don't bother. I'm furious with you."

"Why?" Simon murmured, catching her from behind. "Because of a small injury? Trust me, all your favorite parts are still working." He kissed the side of her neck.

Annabelle stiffened her spine, resisting the embrace. "I couldn't care less if you jumped headfirst into a vat of melted iron, if you're so silly as to go into the foundry with no protective clothing and—"

"Hell-broth." Simon nuzzled into the delicate wisps of her hairline, while one hand coasted upward to find her breast.

"What?" Annabelle asked, wondering if he had just spouted some new profanity.

"Hell-broth . . . that's what they call the melted iron." His fingers circled the reinforced shape of her breast, molded artificially high and stiff within the frame of her corset. "Good God, what do you have on under this dress?"

"My new steam-molded corset." The fashionable garment, imported from New York, had been heavily starched and pressed onto a metal form, giving it more stiffness and structure than the conventionally designed corset.

"I don't like it. I can't feel your breasts."

"You're not supposed to," Annabelle said

with exaggerated patience, rolling her eyes as he brought his hands up to her chest and squeezed experimentally. "Simon . . . your bath . . ."

"What idiot invented corsets in the first place?" he asked grumpily, letting go of her.

"An Englishman, of course."

"It would be." He followed her as she went to shut the valves in the bathing room.

"My dressmaker told me that corsets used to be kirtles, which were worn as a mark of servitude."

"Why are you so willing to wear a mark of servitude?"

"Because everyone else does, and if I didn't, my waist would look as big as a cow's by comparison."

"Vanity, thy name is woman," he quoted, dropping his linens to pad across the tiled floor.

"And I suppose men wear neckties because they are so excessively comfortable?" Annabelle asked sweetly, watching her husband step into the tub.

"I wear neckties because if I didn't, people would think I was even more uncivilized than they already do." Lowering himself with care, for the tub had not been designed for a man of his proportions, Simon let out a hiss of comfort as the hot water lapped around his middle.

Coming to stand beside him, Annabelle ran her fingers over his thick hair, and murmured, "They don't know the half of it. Here—don't lower your arm into the water. I'll help you to wash."

As she lathered him, Annabelle took a plea-

surable inventory of her husband's body. Slowly
her hands coasted over hard planes of muscle,
some places ropy and delineated, others smooth
and solid. Sensual creature that he was, Simon
made no effort to conceal his pleasure, watching her lazily through half-closed eyes. His
breath quickened, though it was still measured,
and his muscles turned iron-hard at the stroke
of her fingertips.

The silence in the tiled room was broken
only by the sluice of water and the sounds of
their breathing. Dreamily, Annabelle tunneled
her fingers through the soapy mat of hair on his
chest, recalling the feel of it on her breasts as
his body moved over hers. "Simon," she whispered.

His lashes lifted, and his dark eyes stared
into hers. One large hand slid over hers, pressing it to the taut contours of his chest. "Yes?"

"If anything ever happened to you, I . . ."
She paused as she heard the sound of vigorous
knocking at the door of the suite. Her reverie
was broken by the intrusive sound. "Hmm . . .
who could that be?"

The interruption caused annoyance to cross
Simon's features. "Did you send for something?"

Shaking her head, Annabelle rose to her feet
and reached for a length of toweling to dry her
hands.

"Ignore it."

Annabelle smiled wryly as the rapping became more insistent. "I don't think our visitor
will give up that easily. I suppose I'll have to go

see who it is." She left the bathing room and closed the door gently, allowing Simon to finish his bath in privacy.

Striding to the entrance of the suite, Annabelle opened the door. "Jeremy!" Her pleasure at her brother's unexpected visit vanished quickly as she saw his expression. His young face was pale and set, and his mouth was clamped in a grim line. He was hatless and coatless, and his hair was in wild disarray. "Jeremy, is something wrong?" she asked, welcoming him into the suite.

"You could say that."

Reading the barely suppressed panic in his gaze, she stared at him with increasing concern. "Tell me what's happened."

Jeremy raked a hand through his hair, causing the thick golden brown strands to stand on end. "The fact is—" He paused with a dumbfounded expression, as if he couldn't believe what he was about to say.

"The fact is *what?*" Annabelle demanded.

"The fact is . . . our mother just stabbed someone."

Annabelle regarded her brother with blank-faced confusion. Gradually a scowl spread across her features. "Jeremy," she said sternly, "this is the most distasteful prank you've ever—"

"It's not a prank! I wish to hell it was."

Annabelle made no effort to hide her skepticism. "Whom is she supposed to have stabbed?"

"Lord Hodgeham. One of Papa's old friends—do you remember him?"

Suddenly, the color drained from Annabelle's face, and a shock of horror went through her. "Yes," she heard herself whisper. "I remember him."

"Apparently he came to the house this evening while I was out with friends—I returned home early—and when I crossed the threshold, I saw blood on the entrance floor."

Annabelle shook her head slightly, trying to take in the words.

"I followed the trail into the parlor," Jeremy continued, "where the cook-maid was in hysterics, and the footman was trying to clean a puddle of blood from the carpet, while Mama stood there like a statue, not saying a word. There was a pair of bloody scissors on the table—the ones she uses for needlework. From what I could get out of the servants, Hodgeham went into the parlor with Mama, there were sounds of an argument, then Hodgeham came staggering out with his hands clasping his chest."

Annabelle's mind began to work at twice its usual speed. She and Philippa had always hidden the truth from Jeremy, who had been away at school whenever Hodgeham had called. As far as Annabelle knew, Jeremy had never been aware that Hodgeham had visited the house. He would be devastated if he realized that some of the money that had paid his school bills had been given in exchange for . . . no, he must not find out. She would have to make up some explanation. Later. The most important thing for now was to protect Philippa.

"Where is Hodgeham now?" Annabelle asked. "How severely was he injured?"

"I have no idea. It seems that he went to the back entrance where his carriage was waiting, and his own footman and driver carried him away." Jeremy shook his head wildly. "I don't know where Mama stabbed him, or how many times, or even why. She won't say—just looks at me as if she can't remember her own name."

"Where is she now? Don't say you just left her at home by herself?"

"I told the footman to watch her every minute, and not to let her—" Jeremy broke off and directed a wary glance to a point beyond Annabelle's shoulder. "Hello, Mr. Hunt. I'm sorry to interrupt your evening, but I've come because—"

"Yes, I heard. Your voice carried to the next room." Simon stood there calmly tucking the tail of a fresh shirt into his trousers, his gaze alert as he stared at Jeremy.

Turning, Annabelle went cold at the sight of her husband. There were times when she forgot how intimidating Simon could be, but at the moment, he looked as ruthless as a killer-for-hire.

"Why did Hodgeham come to the house at such an hour?" Jeremy wondered aloud, his young face fraught with worry. "And why the hell did Mama receive him? And what would have provoked her like that? He must have tricked her somehow. He must have said something about Papa . . . or maybe even made an advance to her, the filthy bastard."

In the tension-riddled silence that followed Jeremy's innocent speculations, Annabelle opened her mouth to say something, and Simon shook his head slightly, silencing her. He turned his attention fully to Jeremy, his voice cool and quiet. "Jeremy, run to the stables at the back of the hotel and have my carriage hitched to a team. And tell them to saddle my horse. After that, go home to collect the carpet and blood-stained clothes and take them to the locomotive works—the first building on the lot. Mention my name, and the manager won't ask questions. There is a furnace—"

"Yes," Jeremy said, understanding immediately. "I'll burn everything."

Simon gave him a short nod, and the boy strode to the door without another word.

As Jeremy left the hotel suite, Annabelle turned toward her husband. "Simon, I . . . I want to go to my mother—"

"You can go with Jeremy."

"I don't know what's to be done about Lord Hodgeham . . ."

"I'll find him," Simon said grimly. "Just pray that his wound is superficial. If he dies, it will be a hell of a lot more difficult to cover up this mess."

Annabelle nodded, biting her lip before she said, "I thought we were finally rid of Hodgeham. I never dreamed that he would dare bother my mother again, after I married you. It seems that nothing will stop him."

He took her shoulders in his hands, and said,

with almost frightening softness, "I'll stop him. You can rest assured about that."

She regarded him with a worried frown. "What are you planning to—"

"We'll talk later. Right now, go fetch your cloak."

"Yes, Simon," she whispered, and sped to her armoire.

When Annabelle and Jeremy arrived at their mother's house, they found Philippa sitting on the stairs, a glass of spirits clutched in her hands. She looked small and almost childlike, and Annabelle's heart twisted in her chest as she stared at her mother's downbent head. "Mama," she murmured, sitting on the step beside her. She laid an arm over her mother's rounded back. Meanwhile, Jeremy assumed a businesslike manner as he enjoined the footman to help him roll up the parlor carpet and convey it to the carriage outside. In the midst of her worry, Annabelle could not help reflecting that he was handling the situation extraordinarily well for a boy of fourteen.

Philippa's head lifted, and she regarded Annabelle with a haunted gaze. "I'm so sorry,"

"No, don't be—"

"Just when I thought everything was finally all right, Hodgeham came here . . . he said that he wanted to continue visiting me, and if I didn't agree, he would tell everyone about the arrangement we'd had. He said he would ruin all of us and make me a figure of public scorn. I cried and pleaded, and he *laughed* . . . then, when he put his hands on me, I felt something give way inside. I saw the scissors nearby, and I couldn't keep from picking them up, and . . . I tried to kill him. I hope I did. I don't care what happens to me now—"

"Hush, Mama," Annabelle murmured, putting an arm around her shoulders. "No one could blame you for your actions—Lord Hodgeham was a monster, and—"

"Was?" Philippa asked numbly. "Does that mean he's dead?"

"I don't know. But everything will be fine regardless—Jeremy and I are here, and Mr. Hunt will not let anything happen to you."

"Mama," Jeremy called, hefting one end of the rolled-up carpet as he and the footman carried it toward the back entrance of the house, "do you know where the scissors are?" The question was asked in such a casual manner that one might have thought he needed them to cut a package string.

"The cook-maid has them, I think," Philippa replied. "She's trying to clean them."

"All right, I'll get them from her." As they progressed down the hall, Jeremy called over his shoulder, "Have a glance over your clothes, will you? Anything with a speck of blood on it has to go."

"Yes, dear."

Listening to the pair of them, Annabelle couldn't help wondering how it was that she and her family were having a casual Thursday night conversation about disposing of murder evidence. And to think that she had felt the slightest bit of superiority over Simon's family . . . she cringed at the thought.

Two hours later, Philippa had finished her drink and was safely tucked into bed; Simon and Jeremy arrived at the town house within minutes of each other. They conferred briefly in the entrance hall. As Annabelle came downstairs, she paused midflight as she saw Simon enfold her brother in a quick, one-armed hug, and tousle his already disheveled hair. The fatherly gesture seemed to reassure Jeremy immensely, and a weary grin came to his face. Annabelle froze as she watched the two of them.

How surprising that Jeremy had accepted Simon so easily, when Annabelle had expected him to rebel against Simon's authority. It gave her a strange feeling to witness the bond that had formed instantly between them, especially knowing that Jeremy's trust was not easily won. She hadn't thought until now what a relief it must be for her brother to have someone strong to lean on, someone who could provide solutions to problems that he was still too young to handle by himself. The yellow light from the entrance hall lamp slid over the clipped dark layers of Simon's hair and gleamed over the high planes of his cheekbones as he looked up at her.

Battening a perplexing swell of emotions, Annabelle descended the rest of the way, and asked, "Did you find Hodgeham? And if so—"

"Yes, I found him." Reaching for the cloak draped over the banister, Simon draped it over her shoulders. "Come, I'll tell you everything on the way home."

Annabelle turned toward her brother. "Jeremy, will you be all right if we leave?"

"I have the situation well in hand," the boy replied with manly confidence.

Simon's eyes glinted with amusement as he fitted his hand behind Annabelle's waist. "Let's go," he murmured.

Once they were in the carriage, Annabelle pelted Simon with questions until he placed his hand over her mouth. "I'll tell you if you can bring yourself to be quiet for a minute or two," he said. She nodded behind his hand, and he grinned, leaning forward to replace his fingers with his mouth. After stealing a quick kiss, he settled back in his seat, his expression turning serious. "I found Hodgeham at his home, being attended by his family physician. And it was a good thing I appeared when I did, as they had already summoned a constable and were waiting for his arrival."

"How did you convince the servants to let you past the front door?"

"I shoved my way into the house and demanded to be taken to Hodgeham immediately. There was so much confusion that no one dared refuse me. I had a footman show me to the upstairs bedroom, where the doctor was stitching Hodgeham's wound." Dark humor infused his expression. "Of course, I could have found the room merely by following the bastard's screams and howls."

"Good," Annabelle said in vehement satisfaction. "Whatever pain Lord Hodgeham is suffering isn't nearly great enough, in my opinion. What was his condition, and what did he say when you appeared in his room?"

One side of Simon's mouth curled in disgust. "It was a shoulder wound—a small one, at that. And most of what he said is better left unrepeated. After letting him rant for a few minutes, I told the doctor to wait in the next room while I had a private talk with Hodgeham. I told him that I was quite sorry to learn of his severe digestive upset—a comment that confused him until I explained that it would be in his best interest to describe his malady to friends and family as a stomach ailment rather than a stab wound."

"And if he didn't?" Annabelle asked with a faint smile.

"If he didn't, then I made it clear that I would carve him up like a side of Yorkshire gammon. And if I ever learned of the slightest rumor that would tarnish your mother's reputation, or that of the family, I would lay the blame at his door, after which there wouldn't be enough of his remains left for a decent burial. By the time I finished with Hodgeham, he was too terrified to breathe. Believe me, he will never approach your mother again. As for the doctor, I compensated him for his visit and persuaded him to banish the episode from his mind. I would have left then, but I had to wait for the constable."

"And what did you tell the constable?"

"I told him there had been a mistake, and he wasn't needed after all. And for his trouble, I told him to go to the Brown Bear tavern after his shift and order as many rounds of ale as he wanted on my credit."

"Thank God." Relieved beyond measure, Annabelle snuggled next to him. She sighed against his shoulder. "What about Jeremy? What will we tell him?"

"It isn't necessary for him to know the truth—it would only hurt and confuse him. As far as I'm concerned, Philippa overreacted to Hodgeham's advances and forgot herself in the moment." Simon caressed the edge of her jaw with the tip of his thumb. "I do have a suggestion, to which I would like you to lend some serious thought."

Wondering if this "suggestion" was going to be a thinly veiled command, Annabelle looked at him suspiciously. "Oh?"

"I think it would be for the best if Philippa put some distance between herself and London—and Hodgeham—until the dust settles."

"How much distance? And where would she go?"

"She can join my mother and sister on their tour of the Continent. They're leaving in just a few days—"

"That is the worst idea I've ever heard," Annabelle exclaimed. "I want her to stay right here, where Jeremy and I can look after her. Second, I can guarantee that *your* mother and sister would be none too pleased—"

"We'll send Jeremy along. He has enough

time before his next school term, and he'll be an excellent escort for all three of them."

"Poor Jeremy . . ." Annabelle tried to envision him escorting the trio of women across Europe. "I wouldn't wish such a fate on my worst enemy."

Simon grinned. "He'll probably learn a great deal about women."

"And none of it pleasant," she retorted. "Why do you think it is necessary to whisk my mother away from London? Does Lord Hodgeham still pose some kind of danger?"

"No," he murmured, gently angling her face upward. "I told you, he'll never dare to approach Philippa again. However, if it turns out that there is any lingering trouble with Hodgeham, I'd prefer to handle it while she is away. Moreover, Jeremy said that she doesn't seem quite herself. Understandable, given the circumstances. A few weeks of touring should make her feel better."

As Annabelle considered the idea, she had to admit that there was some sense in it. It had been a long time since Philippa had gone on any kind of holiday. And if Jeremy went with her, perhaps even the company of the Hunts could be tolerated. As for what Philippa would want . . . she seemed too numb to make any decisions. It seemed likely that she would agree to any plans that Annabelle and Jeremy made. "Simon . . ." she asked slowly, "are you asking for my opinion, or telling me what you've already decided?"

Simon's gaze swept her face in clever assessment. "Which would be more likely to induce you to agree?" He laughed softly as he read the answer in her expression. "Very well . . . I'm asking."

Annabelle smiled wryly and snuggled back into the crook of his shoulder. "Then if Jeremy agrees . . . so will I."

Chapter 25

Annabelle had not asked Simon how Bertha and Meredith Hunt had received the news of their additional traveling companions, and she had certainly not been eager to hear the answer. All that mattered was that Philippa would be far away from London and all reminders of Lord Hodgeham. Annabelle hoped that when her mother returned, she would be refreshed and at ease, and ready to make a new beginning. The trip might even hold some enjoyment for Jeremy, who was looking forward to seeing some of the foreign places he had learned about at school.

With less than a week before their departure, Annabelle threw herself into the project of packing for her mother and brother, trying to anticipate their needs for a six-week journey. Openly amused by the quantity of supplies that Annabelle had purchased for them, Simon remarked that one would think her family was forging through regions of unexplored wilderness rather than lodging in a succession of inns and pensiones.

"Foreign travel can be uncomfortable at times," Annabelle replied, busily stuffing tins of tea and biscuits into a leather satchel. A stack of boxes and parcels towered beside their bed, where she was sorting various articles into organized piles. Among other things, she had collected compounds from the apothecary shop, a pair of down pillows and extra linens, a box of reading material, and a collection of packaged edibles. Holding up a glass jar of preserves, she examined it critically. "The food is different on the Continent—"

"Yes," Simon said gravely. "Unlike ours, it's been known to have flavor."

"And the climate can be unseasonable."

"Blue sky and sunshine? Oh, they'll want to avoid that at all cost."

She responded to his mockery with an arch glance. "Surely you must have better things to do, other than to watch me open boxes."

"Not when you're doing it in the bedroom."

Straightening, Annabelle folded her arms across her chest and regarded him with flirtatious challenge. "I'm afraid you'll have to control your baser urges, Mr. Hunt. Perhaps you hadn't noticed, but the honeymoon has ended."

"The honeymoon doesn't end until I say so," Simon informed her, reaching out to snatch her before she could evade him. He crushed her lips with a dominating kiss and tossed her onto the bed. "Which means there's no hope for you."

Giggling, Annabelle flailed in the tangle of

her skirts until she found herself pinned on the mattress with his body lying over hers. "I have more packing to do," she protested, as he settled between her thighs. "Simon—"

Very little packing was done for the rest of the day.

Eventually, however, Annabelle found herself standing at the door of her family's town house, watching as her mother and brother left in a carriage bound for Dover, where they would meet with the Hunts and cross to Calais.

Simon stood with her, his hand resting comfortingly on her back as the carriage rounded the corner and headed along the main thoroughfare. She waved forlornly after them, wondering how they would manage without her.

Drawing her into the house, Simon closed the door. "This is for the best," he assured her.

"For them or for us?"

"For all parties concerned." Smiling slightly, he turned her to face him. "I predict the next few weeks will pass quickly. And in the meantime you're going to be very busy, Mrs. Hunt. To start with, this morning we're going to meet with an architect about the house plans, then you'll have to decide between two lots that our agent has found in Mayfair."

Annabelle dropped her head on his chest. "Thank God. I've begun to despair of ever leaving the Rutledge. Not that I haven't enjoyed it, mind you, but every woman wants a home of her own, and . . ." She paused as she felt him playing with her pinned-up hair. "Simon," she warned, "don't pull out my pins. It's too much trouble to put my hair back up, and . . ." She sighed and frowned at him as she felt her coiffure loosening and heard the *plink* of crimped wire pins hitting the floor.

"I can't help it." His fingers worked greedily in her unraveling braid. "You have such beautiful hair . . . beautiful everything . . ."

He fitted his mouth to hers in a kiss so warm and coaxing that every rational thought vanished from her mind. Fisting his large hands in her hair, he urged her back against the wall of the entrance hall and entered her with his tongue, feasting leisurely until Annabelle was light-headed and dizzy, her fingers clutching the fabric of his coat sleeves. Gradually his mouth shifted away from hers, and he bit softly at the delicate silk of her throat. He murmured things that shocked her, expressing himself not in flowery phrases, but with the raw simplicity of a man whose lust for her knew no limits. "I have no self-control where you're concerned. Every minute that I'm not with you, all I can think about is being inside you. I hate everything that keeps you separate from me."

Comprehending that she was about to be ravished in the entrance of her family home, Annabelle stumbled back from him, smiling and shivering.

"My bedroom . . ." she managed to say, turning toward the stairs. She began to ascend the flight with quivery legs. After the first few steps, she felt Simon come up behind her swiftly, catching and turning her in his muscular arms. Before she could make a sound, he lifted her and carried her up the rest of the stairs.

Minutes later, as Annabelle lay bonelessly over his body, her cheek nestled on his shoulder, she tried to sort through the bewilderment of her senses. She had never been so satiated, every nerve glazed with pleasure. And yet she had perceived something new in their lovemaking . . . an unattained height that loomed even beyond what they had just experienced . . . some unrealized possibility that hovered just out of reach. A feeling . . . a wish . . . a tantalizing something that had no name. Closing her eyes, Annabelle basked in the closeness of their bodies, while the elusive promise haunted the air like some benevolent spirit.

Increasingly curious about the project that demanded so much of her husband's attention, Annabelle asked Simon if she could visit the locomotive works, only to meet with refusals, diversions, and assorted tactics to keep her from going to the site. Realizing that for some reason Simon did not want to take her to the place, she became increasingly determined. "Just a short visit," she insisted one evening. "All I want is one glimpse of it. I won't touch anything. For heaven's sake, after listening to you discuss the locomotive works so often, aren't I entitled to see it?"

"It's too dangerous," Simon replied flatly.

"You've been telling me for weeks **how** safe it

is, and how there is absolutely no reason for me to worry when you go there . . . and now you're saying that it's dangerous?"

Realizing his tactical error, Simon scowled.

He paced around the parlor, frustration evident in every taut line of his body. He stopped before the settee on which she reposed and towered over her. "Annabelle," he said gruffly, "visiting the foundry is like looking through the doors of hell. The place is as safe as we can make it, but even so, it's a noisy, rough, dirty business. And yes, there is always a chance of danger, and you . . ." He stopped and dragged his fingers through his hair, and looked around impatiently, as if it was suddenly difficult for him to meet her gaze. With an effort, he forced himself to continue. "You're too important for me to risk your safety in any way. It's my responsibility to protect you."

Annabelle's eyes widened. She was touched and more than a little surprised by his admission that she was important to him. As they stared at each other, she was conscious of a peculiar tension . . . not unpleasant, but disquieting nonetheless. Leaning the side of her head against her hand, she studied him intently. "You're entirely welcome to protect me," she murmured. "However, I don't want to be locked in an ivory tower." Sensing his inner struggle, she continued reasonably. "I want to know more about what you do during the hours that you're away from me. I want to see the place that is so important to you. Please."

Simon brooded silently for a moment. When

he replied, there was an unmistakable thread of surliness in his tone. "All right. Since it's obvious that I'll have no peace otherwise, I'll take you there tomorrow. But don't blame me when you're disappointed. I warned you what to expect."

"Thank you," Annabelle said in satisfaction, giving him a sunny smile that dimmed somewhat at his next words.

"Fortunately, Westcliff will be visiting the foundry tomorrow as well. It will be a good opportunity for the two of you to become better acquainted."

She still hadn't forgiven the earl for his cutting remarks about her and his prediction that marriage to her would ruin Simon's life. However, if Simon thought that the prospect of being in the company of a pompous ass like Westcliff would dissuade her, he was mistaken. Pasting a thin smile on her face, she spent the rest of the evening thinking what a pity it was that a wife could not choose her husband's friends for him.

Late the next morning, Simon took Annabelle to the nine-acre site of the Consolidated Locomotive works. The rows of cavernous buildings were fitted with myriads of jutting smokestacks, spewing out smoke that drifted over truck yards and intersecting walkways. The scale of the locomotive works was even larger than Annabelle had expected, housing equipment so mammoth in scale that she was nearly rendered speechless at the sight. The first place they visited was the assembly shop, where nine locomotive engines were in various stages of production.

Next they went to the pattern shop, where drawings of parts were carefully examined and wooden prototypes constructed according to specifications. Later, as Simon explained to her, the wooden patterns would be used to make molds, into which molten iron would be poured and cooled. Fascinated, Annabelle asked a slew of questions about the casting process and how the hydrostatic riveting machines and presses worked, and why quickly cooled iron was stronger than slow-cooled.

Despite Simon's initial misgivings, he seemed to enjoy touring her through the buildings, smiling occasionally at her absorbed expression. He guided her carefully into the foundry, where she discovered that his description of it as a glimpse into hell was not the exaggeration it had seemed. It had nothing to do with the condition of the workers, who seemed to be well treated, nor was it because of the buildings, which were relatively organized. Rather, it was the nature of the work itself, a kind of coordinated bedlam in which fumes and thundering noise and the red glow of roaring furnaces provided a seething backdrop for heavily clothed workers bearing brands and mallets. Moving through the labyrinth of fire and steel, the foundrymen ducked beneath massive pivoting cranes and vats of hell-broth, and paused casually to allow huge plates of metal to swing across their paths. Annabelle was aware of a few curious glances cast her way, but for the most part, the foundrymen were too intent on their work to allow for distractions.

Traveling cranes were set all through the center of the foundry, hoisting trucks filled with pig iron, scrap iron, and coke to the tops of cupola stacks more than twenty feet high. The iron mixture was loaded at the top of the cupolas, where it was melted and forced into gigantic ladles and poured into molds by additional cranes. Odors of fuel, metal, and human sweat imparted a hazy weight to the air. As Annabelle watched the melted iron being transferred from vats to molds, she drew instinctively closer to Simon.

Buffeted by the relentless shrieks and moans of bending metal, the startling hiss of steam-powered machinery, and the echoing jolts of a great hammer being operated by six men, Annabelle found herself flinching with each new assault on her ears. Instantly, she felt Simon's arm slide around her back, while he engaged in a friendly, half-shouted conversation with the flange-shop manager, Mr. Mawer.

"Have you caught sight of Lord Westcliff yet?" Simon asked. "He had planned to arrive at the foundry at noon—and I've never known him to be late before."

The middle-aged foundryman blotted his sweating face with a handkerchief as he replied. "I believe the earl is at the assembly yard, Mr. Hunt. He had a concern about the dimensions of the new cylinder castings, and he

wanted to inspect them before they were bolted
into place."

Simon glanced down at Annabelle. "We'll go
outside," he told her. "It's too damned hot and
noisy to wait for Westcliff in here."

Relieved at the prospect of escaping the relentless clamor of the foundry, Annabelle
agreed immediately. Now that she had gotten
a thorough look at the place, her curiosity was
satisfied, and she was ready to leave—even if
that mean having to spend time in the company
of Lord Westcliff. As Simon paused to exchange
a few last words with Mawer, she watched as a
steam-powered blower was employed to force
air into the large central cupola. The blast of
air caused hot metal to run into carefully positioned ladles, each one containing a thousand
pounds of unstable liquid.

A particularly large heap of scrap iron was
dumped into the charging door at the top of the
cupola . . . too large, apparently, for the fore-
man shouted angrily at the foundryman who
had loaded the truck. Narrowing her eyes,
Annabelle observed them intently. A few rough
shouts of warning from the men at the top of the
gallery heralded another air blast of the steam
blower . . . and this time, disaster struck. Boiling iron swiftly overran the ladles and dropped
in bubbling wads from the cupola, some of it
catching in the traveling cranes. Simon paused
in midconversation with the flange-shop manager, both of them glancing upward at the same
time.

"*Jesus*," she heard Simon say, and she had

one flashing glimpse of his face before he shoved her to the ground and covered her with his own body. At the same time, two pumpkin-sized clots of hell-broth dropped into the cooling troughs below, setting off a series of instantaneous explosions.

The impact of the blasts was like a succession of full body blows. Annabelle had no breath to cry out as Simon hunched over her, his shoulders curving in a shield over her head. And then—

Silence.

At first it seemed the motion of the earth itself had been brought to a jarring halt. Disoriented, Annabelle blinked to clear her vision, and was assaulted by the harsh brilliance of fire, the looming shapes of machinery silhouetted like monsters from the illustrations of a medieval tome. Intermittent blasts of heat struck her with such force that they threatened to peel the flesh from her bones. Flurries of metal chips and filings flew through the air as if they had been shot from a gun. She was surrounded by a whirl of movement and chaos, all of it blanketed in stunning quiet. Suddenly, there was a popping sensation in her ears, and they were filled with a tinny, high-pitched tone.

She was being pulled from the floor. Simon gave a hard tug to her arms, bringing her up in one powerful motion. Helpless against the force of momentum, she landed against his chest. He was saying something to her . . . she could almost make out the sound of his voice, and she began to hear the bursts of smaller explosions and the roaring undercurrent of fire as it fed hungrily on the building. Staring at Simon's hard face, she tried to comprehend his words, but she was distracted by the sting of more hot metal chips that peppered her face and neck like a swarm of nasty biting insects. Driven by instinct rather than reason, she couldn't stop herself from swatting foolishly at the air with her hand.

Simon shoved and dragged her through the pandemonium while trying to protect her with his body. An elephantine boiler barrel rolled gently before them, placidly crushing everything in its path. Cursing, Simon jerked Annabelle backward as the object rumbled by. There were men everywhere, shoving and swarming and shouting, white-eyed with the will to survive as they headed to the entryways on both ends of the building. A new set of eruptions shook the foundry, accompanied by rough cries. It was too hot to breathe, and Annabelle wondered dazedly if they would be roasted alive before they reached the door of the foundry.

Simon bent and hoisted her over his shoulder, carrying her over toppled cranes and collapsed equipment, with his arm clamped tightly around her knees. Dangling helplessly, Annabelle saw bloody holes in his coat, and realized that the blast had embedded metal filings and splinters in his back as he had covered her with his body. Crossing obstacle after obstacle, Simon finally reached the triple-width doors and set Annabelle on her feet. He star-

tled her by pushing her firmly toward someone, shouting for him to take her. Twisting,
Annabelle discovered that Simon had given her
over to Mr. Mawer. "Take her outside," Simon
commanded hoarsely. "Don't stop until she's
completely clear of the building."

"Yes, sir!" The shop manager seized Annabelle in an unbreakable hold.

As she was compelled forcibly toward the entrance, Annabelle looked back wildly at Simon.
"What are you going to do?"

"I have to make certain that everyone
gets out."

A thrill of horror went through her. "No!
Simon, come with me—"

"I'll be out in five minutes," he said brusquely.

Annabelle's face contorted, and she felt tears
of terrified fury spring to her eyes. "In five
minutes the building will have burned to the
ground."

"Keep going," he said to Mawer, and turned
away.

"Simon!" she screeched, balking as she saw
him disappear back into the foundry. The ceiling was rippling with blue flame, while the
machinery in the building shrieked as it was
warped by intense heat. Smoke poured from the
doorways, erupting in black blossoms that contrasted weirdly with the white clouds overhead.
Annabelle quickly discovered that resisting
Mawer's superior hold was useless. She drew in
deep lungfuls of outside air, coughing as her ir-
ritated lungs tried to expel the taint of smoke.

Mawer didn't pause until he had deposited her on a graveled walkway, delivering a firm order to stay where she was.

"He'll come out," he told her shortly. "You stay here and watch for him. Promise you won't move, Mrs. Hunt—I must try and account for all my men, and I don't need extra trouble from you."

"I won't move," Annabelle said automatically, her gaze fixed on the foundry entrance. "Go."

"Yes, ma'am."

She was motionless as she stood on the gravel, staring dazedly at the doorway of the foundry while a furor of activity raged around her. Men passed her at a dead run, while others crouched over the wounded. A few, like her, stood as still as statues, watching the blaze with empty gazes. The fire roared with a force that made the ground vibrate, gaining new and angry life as it consumed the foundry. A hand-pump engine pulled by two dozen men rolled close to the building—it must have been kept on the site for emergencies, as there had not been sufficient time to send for outside help. Frantically, the men sought to connect a leather siphon hose to an underground water cistern. Taking hold of long side handles, they began to pump in concerted effort, producing enough pressure in the engine's air chamber to send a stream of water a hundred feet in the air. The effort was pitifully inconsequential against the magnitude of the inferno.

Each minute that Annabelle waited took the toll of a year. She felt her lips moving, shaping silent words . . . *Simon, come out . . . Simon, come . . .*

A half dozen forms staggered from the entrance, their faces and clothes smoke-blackened. Annabelle's gaze raked over the emerging men. Perceiving that her husband was not among them, she switched her attention to the hand engine. The men had directed the hose to the adjoining building, drenching it in an effort to keep the fire from spreading. Annabelle shook her head in disbelief as she realized that they had given the foundry up for lost. They were surrendering all its contents . . . including anyone who may have been trapped inside. Galvanized into action, she ran to the other side of the foundry, desperately scanning the crowd for any sign of her husband.

Catching sight of one of the shop managers, who was taking inventory of the evacuated foundrymen, Annabelle hurried to him. "Where is Mr. Hunt?" she asked sharply, having to repeat the question before she had caught his attention.

He barely spared her a glance as he replied with distracted impatience. "There was another collapse inside. Mr. Hunt was helping to free a foundryman who was pinned by debris. He hasn't been seen since."

Despite the blistering heat that radiated from the foundry, Annabelle felt cold from her skin to her bones. Her mouth trembled. "If he was able to come out," she said, "he would have by now. He needs help. Can someone go in there to find him?"

The shop manager looked at her as if she was a madwoman. "*In there?* It would be suicide." Turning away from her, he went to a man who had collapsed to the ground, and bent to shove a wadded-up coat beneath his head. When he thought to spare a glance back at the space where Annabelle had been, it was empty.

Chapter 26

If anyone had noticed that a woman was plunging into the building, they did not try to stop her. Covering her mouth and nose with a handkerchief, Annabelle made her way through billows of acrid smoke that drew streams of water from her squinting eyes. The fire, which had begun at the other side of the foundry, was eating its way across the rafters in voluptuous ripples of blue and white and yellow. More frightening than the scalding heat was the noise; the growling flames, the screeches and groans of bending metal, the clangs of heavy machinery as it snapped like children's toys being crushed underfoot. Liquid metal popped and sprayed in occasional bursts of grapeshot.

Picking up her skirts in awkward bunches, Annabelle stumbled over the smoldering knee-deep rubble, calling out for Simon, her voice muted in the cacophany. Just as she despaired of finding him, she caught sight of movement in the rubble.

Crying out, she hurried to the long, fallen form. It was Simon, alive and conscious, his leg trapped beneath the steel shaft of a fallen crane. As he saw her, his soot-smeared face contorted with horror, and he struggled to a half-sitting position. "Annabelle," he said hoarsely, pausing as he was wracked with coughing. "Dammit, *no*—get out of here! What the hell are you doing?"

She shook her head, unwilling to waste breath in arguing. The crane was too heavy for either of them to move—she had to find something . . . some makeshift lever to dislodge it. Wiping her burning eyes, she hunted through a pile of castings and broken stone and a heap of counterbalance weights. Everything was covered with layers of oil and soot that caused her feet to slip as she moved through the wreckage. A row of driving wheels rested against the shuddering wall, some of them taller than she. She made her way toward them and found a stack of axles and connecting rods as thick as her fist. Grasping one of the heavy, grease-coated rods, she tugged it from the stack and dragged it back to her husband.

One glance at Simon left no doubt that if he could have gotten his hands on her, he would have murdered her on the spot. "Annabelle," he roared, between spasms of coughing, "get out of this building *now!*"

"Not without you." She fumbled with a wooden block that had been placed at the end of a hydrostatic ram.

Twisting and tugging at his pinned leg,

Simon showered her with threats and profanities while she lugged the wooden block over to him and shoved it against the crane.

"It's too heavy!" he snarled, as she struggled with the connecting rod. "You can't budge it! Get out of here. *Damn you*, Annabelle—"

Grunting with effort, she braced the rod on the wooden block and wedged the end of it beneath the crane. She pushed down, using all her weight. The crane remained solidly in place, indifferent to her efforts. With a gasp of frustration, she struggled with the lever, until the rod creaked in protest. It was no use—the crane would not move.

A loud crack went off, and iron shards flew through the air, causing her to duck and cover her head. She felt a blow against her arm, striking with enough force to send her to the ground. An aching burn penetrated her upper arm, and she glanced down to discover that a metal chip had lodged in her flesh, provoking a splash of brilliant red blood. Crawling to Simon, she felt him snatch her against his chest, shielding her until the shower of iron pellets had abated. "Simon," she panted, drawing back to look into his fume-reddened eyes, "you always carry a knife. Where is it?"

Simon went still as the import of the question struck him. For a split-second she saw him weigh the possibility, then he shook his head. "No," he rasped. "Even if you could manage to sever the leg, you couldn't drag me out of here." He shoved her away from him. "There's no time left—you have to get out of the damned foundry." As he saw the refusal on her face, his features twisted with hideous fear, not for himself but for her. "My God, Annabelle," he grated, finally reduced to begging, "don't do this. Please. If you care for me at all—" A shuddering cough tore through his body. "Go. *Go.*"

For an instant Annabelle wanted to obey him, as the desire to escape the hellish nightmare of the burning foundry nearly overwhelmed her. But as she staggered to her feet, and looked down at him, so large and yet so defenseless, she could not make herself walk away. Instead she picked up the connecting rod once more, and hoisted it back onto the wooden block, while pain shot through her injured shoulder. Blood thundered in her ears, making it impossible to distinguish Simon's outburst from the din of the shuddering building around them. And that was likely a good thing, as he looked insane with fury. She pulled and hung on the lever, while her tortured lungs pulled in choking air and spasmed in response. The scene blurred around her, but she continued to exert her remaining strength on the iron bar, her slight weight straining to move it.

All of a sudden she felt something grasp the back of her dress. Had she any breath left to scream, she would have. Startled out of her wits, Annabelle went stiff as she was hauled backward, and her hands were pried from the bar. Choking and sobbing, she stared through smoke-blinded eyes at the lean, dark shape behind her. A cool voice reverberated in her ear.

"I'll lift the crane. Go pull his leg free at my command."

She recognized his autocratic tone even before his face registered. *Westcliff*, she thought in amazement. It was indeed the earl, his white shirt torn and filthy, his features streaked with soot. Yet for all his dishevelment, he looked calm and capable as he motioned for her to go to Simon. Hefting the iron bar with ease, he deftly adjusted the lever beneath the crane shaft. Although he was only of medium height, his lean body was solid and superbly fit, conditioned by years of punishing physical exertion. As Westcliff pushed downward with a mighty shove, Annabelle heard the squeaks and groans of bending metal, and the massive crane eased upward a few crucial inches. The earl barked at Annabelle, who frantically tugged at Simon's leg, ignoring his groan of agony as he rolled from beneath the crushing object.

Lowering the crane with a massive *thud*, Westcliff came to help Simon struggle to his feet, wedging a solid shoulder beneath his arm to support his injured side. Annabelle took the other side and winced as Simon seized her in a punishing grip. Smoke and heat overwhelmed her, making it impossible to see or breathe or think. Continuous coughing rattled her slender frame. Had she been left to her own devices, she would never have been able to find her way out of the foundry. She was hauled and pushed forward by Simon's brutal grasp, occasionally lifted from her feet as they crossed the wreckage on the ground, her shins and ankles and knees battered painfully. The torturous journey seemed to last forever, their progress incremental, while the foundry shook and roared like a beast hovering over its injured prey. Annabelle's mind swam. She fought to stay conscious, while her vision was filled with glittering sparks and an inviting darkness that loomed just beyond them.

She never remembered the moment they emerged from the foundry with smoking clothes and singed hair and heat-parched faces . . . all she could recall later was that there were countless pairs of hands reaching for her, and her aching legs were suddenly relieved of the burden of her own weight. Collapsing slowly into someone's arms, she felt herself being lifted while her lungs worked greedily to collect clean air. A dripping, brackish cloth passed over her face, and unfamiliar hands reached inside her dress to unfasten her corset. She couldn't even bring herself to care. Blanketed in an exhausted stupor, she surrendered to the rough ministrations and gulped the contents of a metal dipper that was pressed to her mouth.

When Annabelle finally came to herself, she blinked repeatedly to let the assuaging fluids spread across the stinging surface of her eyeballs. "Simon . . . ?" she mumbled, struggling upward. She was gently subdued.

"Rest for another minute," came a gravelly voice. "Your husband is fine. A bit battered and scorched, but definitely salvageable. I don't even think his damned leg is broken."

As full awareness seeped over her, she realized in sluggish amazement that she was half-sitting in Lord Westcliff's lap, on the ground, with her gown partly undone. Glancing up into the earl's harsh-planed face, she saw that his tanned complexion was streaked with black, and his hair was rumpled and filthy. The usually impeccable earl looked so sympathetic and disheveled and approachably human that she barely recognized him.

"Simon . . ." she whispered.

"He is being loaded into my carriage as we speak. Needless to say, he is rather impatient for you to join him. I am taking the both of you to Marsden Terrace—I've already sent for a doctor to meet us there." Westcliff shifted her a little higher in his arms. "Why did you go in after him? You could have been a very wealthy widow." The question was asked not with mockery, but with a gentle interest that confused her.

Rather than answer, Annabelle turned her attention to a bloody blotch on his shoulder. "Hold still," she murmured, using her broken fingernails to grasp the end of a needle-thin metallic shard that protruded from his shirt. She tugged it out quickly, and Westcliff's face twitched with pain.

Regarding the shard as she held it up for him to see, the earl shook his head ruefully. "God. I hadn't noticed that."

Enclosing the object in her fingers, Annabelle asked warily, "Why did *you* go in, my lord?"

"Having been informed that you had dashed

into a burning building to fetch your husband, I thought you might like some help."

Carefully, Westcliff helped her to sit up. Keeping his arm behind her back, he closed the fastenings of her dress with a deft, impersonal touch, while he contemplated the full-bore devastation of the foundy. "Only two men perished, and one still unaccounted for," he murmured. "Miraculous, considering the scope of the disaster."

"Does this mean the end of the locomotive works?"

"No, I expect that we'll rebuild as soon as possible." The earl stared kindly into her exhausted face. "Later you might describe to me what happened. For now, allow me to take you to the carriage."

Annabelle gasped a little as he stood and lifted her in his arms. "Oh—there's no need—"

"It's the least I can do." Westcliff flashed another rare smile as he carried her with facile strength. "I have some amends to make, where you're concerned."

"You mean because you now believe that I actually care about Simon, instead of having just married him for his money?"

"Something like that. It seems I was mistaken about you, Mrs. Hunt. Please accept my humble apology."

Suspecting that the earl was rarely given to making apologies of any kind, much less humble ones, Annabelle linked her arms around his neck. "I suppose I'll have to," she said grudgingly, "since you saved our lives."

He shifted her more comfortably in his arms. "Shall we cry pax, then?"

"Pax," she agreed, and coughed against his shoulder.

While the doctor visited Simon in the master bedroom of Marsden Terrace, Westcliff took Annabelle aside and personally tended to the wound in her upper arm. After tweezing out the metal chip that was half-buried in her skin, he doused the area with alcohol while Annabelle screeched in pain. He dabbed the cut with salve, bandaged it expertly, and gave her a glass of brandy to dull her discomfort. Whether he had added something to the brandy, or pure exhaustion had amplified its effects, Annabelle would never know. After downing two fingers of the dark amber liquid, she felt woozy and light-headed. Her voice was distinctly slurred as she told Westcliff that the world was fortunate that he hadn't gone into the medical profession, which he gravely acknowledged was probably true. She staggered off drunkenly to find Simon, and was firmly dissuaded by the housekeeper and a pair of housemaids, who seemed intent on washing her. Before Annabelle quite knew what had happened, she had been bathed and changed into a nightgown purloined from Westcliff's elderly mother and was lying in a soft, clean bed. As soon as she closed her eyes, she sank into a helpless slumber.

To Annabelle's chagrin, she awoke quite late the next morning, struggling to gather where she was and what had happened. The moment her thoughts touched on Simon, she floundered out of bed, paying no heed to her handsome surroundings as she padded barefoot into the hall. She crossed the path of a housemaid, who looked mildly startled by the appearance of a woman with wild, unbound hair, a scratched and reddened face, and an ill-fitting nightgown . . . a woman, who, in spite of a thorough washing the night before, was still strongly scented of foundry smoke.

"Where is he?" Annabelle asked without prelude.

To the housemaid's credit, she comprehended the abrupt query and directed Annabelle to the master bedroom at the end of the hall.

Coming to the open doorway, Annabelle saw Lord Westcliff standing by the side of the huge bed, where Simon was sitting up against a stack of pillows. Annabelle winced as she saw the profusion of plasters affixed to his arms and chest, having some idea of the discomfort that he must have endured in having so many metal pellets removed. The two men stopped talking as soon as they became aware of her presence.

Simon's gaze locked on her face and held with unnerving intensity. An invisible swell of emotion filled the room, drowning them both in acute tension. As Annabelle stared into her husband's granite-hard face, no words seemed appropriate. If she spoke to him just then, it was either going to be puerile hyperbole or inane understatement. Absurdly grateful for Westcliff's presence as a temporary buffer, Annabelle addressed her first comment to him.

"My lord," she said, inspecting the cuts and burns on his face, "you look like the loser in a tavern brawl."

Coming forward, Westcliff took her hand and executed an impeccable bow over it. He surprised her by pressing a chivalrous kiss to the back of her wrist. "Had I ever participated in a tavern brawl, madam, I assure you that I would not have lost."

That drew a grin from Annabelle, who could not help reflecting that twenty-four hours ago, she had despised his arrogant aplomb, whereas now it seemed almost endearing. Westcliff released her hand after giving it a reassuring squeeze. "With your permission, Mrs. Hunt, I will withdraw. No doubt you have a few things to discuss with your husband."

"Thank you, my lord."

As the earl left and closed the door, Annabelle approached the bedside. Simon looked away from her with a scowl, the bold structure of his profile gilded with sunlight.

"Is your leg broken?" Annabelle asked huskily.

Simon shook his head, concentrating on the ornately flowered paper that covered the bedroom wall. He spoke in a smoke-ravaged voice. "It will be fine."

Annabelle's gaze touched on him, lingering on the heavy musculature of his arms and chest, the long fingers of his hand, the way a lock of dark hair fell over his brow. "Simon," she asked softly. "Won't you look at me?"

His eyes narrowed as he turned to pin her

with a hostile stare. "I'd like to do more than look at you. I'd like to throttle you."

It would have been ingenuous for Annabelle to ask why, since she already knew. Instead, she waited with forced patience, while Simon's throat worked violently. "What you did yesterday was unforgivable," he finally muttered.

She gave him a startled glance. "What?"

"Lying there in that hell-pit, I made what I thought would be the last request of my life. And you refused."

"As things turned out, it wasn't your last request," Annabelle replied warily. "You survived, and so did I, and now everything is fine—"

"It is *not fine*," Simon snapped, his face darkening with rising fury. "For the rest of my life I will remember how it felt to know that you were going to die along with me, while I couldn't do a damned thing to stop you." He averted his face as his breath turned harsh with unwanted emotion.

Annabelle reached for him, then checked herself, her hands suspended in the air between them. "How could you ask me to leave you there, hurt and alone? I couldn't."

"You should have done as I told you!"

Annabelle didn't flinch, understanding the fear that seethed beneath his anger. "*You* wouldn't have left had it been me on the foundry floor—"

"I knew you were going to say that," he said in savage disgust. "Of course I wouldn't have left you. I'm the man. A man is supposed to protect his wife."

"And a wife is supposed to be a helpmate," Annabelle countered.

"You were not helping me," Simon bit out. "You were putting me through agony. Dammit, Annabelle, why didn't you obey me?"

She took a deep breath before replying. "Because I love you."

Simon continued to look away from her, while the soft words sent a visible shock through him. His large hand tightened into a fist on the coverlet as his defenses began to crack visibly. "I would die a thousand times over," he said, a tremor in his voice, "to spare you the slightest harm. And the fact that you were willing to throw your life away in a completely pointless sacrifice is more than I can bear."

Annabelle's eyes stung as she stared at him, while need and inexhaustible tenderness gathered like an ache in her body. "I realized something," she said huskily, "when I was standing outside the foundry, watching it burn and knowing you were inside." She swallowed hard against the thickness in her throat. "I would rather have died in your arms, Simon, than face a lifetime without you. All those endless years . . . all those winters, summers . . . a hundred seasons of wanting you and never having you. Growing old, while you stayed eternally young in my memories." She bit her lip and shook her head, while her eyes flooded. "I was wrong when I told you that I didn't know where I belonged. I do. With you, Simon. Nothing matters except being with you. You're stuck with me forever, and I'll *never* listen when you tell me to go." She managed a tremulous smile. "So you may as well stop complaining and resign yourself to it."

With startling suddenness, Simon turned to snatch her against him. He buried his face in the tangled skein of her hair. His voice came out in an anguished growl.

"My God, I can't stand this! I can't let you go out every day, fearing every minute that something might happen to you, knowing that every ounce of sanity I've got left is hinged on your well-being. I can't feel this way . . . it's too strong . . . oh, *hell*. I'll turn into a raving lunatic. I'll never be of use to anyone again. If I could just reduce it somehow . . . love you only half this much . . . I might be able to live with it."

Annabelle laughed shakily at his rough confession, while a hot rush of joy spilled through her. "But I want all your love," she said. As Simon drew his head back to look at her, his expression knocked the breath from her lungs. It took her several seconds to recover. "All your heart and mind," she continued with a crooked smile, and lowered her voice provocatively. "All your body, too."

Simon trembled and stared at her radiant face as if he would never be able to tear his gaze away. "That's reassuring. Since you seemed more than eager to saw off my leg with a pocketknife yesterday."

Annabelle's mouth quirked, and she stroked her fingertips over his hairy chest, playing with the glinting dark strands. "My intention was to preserve the largest possible portion of you, and get you out of that place."

"At that point I might have let you, had I thought it would work." Simon caught her hand in his, and pressed his cheek against her abraded palm. "You're a strong woman, Annabelle. Stronger than I would have believed."

"No, it's my love for you that is strong." Sliding him a glance of sparkling mischief from beneath her lashes, Annabelle murmured, "I wouldn't be able to saw off just *anyone's* leg, you know."

"If you ever risk your life again, for any reason, I'm going to strangle you. Come here." Gripping his hand behind her head, Simon pulled her forward. When their noses were nearly touching, he took a deep breath, and said, "I love you, dammit."

She brushed her lips teasingly against his. "How much?"

He made a slight sound, as if the soft kiss had affected him intensely. "Without limit. Beyond forever."

"I love you more," Annabelle said, and brought her mouth to his. She felt a surge of exquisite pleasure, accompanied by the elusive sense of completeness, of perfect fulfillment, that they had never quite reached before. She was floating in warmth, as if her soul was bathed in light. Drawing back, she saw from the stunned brilliance in Simon's gaze that he had felt it, too.

There was a new, wondering note in his voice as he said, "Kiss me again."

"No, I'll hurt you. I'm leaning on your leg."

"That's not my leg," came his roguish reply, making her laugh.

"You perverse man."

"You're so beautiful," Simon whispered. "Inside and out. Annabelle, my wife, my sweet love . . . kiss me again. And don't stop until I tell you to."

"Yes, Simon," she murmured, and cheerfully obeyed.

Epilogue

"...No, that's not the best part," Annabelle said animatedly, waving a handful of pages in a gesture for the Bowmans to be quiet. The three women lounged in Annabelle's suite at the Rutledge, dangling their stockinged feet as they sipped glasses of sweet wine. "Let me read on ... *'As we stopped in the Loire Valley to view a sixteenth-century chateau that is undergoing restoration, Miss Hunt made the acquaintance of an unmarried English gentleman, Mr. David Keir, who is accompanying his two younger cousins on their Grand Tour. Apparently he is an art historian, engaged in writing a scholarly work on something-or-other, and he and Miss Hunt found much to discuss. According to the mothers—from now on that is how I shall refer to Mama and Mrs. Hunt, as they are always in each other's company and appear to have divided one brain between themselves—'* "

"Good God," Lillian exclaimed with a

laugh, "does your brother have to write in such long sentences?"

"Hush!" Daisy admonished. "Jeremy was about to say what the mothers think of Mr. Keir! Go on, Annabelle."

" '—*they are of the unified opinion that Mr. Keir is a prepossessing and well-favored gentleman*—' " Annabelle read.

"Does that mean handsome?" Daisy asked.

Annabelle grinned. "Decidedly. And Jeremy goes on to say that Mr. Keir has asked permission to write to Meredith, and he intends to call on her when she returns to London!"

"How lovely!" Daisy exclaimed, extending her glass to Lillian. "Pour me another, dear—I want to drink to Meredith's future happiness."

They all drank obligingly, and Annabelle set the letter aside with a pleased sigh. "I wish I could tell Evie."

"I miss Evie," Lillian said with a surprising wistfulness. "Perhaps soon her jailers—pardon, her family—will allow us to visit."

"I have an idea," Daisy commented. "When father comes from New York next month, we'll have to go with him for another visit to Stony Cross. Naturally, Annabelle and Mr. Hunt will be invited, because of their friendship with Lord Westcliff. Perhaps we can ask that Evie and her aunt be included, too. Then we can have an official wallflower meeting—not to mention another Rounders game."

Annabelle groaned theatrically, downing her wine in a large gulp. "God help me." Placing her glass on a nearby table, she fished in her pocket for a tiny paper packet with an object folded inside. "That reminds me—Daisy, will you do a favor for me?"

"Of course," the girl replied promptly and opened the paper. Her face wrinkled in curiosity as she saw a needlelike piece of metal. "What in heaven's name is this?"

"I pulled that from Lord Westcliff's shoulder on the day of the foundry fire." She grinned at their appalled expressions as they saw the long iron shard. "If you wouldn't mind, take it with you to Stony Cross and toss it into the wishing well."

"What should I wish for?"

Annabelle laughed softly. "Make the same wish for poor old Westcliff that you did for me."

"Poor old Westcliff?" Lillian snorted, and regarded the two of them suspiciously. "What *was* the wish that you made for Annabelle?" she demanded of her younger sister. "You never told me."

"I never told Annabelle, either," Daisy murmured, regarding Annabelle with a curious smile. "How do you know what it was?"

Annabelle grinned back at her. "I figured it out." Curling her legs beneath her, she leaned forward and murmured, "Now, about finding a husband for Lillian . . . I have a rather interesting notion . . ."

Keep reading for a sneak peek at the
latest novel in the *Ravenels* series

Devil in Disguise

by Lisa Kleypas

Coming soon from Avon Books

Chapter 1

"MacRae is as angry as a baited bear," Luke Marsden warned as he entered the office. "If you've never been around a Scotsman in a temper, you'd better brace yourself for the language."

Lady Merritt Sterling looked up from her desk with a faint smile. Her brother was a fine sight, with his windblown dark hair and his complexion infused with color from the brisk autumn air. Like the rest of the Marsden brood, Luke had inherited their mother's long, elegant lines. Merritt, on the other hand, was the only one out of the half-dozen siblings who'd ended up short and full-figured.

"I've spent nearly three years managing a shipping firm," she pointed out. "After all the time I've spent around longshoremen, nothing could shock me now."

"Maybe not," Luke conceded. "But Scotsmen have a special gift for cursing. I had a friend at Cambridge who knew at least a dozen different words for testicles."

Merritt grinned. One of the things she enjoyed most about Luke, the youngest of her three brothers, was that he never shielded her from vulgarity or treated her like a delicate flower. That, among other reasons, was why she'd asked him to take over the management of her late husband's shipping company, once she'd taught him the ropes. He'd accepted the offer without hesitation. As the third son of an earl, his options had been limited, and as he'd remarked, a fellow couldn't earn a living by sitting around looking picturesque.

"Before you show Mr. MacRae in," Merritt said, "you might tell me why he's angry."

"To start with, the ship he chartered was supposed to deliver his cargo directly to our warehouse. But the dock authorities turned it away because all the berths were full. So it was just unloaded four miles inland, at Deptford Buoys."

"That's the usual procedure," Merritt said.

"Yes, but this isn't the usual cargo."

She frowned. "It's not the timber shipment?"

Luke shook his head. "Whisky. Twenty-five thousand gallons of extremely valuable single malt from Islay, still under bond. They've started the process of bringing it here in barges, but they say it will take three days for all of it to reach the warehouse."

Merritt's frown deepened. "Good Lord, all

that bonded whisky can't sit at Deptford Buoys for three days!"

"To make matters worse," Luke continued, "there was an accident."

Her eyes widened. "What kind of accident?"

"A cask of whisky slipped from the hoisting gear, broke on the roof of a transit shed, and poured all over MacRae. He's ready to murder someone—which is why I brought him up here to you."

Despite her concern, Merritt let out a snort of laughter. "Luke Marsden, are you planning to hide behind my skirts while I confront the big, mean Scotsman?"

"Absolutely," he said without hesitation. "You like them big and mean."

Her brows lifted. "What in heaven's name are you talking about?"

"You love soothing difficult people. You're the human equivalent of table syrup."

Amused, Merritt leaned her chin on her hand. "Show him in, then, and I'll start pouring."

It wasn't that she *loved* soothing difficult people. But she definitely liked to smooth things over when she could. As the oldest of six children, she'd always been the one to settle quarrels among her brothers and sisters, or come up with indoor games on rainy days. More than once, she'd orchestrated midnight raids on the kitchen pantry or told them stories when they'd sneaked to her room after bedtime.

She sorted through the neat stack of files on her desk and found the one labeled "MacRae Distillery."

Not long before her husband, Joshua, had died, he'd struck a deal to provide warehousing for MacRae in England. He'd told her about his meeting with the Scotsman, who'd been visiting London for the first time.

"Oh, but you must ask him to dinner," Merritt had exclaimed, unable to bear the thought of a stranger traveling alone in an unfamiliar place.

"I did," Joshua had replied in his flat American accent. "He thanked me for the invitation but turned it down."

"Why?"

"MacRae is somewhat rough-mannered. He was raised on a remote island off the west coast of Scotland. I suspect he finds the prospect of meeting the daughter of an earl overwhelming."

"He needn't worry about that," Merritt had protested. "You know my family is barely civilized!"

But Joshua replied that her definition of "barely civilized" was different from a rural Scotsman's, and MacRae would be far more comfortable left to his own devices.

Merritt had never dreamed that when she and Keir MacRae finally met, Joshua would be gone, and she would be the one managing Sterling Enterprises.

Her brother came to the doorway and paused at the threshold. "If you'll come this way," he said to someone outside the room, "I'll make introductions and then—"

Keir MacRae burst into the office like a force

of nature and strode past Luke, coming to a stop on the other side of Merritt's desk.

Looking sardonic, Luke went to lean against the doorjamb and folded his arms. "On the other hand," he said to no one in particular, "why waste time with introductions?"

Merritt stared in bemusement at the big, wrathful Scotsman. He was an extraordinary sight, more than six feet of muscle and brawn dressed in a thin wet shirt and trousers that clung as if they'd been glued to his skin. An irritable shiver, almost certainly from the chill of evaporating alcohol, ran over him. Scowling, he reached up to remove his flat cap, revealing a shaggy mop of hair, several months past a good cut. The thick locks were a beautiful cool shade of amber shot with streaks of light gold.

He was handsome despite his unkempt state. *Very* handsome. His blue eyes were alert with the devil's own intelligence, the cheekbones high, the nose straight and strong. A tawny beard obscured the line of his jaw—perhaps concealing a weak chin?—she couldn't tell. Regardless, he was a stunner.

Merritt wouldn't have thought there was a man alive who could fluster her like this. She was a confident and worldly woman, after all. But she couldn't ignore the flush rising from the high-buttoned neck of her dress. Or the way her heart had begun to pound like a clumsy burglar trampling the flower bed.

"I want to speak to someone in charge," he said brusquely.

"That would be me," Merritt said with a quick smile, coming around the desk. "Lady Merritt Sterling, at your service." She extended her hand.

MacRae was slow to respond. His fingers closed over hers, cool and slightly rough.

The sensation raised the hairs on the back of her neck, and she felt something uncoil pleasantly at the pit of her stomach.

"My condolences," he said gruffly, releasing her hand. "Your husband was a good man."

"Thank you." She took a steadying breath. "Mr. MacRae, I'm so sorry for the way your delivery has been botched. I'll submit paperwork to make sure you're exempted from the landing charges and wharfage rates, and Sterling Enterprises will handle the lighterage fees. And in the future, I'll make sure a berth is reserved on the day your shipment is due."

"There'll be no fookin' future shipments if I'm to be put out of business," MacRae said. "The excise agent says every barrel of whisky that hasn't been delivered to the warehouse by midnight will no longer be under bond, and I'm to be paying duties on it immediately."

"What?" Merritt shot an outraged glance at her brother, who shrugged and shook his head to indicate he knew nothing about it. This was deadly serious business. The government's regulations about storing whisky under bond were strictly enforced, and violations would earn terrible penalties. It would be bad for her business, and disastrous for MacRae's.

"No," she said firmly, "that will not happen." She went back behind the desk, took her chair and sorted rapidly through a pile of authorizations, receipts and excise forms. "Luke," she said, "the whisky must be transported here from Deptford Buoys as fast as possible. I'll persuade the excise officer to give us at least 'til noon tomorrow. Heaven knows he owes us that much, after the favors we've done him in the past."

"Will that be enough time?" Luke asked, looking skeptical.

"It will have to be. We'll need every barge and lighter vessel we can hire, and every able-bodied man—"

"No' so fast," MacRae said, slapping his palms firmly on the desk and leaning over it.

Merritt started at the sound and glanced up into the face so close to hers. His eyes were a piercing shade of ice blue, with faint whisks at the outer corners, etched by laughter and sun and sharp windy days.

"Yes, Mr. MacRae?" she managed to ask.

"Those clodpates of yours just spilled one hundred and nine gallons of whisky over the wharf, and a good portion over me in the bargain. Damned if I'll be letting them bungle the rest of it."

"Those weren't our clodpates," Luke protested. "They were lightermen from the barge."

To Merritt, her brother's voice sounded as if it were coming from another floor of the building. All she could focus on was the big, virile male in front of her.

Do your job, she told herself sternly, ripping

her gaze from MacRae with an effort. She spoke to her brother in what she hoped was a professional tone. "Luke, from now on, no lightermen are to set foot on the hoisting crane platform. Only our men will be allowed to operate the equipment." She turned back to MacRae. "My employees are experienced at handling valuable cargo," she assured him. "They'll be the only ones allowed to load your whisky onto the crane and stock it in the warehouse. No more accidents—you have my word."

"How can you be sure?" MacRae asked, one brow lifting in a mocking arch. "Will you be managing the operation yourself?"

The way he asked, sarcasm wrapped in silk, elicited an odd little pang of recognition, as if she'd heard him say something in just that tone before. Which made no sense, since they'd never met until this moment.

"No," she said, "my brother will manage it from start to finish."

Luke let out a sigh as he realized she'd just committed him to working through the night. "Oh, yes," he said acidly. "I was just about to suggest that."

Merritt looked at MacRae. "Does that meet with your approval?"

"Do I have a choice?" the Scotsman countered darkly, pushing back from the desk. He tugged at the damp, stained fabric of his shirt. "Let's be about it, then."

He was cold and uncomfortable, Merritt thought, and he reeked of cask-strength single malt. Before he returned to work, he needed the opportunity to tidy himself. "Mr. MacRae," she asked gently, "where are you staying while you're in London?"

"I was offered the use of the flat in the warehouse."

"Of course." A small, utilitarian set of rooms at their bonded warehouse had been installed for the convenience of vintners and distillers who wished to blend and bottle their products on the premises. "Has your luggage been taken there yet?"

" 'Tis still on the docks," MacRae replied curtly, clearly not wanting to be bothered with trivial issues when there was so much to be done.

"We'll collect it right away, then, and have someone show you to the flat."

"Later," he said.

"But you'll need to change your clothes," Merritt said, perturbed.

"Milady, I'm going to work through the night beside longshoremen who won't give a damn how I look or smell."

Merritt should have let the matter go. She knew that. But she couldn't resist saying, "The docks are very cold at night. You'll need a coat."

MacRae looked exasperated. "I have only the one, and 'tis drookit."

Merritt gathered "drookit" meant thoroughly soaked. She told herself that Keir MacRae's well-being was none of her concern, and there was urgent business requiring her attention. But . . . this man could use a bit of looking after. Having grown up with three brothers, she was well familiar with the surly, hollow-eyed look of a hungry male.

Luke was right, she thought wryly. *I do like them big and mean.*

"You can't very well leave your luggage sitting out in public," she said reasonably. "It will only take a few minutes for me to fetch a key and show you to the flat." She slid a glance to her brother, who joined in obligingly.

"Besides, MacRae," Luke added, "there's nothing you can accomplish until I've had a chance to organize the men and hire extra barge crew."

The Scotsman pinched the bridge of his nose and rubbed the corners of his eyes. "You can't show me to the flat," he told Merritt firmly. "No' without a chaperone."

"Oh, no need to worry about that. I'm a widow. I'm the one who chaperones others."

MacRae gave Luke an expectant stare.

Luke wore a blank expression. "Are you expecting me to say something?"

"You will no' forbid your sister to go off alone with a stranger?" MacRae asked him incredulously.

"She's my older sister," Luke said, "and she employs me, so . . . no, I'm not going to tell her a damned thing."

"How do you know I won't insult her virtue?" the Scotsman demanded in outrage.

Luke lifted his brows, looking mildly interested. "Are you going to?"

"*No.* But I *could!*"

Merritt had to gnaw the insides of her lips to restrain a laugh. "Mr. MacRae," she soothed, "my brother and I are both well aware that I have nothing at all to fear from you. On the contrary, it's common knowledge that Scotsmen are trustworthy and honest, and . . . and simply the *most* honorable of men."

MacRae's scowl eased slightly. After a moment, he said, "'Tis true that Scotsmen have more honor per man than other lands. We carry the honor of Scotland with us wherever we go."

"Exactly," Merritt said. "No one would doubt my safety in your company. In fact, who would dare utter one offensive word, or threaten any harm to me, if you were there?"

MacRae seemed to warm to the idea. "If someone did," he said vehemently, "I'd skin the bawfaced bastard like a grape and toss him onto a flaming dung heap."

"There, you see?" Merritt exclaimed, beaming at him. "You're the perfect escort." Her gaze slid to her brother, who stood just behind MacRae.

Luke shook his head slowly, amusement tugging at the corners of his lips before he mouthed two silent words to her:

Table syrup.

She ignored him. "Come, Mr. MacRae—we'll have your affairs settled in no time."

Keir couldn't help following Lady Merritt. Since the moment he'd been drenched in fifty-proof whisky on the docks, he'd been chilled to the marrow of his bones. But this woman, with her quick smile and coffee-dark eyes, was the warmest thing in the world.

They went through a series of handsome rooms lined with wood paneling and paintings of ships. Keir barely noticed the surroundings. His attention was riveted by the shapely figure in front of him, the intricately pinned-up swirls of her hair, the voice dressed in silk and pearls. How good she smelled, like the kind of expensive soap that came wrapped in fancy paper. Keir and everyone he knew used common yellow rosin soap for everything: floors, dishes, hands, and body. But there was no sharpness to this scent. With every movement, hints of perfume seemed to rise from the rustling of her skirts and sleeves, as if she were a flower bouquet being gently shaken.

The carpet underfoot had been woven in a pattern beautiful enough to cover a wall. A crime, it was, to tread on it with his heavy work boots. Keir felt ill at ease in such fine surroundings. He didn't like having left his men, Owen and Slorach, out on the wharf. They could manage without him for a while, especially Slorach, who'd worked at his father's distillery for almost four decades. But this entire undertaking was Keir's responsibility, and the survival of his distillery depended on it. Making sure the bonded whisky was installed safely in the warehouse was too important to let himself be distracted by a woman.

Especially this one. She was educated and

well-bred, the daughter of an earl. Not just any earl, but Lord Westcliff, a man whose influence and wealth was known far and wide. And Lady Merritt was a power in her own right, the owner of a shipping business that included a fleet of cargo steamers as well as warehouses.

As the only child of elderly parents, Keir had been given the best of what they'd been able to provide, but there had been little in the way of books or culture. He'd found beauty in seasons and storms, and in long rambles over the island. He loved to fish and walk with his dogs, and he loved making whisky, the trade his father had taught him.

His pleasures were simple and straightforward.

Lady Merritt, however, was neither of those things. She was an altogether different kind of pleasure. A luxury to be savored, and not by the likes of him.

But that didn't stop Keir from imagining her in his bed, all flushed and yielding, her hair a blanket of dark silk over his pillow. He wanted to hear her pretty voice, with that high-toned accent, begging him for satisfaction while he rode her long and slow. Thankfully she had no idea of the lewd turn of his thoughts, or she would have fled from him screaming.

They came to an open area where a middle-aged woman with fair hair and spectacles sat in front of a machine on an iron stand.

"My lady," the woman said, standing up to

greet them. Her gaze flicked over Keir's unkempt appearance, taking in his damp clothes and the lack of a coat. A single twitch of her nose was her only recognition of the potent smell of whisky. "Sir."

"Mr. MacRae," Lady Merritt said, "this is my secretary, Miss Ewart." She gestured to a pair of sleek leather chairs in front of a fireplace framed by a white marble mantel. "Would you like to sit over there while I speak with her?"

No, he wouldn't. Or rather, he couldn't. It had been days since he'd had a decent rest. If he sat even for a few minutes, exhaustion was likely to overtake him.

Keir shook his head. "I'll stand."

Lady Merritt gazed at him as if he and his problems interested her more than anything else in the world. The private tenderness in her eyes could have melted an icehouse in the dead of winter. "Would you like coffee?" she suggested. "With cream and sugar?"

That sounded so good, it almost weakened his knees. "Aye," he said gratefully.

In no time at all, the secretary had brought out a little silver tray with a coffee service and a footed porcelain mug. She set it on a table, where Lady Merritt proceeded to pour the coffee and stir in cream and sugar. Keir had never had a woman do that for him before. He drew closer, mesmerized by the graceful movements of her hands.

She gave him the mug, and he wrapped

his fingers around it, relishing the radiant heat. Before drinking, however, he warily inspected the half-moon-shaped ledge at the rim of the cup.

"A mustache cup," Lady Merritt explained, noticing his hesitation. "That part at the top guards a gentleman's upper lip from the steam, and keeps mustache wax from melting into the beverage."

Keir couldn't hold back a grin as he lifted the cup to his lips. His own facial hair was close-trimmed, no wax necessary. But he'd seen the elaborate mustaches affected by wealthy men who had the time every morning to twirl and wax the ends into stiff little curls. Apparently the style required the making of special drinking mugs for them.

The coffee was rich and strong, possibly the best he'd ever had. So delicious, in fact, that he couldn't stop himself from downing it in just a few gulps. He was too famished to sip like a gentleman. Sheepishly he began to set the cup back on the tray, deciding it would be rude to ask for more.

Without even asking, Lady Merritt refilled his cup and prepared it again with sugar and cream. "I'll be but a moment," she murmured, before going to confer with the secretary.

Keir drank it down more slowly this time, and set the cup down. While the women talked, he meandered back to the desk to have a look at the shiny black contraption. A typewriter. He'd seen advertisements of them in newspapers. Intrigued, he bent to examine the alphabet keys mounted on tiny metal arms.

After the secretary left the room, Lady Merritt came to stand by Keir's side. Noticing his interest in the machine, she inserted a small sheet of letter paper and turned a roller to position it. "Push one of the letters," she invited.

Cautiously Keir touched a key, and a metal rod rose to touch an inked ribbon mounted in front of the paper. But when the arm lowered, the page was still blank.

"Harder," Lady Merritt advised, "so the letter plate strikes the paper."

Keir shook his head. "I dinna want to break it." The typewriter looked fragile and bloody expensive.

"You won't. Go on, try it." Smiling at his continued refusal, she said, "I'll type your name, then." She hunted for the correct keys, tapping each one firmly. He watched over her shoulder as his name emerged in tiny, perfect font.

Mr. Keir MacRae

"Why are the letters no' in alphabetical order?" Keir asked.

"If you type letters that are too close together, such as *S* and *T*, the metal arms jam together. Arranging the alphabet this way helps the machine operate smoothly. Shall I type something else?"

"Aye, your name."

A dimple appeared in her soft cheek as she

complied. All Keir's attention was riveted on the tiny, delectable hollow. He wanted to press his lips there, touch his tongue to it.

Lady Merritt Sterling, she typed.

"Merritt," he repeated, testing the syllables on his lips. " 'Tis a family name?"

"Not exactly. I was born during a storm, on a night when the doctor wasn't available, and the midwife was in her cups. But the local veterinarian, Dr. Merritt, volunteered to help my mother through her labor, and they decided to name me after him."

Keir felt a smile tugging at the corners of his mouth. Although he was half-starved and had been in the devil's own mood for most of the day, a feeling of well-being began to creep over him.

As Lady Merritt turned the roller to free the paper, Keir caught a glimpse of her inner wrist, where a tracery of blue veins showed though the fine skin. Such a delicate, soft place. His gaze traveled along her back, savoring the full, neat curves of her, the trim waist and flared hips. The shape of her bottom, concealed by artfully draped skirts, he could only guess at. But he'd lay odds it was round and sweet, perfect to pat, squeeze, stroke—

As desire surged in his groin and tautened his flesh, he bit back a curse. He was in a place of business, for God's sake. And she was a widow who should be treated with dignity. He tried to focus on how fine and cultured she was, and how much he respected her. When that didn't work, he thought very hard about the honor of Scotland.

A little lock of hair had slipped free of the complex arrangement of loops and swirls at the back of her head. The dark tendril lay against the back of her neck, curling at the end like a finger inviting him closer. How tender and vulnerable the nape of her neck looked. How good it would feel to nuzzle her there, and bite softly until she quivered and arched back against him. He would—

Bloody hell.

Desperately hunting for distractions, Keir glanced at their surroundings. He caught sight of a small but elaborately framed painting on one wall.

A portrait of Joshua Sterling.

That was enough to cool his lust.

The secretary had returned. Lady Merritt discarded the piece of typing paper in a little painted metal waste bin and went to speak with her.

Keir's gaze fell to the contents of the bin. As soon as the women's backs were turned, he reached down to retrieve the typed page, folded it into a small square, and slid it into his trouser pocket.

He wandered to the painting for a closer look.

Joshua Sterling had been a fine-looking man, with rugged features and a level gaze. Keir remembered having liked him a great deal, especially after they'd discovered they both loved fly-fishing. Sterling had mentioned learning to fly cast in the streams and lakes around his native Boston, and Keir had invited him to visit Islay someday and fish for sea trout. Sterling had assured Keir he would take him up on the offer.

Poor bastard.

Sterling had reportedly died at sea. A shame, it was, for a man to have been taken in his prime, and with such a wife waiting at home. From what Keir had heard, there were no children from the union. No son to carry on his name and legacy.

He wondered if Lady Merritt would marry again. There was no doubt she could have any man she wanted. Was that why she planned to give her younger brother charge of Sterling Enterprises? So she could take part in society and find a husband?

Her voice interrupted his thoughts.

"I've always thought that portrait made my husband appear a bit too stern." Lady Merritt came to stand beside Keir. "I suspect he was trying to appear authoritative, since he knew the painting was intended for the company offices." She smiled slightly as she contemplated the portrait. "Perhaps someday I'll hire an artist to add a twinkle in his eyes, to make him look more like himself."

"How long were you married?" Keir was surprised to hear himself ask. As a rule, he rarely asked about people's personal business. But he couldn't help being intensely curious about this woman, who was unlike anyone he'd ever met.

"A year and a half," Lady Merritt replied. "I met Mr. Sterling when he came to London to establish a branch of his shipping firm." She paused. "I never imagined I would someday be running it."

"You've done very well," Keir commented, before it occurred to him that it might seem presumptuous, offering praise to someone so far above him.

Lady Merritt seemed pleased, however. "Thank you. Especially for not finishing that sentence with '. . . for a woman,' the way most people do. It always reminds me of the Samuel Johnson quote about a dog walking on its hind legs: 'it's not done well, but one is surprised to find it done at all.' "

Keir's lips twitched. "There's more than one woman who successfully runs a business on Islay. The button maker, and the butcher—" He broke off, wondering if he'd sounded condescending. "Although their shops can't be compared to a large shipping firm."

"The challenges are the same," Lady Merritt said. "Assuming the burden of responsibility, taking risks, evaluating problems . . ." She paused, looking wry. "I'm sorry to say that mistakes still happen under my leadership. Your shipment being a case in point."

Keir shrugged. "Ah, well. There's always a knot somewhere in the rope."

"You're a gentleman, Mr. MacRae." She gave him a smile that crinkled her nose and tip-tilted her eyes. It made him a wee bit dizzy, that smile. It fed sunshine into his veins. He was dazzled by her, thinking she could have been some mythical creature. A fairy or even a goddess. Not some coldly aloof and perfect goddess . . . but a small and merry one.